GUNNING FOR TROUBLE

Buckskin was almost at the saloon when three mounted men stormed down the street toward him, their guns out. They saw Buckskin and all turned sharply and headed for him, their weapons up and firing. Buckskin jerked the big black to the side and rode hell bent for breakfast down the alley beside the saloon, turned back the way he had come and pounded hard down the street and into the flatness of the Wyoming prairie.

For a moment the three riders from town lost him, then they came out from behind some buildings, saw him and fired two rifle shots at him.

The Buckskin Series:

RIFLE RIVER
GUNSTOCK
PISTOLTOWN
COLT CREEK
GUNSIGHT GAP
TRIGGER SPRING
CARTRIDGE COAST
BOLT ACTION
TRIGGER GUARD
RECOIL
DOUBLE BUCKSKIN
GUNPOINT
LEVER ACTION
SCATTERGUN
WINCHESTER VALLEY
GUNSMOKE GORGE
REMINGTON RIDGE
SHOTGUN STATION
PISTOL GRIP
BUCKSKIN SPECIAL EDITION:
    THE BUCKSKIN BREED
PEACEMAKER PASS
SILVER CITY CARBINE
CALIFORNIA CROSSFIRE
BUCKSKIN DOUBLE EDITION:
    HANGFIRE HILL/CROSSFIRE COUNTRY
COLT CROSSING
POWDER CHARGE
LARAMIE SHOWDOWN

BOUNTY HUNTER'S MOON
BUCKSKIN

KIT DALTON

LEISURE BOOKS   NEW YORK CITY

A LEISURE BOOK

July 1989

Published by

Dorchester Publishing Co., Inc.
276 Fifth Avenue
New York, NY 10001

Copyright©1989 by Chet Cunningham/Book Crafters

All rights reserved. No part of this book may be reproduced or transmitted in any form or by any electronic or mechanical means, including photocopying, recording, or by any information storage and retrieval system, without the written permission of the Publisher, except where permitted by law.

The name "Leisure Books" and the stylized "LB" with design are trademarks of Dorchester Publishing Co., Inc.

Printed In the United States of America.

One

Buckskin Lee Morgan charged hard down the shallow gully and kicked the big roan into a thin shield of brush and trees at the midpoint along the straight section. He spurred her through the brush into the heavier timber until he was out of sight but still could see the ravine. He held the roan in check behind the sprinkling of piñon pine and watched his back trail.

The bastard who had been chasing him for the past three days was still back there, Buckskin knew. He had done his best to out-ride and out-maneuver the guy, but he held onto the trail like a totally devoted lawman. But the tracker wasn't a sheriff or marshall. He was a common bounty grabber. He hunted men down and took them back dead or alive to get the reward.

A man rode around the sharp corner of the

ravine, his sturdy black sliding on the gravel which made it seem that was the reason Buckskin's shot missed him. The bounty hunter pumped three shots in return fire at the spot where he saw the pall of blue smoke from Buckskin's warning shot. By the time Morgan eased his mount out from behind the pair of piñon pines, both the bountyman and the horse had clattered down the ravine and around a small bend putting them out of sight.

Buckskin Lee Morgan rode ahead again to get the trail in sight. Now the chaser became the chased. Buckskin caught a flash of the rider as he galloped around another twist in the gully 50 yards ahead.

Morgan worked down through the light stand of timber and brush, keeping the ravine to his right, watching for an opening where he could see the man on the black with the gray hat and denim jacket.

For three days the bounty hunter had followed Buckskin, now the tables were reversed and the man on the big roan enjoyed the feeling. He caught sight of the bounty hunter three more times as they wound down out of the timber until the land was almost bare of trees. They were in a small valley somewhere in the Medicine Bow Mountains of Wyoming Territory.

Morgan had been heading for Rawlins and a job, but the man with the poster that held a picture of his face, and the ugly words Dead or Alive under it, and the $2,000 reward, had caused him to take a detour.

Buckskin looked out from the brush, but

couldn't spot the other man or his horse. He had to be out there. A red tailed hawk sailed through the small thermals of hot rising air, then swept down to land on a shrub 100 hards out in the valley.

Suddenly it shrieked in surprise and anger, lifted up sharply from the bush and flew away. Buckskin concentrated on the spot and soon saw movement. Morgan dropped off his horse, took his rifle and bellied down in the hot afternoon sun beside a two-foot high boulder and peered around it. Again something moved and Morgan decided it had to be the horse in dappled sunshine. Where was the bounty hunter?

His answer came almost at once with the crack of a heavy rifle and the death scream of his roan horse just behind him. Buckskin looked up as the big animal crashed sideways, eyes already glassy, a gout of blood on the side of her head and all four feet kicking furiously in a death struggle that ended quickly.

Buckskin Lee Morgan rolled to the side and looked for the blue smoke. Someday someone would invent smokeless powder so a gunman wouldn't give away his position with every shot.

He saw the haze beside a smooth rock near where he had spotted the black horse. But there was no sign of the gunman. Fire and move, the man had learned his basic infantry training lessons well. Buckskin swept his eyes over the area, a small section at a time, searching for a place nearby to where the gunman had moved. He found it on the fourth pass.

Just then the sun glinted off a rifle barrel and

Buckskin lifted his Spencer repeating carbine and fired a shot into the space just over the rifle. At once he jolted behind the rock as three hot lead slugs dug into the rock and another one ricocheted away.

"Give it up, Morgan," a voice called. "You're on foot now, 40 miles from town. All I've got to do is run you down and pack your body out to Arizona, or get a U.S. Marshall to swear that you're dead and I killed you. Give it up and go back for a trial."

Buckskin Lee Morgan didn't give away his position. He kept quiet. The bounty hunter had to try to get to his black horse sooner or later. He couldn't wait until dark, but Buckskin could. Morgan eased out to the edge of the rock to keep the area in sight. He saw where he figured the gunman had moved to and figured out how he probably would work back to his horse.

Morgan zeroed in on a twelve foot bare spot that he guessed the bounty hunter would have to cross to get to his black. Morgan had learned patience early in life. It served him well now. Nearly a half hour passed with no words spoken by either of them before Morgan saw the man begin an Indian move across the open area.

Then the man lost his nerve and lifted up to run. Buckskin Morgan's first round clipped his right leg, and his second missed forward before the figure dove into what must be another ravine that protected the horse.

"Bastard!" the man shouted. "Now for damn sure I'm going to kill you and take you into Cheyenne. The Marshall there will give me a certified death certificate on you. Bastard, you shot my leg."

Buckskin checked the sky. Another half hour and it would be dark. Not even this guy could track a man on foot in this kind of country. He'd get his sack of supplies from the horse and the saddlebags with his clothes and ammunition and go back to the woods. By daylight he would be 30 miles away and this bounty hunter would never find him.

Maybe. What were the alternatives? Buckskin began to grin. Maybe he wouldn't walk away after all. He watched the bounty hunter's location.

He even knew his name, Alonzo Warnick. He had seen the man in Cheyenne where Morgan had stopped for supplies. He had bought Morgan a beer in a saloon and talked all friendly. Then when they got outside Warnick had tried to draw his six-gun on Morgan who knocked it out of his hand. Warnick had yelled at two men going by to help him, claiming to be a town marshall from Arizona. The Wyoming cowboys laughed at him and went into a saloon.

Morgan had knocked Warnick down, taken his gun and ridden out of town. He should have killed the poster hunter right there.

It was nearly dusk. The tracker would have no chance of following a trail at night, even if he had a lantern, not through the scrub oak, mountain mahogany and some weathered piñon pine in this part of Wyoming. Behind them the country got rougher and swept up into the tops of the Medicine Bow Mountains. Ahead the land eased down to faint beginnings of the flat, wide Laramie Valley fifteen miles away.

Buckskin Morgan watched Warnick who now worked his horse carefully down the ravine. There was no chance for a good shot at either horse or man. The dry watercourse they were in fed runoff water from spring rains and snow melt into a year-round creek a half mile down the gentle slope.

Morgan claimed his foodstuffs and saddlebags from the dead horse. He wasn't going to lug the heavy saddle with him. He moved cautiously toward the ravine. It was deeper than he had guessed and soon he was walking down it, followig the prints of the bounty hunter's horse.

Soon it would be dark. Then he would move ahead cautiously. From the way this man operated, Morgan guessed that he would find a good place to camp as soon as he hit the creek. Then in the morning he would circle, pick up any tracks he found, and plan a leisurely ride-down of his victim.

Time for a change of plans for Alonzo Warnick. He would make a fire, Buckskin was almost sure. The man didn't seem to be enough of a woodsman to know that a fire would be like a beacon signal leading anyone in the area directly to him. As soon as he started a fire he would build it bigger than needed and it would make a lot of smoke.

Buckskin could smell smoke a mile away even if he was upwind of it. After living in the outdoors so much, he could catch the briefest whiff of wood smoke out in the open.

Now it was dark. The moon gave a little light, but twice Morgan fell with a clatter of rocks. He hoped he was far enough away so Warnick wouldn't hear him. He was more careful after that, working slowly down the gully. A half hour later he smelled smoke. A short time more and he saw the flames of a fire less then 100 yards ahead.

The six-footer took off his hat and scrubbed blondish hair back out of his eyes. He was clean shaven, and now watched the bounty hunter's fire from clear brown eyes.

Twice today Buckskin Morgan had touched the Spencer repeating carbine and almost pulled it from the leather boot on the right side of his saddle. Two clean shots and the deadly danger the man presented to Buckskin could be gone forever. But Buckskin had resisted the easy solution. Besides, he didn't like killing a man from ambush—it wasn't his style.

A good stand-up shootout would be better—or even a fight with knives in a dark alley—but he wouldn't gun a man down from hiding, even though that man might do exactly the same thing to him.

Buckskin could see the bountyman moving around the fire. Warnick had picked up Morgan's trail just outside of Cheyenne, Wyoming Territory, three days ago, and had hung on like fresh pitch off a pine tree. Buckskin wondered which Wanted poster the man had, the one from Idaho, or the one from Arizona.

Both of them were frauds. The Idaho warrant and poster were cooked up by the crooked sheriff near Boise who had been bedeviling Buckskin for five years. Buckskin still owned the Spade Bit Ranch his father, William "Buckskin" Frank Leslie, had left him. The Sheriff and his legal outlaws wanted the place. The Wanted poster for some imagined crime was their way of eliminating the legal owner.

The problem in Arizona had gotten out of hand. It had been a fair fight. Every man in the saloon had said so. The young man had been drunk and crude and pushed over Buckskin's poker table and swung at him and then demanded that they shoot it out, right there. The kid had provoked the fight and Buckskin had even let him shoot first.

He'd missed and Buckskin wounded him in the shoulder instead of killing him. But the damn fool kept shooting so Buckskin had to shoot again. The Sheriff listened to the witnesses and agreed that it was self defense and let him go. A month later the local District Attorney came back to town from the state capital and swore out a warrant on Buckskin. The crazy gunman Buckskin had killed was the district attorney's brother. So much for Arizona Territorial justice. The lawman had printed up the Wanted poster with a $2,000 reward.

$2,000 was over six years' pay for a cowboy or a clerk in a store. Most farmers never saw $100 in cash money for any year's work. It was enough money to put a whole pack of full time bounty hunters watching for Buckskin Lee Morgan.

There had been a bounty hunter or two who bothered Buckskin in the four or five years the

Wanteds had been out, but no one had been this close before.

Buckskin wished the man would simply ride away. He remembered the better idea he had thought of before and a grin slashed across his face as he pondered it. Buckskin nodded and set his jaw.

He moved up on the fire slowly. He left his sack of possibles beside a small willow at the edge of the little creek, and checked out the campsite again. Warnick had left his horse back from the fire. He was evidently cooking something. Morgan could not smell any coffee boiling.

Buckskin grinned. It was going to be a few days before Warnick found his way back to town. By his best calculations they were about 40 miles west of Laramie and close to 60 miles on to Rawlins. Either direction would be a fine hike. But it could be worse, which fit well into Buckskin Morgan's plans for the bounty chaser.

He moved up slowly, working through the brush with the fire as his beacon. When he was 50 yards away he could see the small camp Warnick had made. He was directly on the bank of the creek. His saddle and bridle lay nearby and a white flour sack of provisions had been opened and arranged on the spread out sack near the fire.

Warnick had not bothered with a forked stick spit. Buckskin was not sure if the fire was for cooking or just for staying warm. The weather was usually chilly in the Medicine Bow Mountains this early in the spring. The snow was long since gone, and some wild flowers had grown, but the nights were still nippy.

Buckskin moved closer, not breaking a twig, not putting his foot down until he was sure nothing under it would make a sound. He paused now beside a juniper with a twisted trunk that would hide him if Warnick looked his way. He had come to within 30 feet of the man.

Warnick sat facing the small fire, adding sticks as it burned down. When Buckskin was only ten feet away from the man, in the open area beside the creek, he pulled out his Colt .45 and cocked the hammer.

The click the weapon made as it locked in full cock jolted through the air space around the two men like a gong. Warnick turned his head slowly. His hands were in sight and he had no gun in either one.

"Go ahead, kill me, Morgan. That's what you're trying to do. Let's get it over with."

"Warnick, if I wanted you dead, you would have been in your grave by now in Cheyenne."

"Then I don't understand."

"That fits. I want you to get your six-gun and rifle and put them on the ground in my direction as far as you can reach. You try to shoot and you're a dead man. I'd hate to have to blow your head off now after I've been so good to you."

"By letting me live?"

"Right. That's about as good as I'm going to get. Put the weapons over here, then take off your boots."

"My boots?"

"Yep."

Warnick put a well used pistol beside his

Remington rifle and slid away from them.

"Now the boots, and your pants."

When Buckskin lifted onto the back of the big black gelding ten minutes later, Alonzo Warnick sat beside his fire shivering. He had only his blanket and his underwear left. A makeshift bandage tied up a shallow bullet wound on his left leg.

"What the hell am I supposed to do now?" Warnick snapped.

"Just be glad you're alive. I told you neither of those Wanted posters are worth a thing."

"Yeah, sure. Every man I've brought in during the past ten years has said the same thing."

"You want me to make dead certain you don't bother me any more?" Buckskin asked, pulling his Colt .45.

Warnick looked at Buckskin closely, then slowly shook his head. "No sir, Mr. Morgan. I surely do not want that."

"Good. You have a nice walk, Mr. Warnick. I'd suggest east to Laramie. Only about 40 miles that way. Couple of days and you'll be back among people with their pants on."

Buckskin let a grin break up his stern face, pulled the black's head around and turned west. He should be in Rawlins sometime tomorrow late, if he pushed it.

"You have a good walk into town, Mr. Warnick. You better go into another line of work. If I see you coming after me again, I'll blow your head off."

Warnick shivered from the cold so much he could hardly talk. His face twisted in anger.

"That Arizona Wanted says Dead or Alive. You'll never see me, Morgan, not before I blow your brains out. Every time you turn around you'll be watching for me."

"Maybe, Warnick. But at least not until you find a gun and find your way back to town."

Morgan rode out and continued through the moonlight down a long valley to a river he figured should be the North Platte. It ran north here and would lead him almost into Rawlins. That's where he was heading when Warnick had sidetracked him.

In Rawlins he had a job, and the current thinness of his wallet made some profit yielding work of prime importance.

Buckskin reset the black low crowned cowboy hat on his head and settled in the new saddle. He had a long ride ahead of him.

Two

Hartley J. Minderhausen stared out the window of his office on the third floor of the Minderhausen Brewery in Rawlins, Wyoming Territory. He was a short, stout German immigrant who had been in the country only ten years but had mastered the English language, transferred his brewery skills to America, and developed one of the biggest breweries in the mid-west.

The glorious railroad had made it possible. Before then he had simply one of the best breweries in Chicago. A chance trip to Rawlins in 1869, just after the railroad went through there, led him to discover the fresh water springs and the delightful taste of the water.

He moved Minderhausen Breweries to Rawlins and quickly captured the local beer market and soon was shipping his brew by rail to towns large and small up and down the Union Pacific rail lines. He sent his brew as far as Denver to the south and to Omaha.

He was considered by the local population as something of a marvel. Most small towns had at least one local brewery and often two or three. He had put dozens of them out of business with his finer product at a lower price.

Now Minderhausen folded his hands together on his round belly and stared at the railroad west. He was sure the kidnappers had taken Herta west, perhaps getting on the train at the next stop.

But he had checked with the railroad people. They had reported no special stops to the west. He growled deep in his throat. Herta was all he had left. His beloved wife had died a year before they came to America. Now his Herta was gone!

Minderhausen stood five-feet five-inches tall and weighed nearly 200 pounds. His black hair had streaks of gray and his full moustache and beard was now as much gray and white as it was black. He kept it trimmed an inch long and it framed his face making him look more like a university professor than a brewmaster.

He slammed his fist into his open palm and turned to the office door. "Hans!" he bellowed.

Within a few seconds the door opened and a tall, thin blond man hurried into the room, a pad of paper and pencil in his hand. He said nothing but stood quietly waiting for orders.

"Anything yet?"

"No, sir. We have no word from Mr. Morgan other than that he was on his way and hoped to arrive sometime tomorrow."

"No changes from him?"

"No, sir."

"Anything comes in, you let me know."

"Yes, sir!"

Minderhausen nodded at the tall man and he hurried out of the room.

The master brewer and rich brewery owner went back to the large leather chair with the high back that rocked and swung around as well and leaned back closing his eyes. But he could rest only a few seconds. Then he pushed forward on the desk and stared at a picture of his daughter that had been hand colored to show her masses of blonde hair, her round smiling face and a slender form in a formal gown.

"How could anyone kidnap such a perfect little lady?" Minderhausen asked softly of himself. He had received no word from her, nor any letter or demands from her kidnappers. She was there in the heart of his family one moment, and the next gone without a word, without a trace.

The local sheriff had been no help at all. They had watched around town, but in a place as small as Rawlins it would be hard to hide anyone. There were fewer than 2,000 people there, including all of the railroad workers. It was a division point for the Union Pacific, with many shops and repair facilities and storage yards.

Where could she have gone? Where would his princess vanish to without even telling him? She must have been kidnapped.

He left the office with only a cursory wave at Hans, his male secretary and office manager. He wandered through the offices that handled the purchasing, the brewing and the sales for his small kingdom. Now and then he waved or nodded to an employee. He had hired as many German immigrants as he could find. They were good workers, understood him and his Germanic methods and they felt at home here.

Soon he left the business and had his carriage driver take him home to his big house on the highest point in Rawlins. He went to his door and found it opened quickly for him by his housekeeper. He could afford a butler and several maids, but he preferred just to have a housekeeper who was also a great cook.

Serilda smiled and welcomed him in German and he smiled. He kissed her on the cheek.

"Serilda, you must practice your English as well. To become successful in America you must speak the good English as I do."

"Yes, yes. I practice." She smiled at him and Minderhausen caught her hand and walked into his first floor den. They sat on the couch there and he kissed her lips tenderly.

"You are troubled about Herta," she said softly in German. "I try to tell you not to worry. She is safe, I am sure."

"She spoke to you before she left?"

"No, but I am sure. Let me make you feel better." She picked up his hand and put it on her breasts which pressed hard against the thin material of her blouse.

His hand lay there for a moment, then it began to move, to caress the mounds through the cloth. Serilda undid the buttons down the front of her blouse and let her breasts surge out from their bondage.

"You are so good to me, Serilda, so good." Then he was kissing her bare bosom, licking the white flesh, breathing in the soft scent of her and at last biting her nipples until they swelled and filled with hot blood, standing twice as tall as they had moments before.

He lay on the couch, pulling her over the top of him until one of her orbs nestled in his mouth and he moaned in delight and satisfaction.

One of her hands found its way between their bodies and rubbed the hardness at his crotch. Serilda knew exactly what the chunky man wanted, and precisely how to please him.

She had come to work at the Minderhausen mansion six months ago, just after her eighteenth birthday, and knew of his reputation for helping German immigrants.

After two months she had replaced the much older cook, who was Irish, and a month later she had gone to his bedroom one night and slipped into bed beside him, then awoke him and they made love for the first time. Now two or three times a week she comforted him.

"You are too good to me, Serilda, much too good."

They had talked about what would happen if she became pregnant. He had maintained steadfastly that he would then marry her, and Serilda glowed with happiness and urged him to come to bed with her at every chance.

He pushed her off him and undressed her, constantly amazed at her sleek, young body, her big breasts yet with no sag, and her flat little tummy. He bent and kissed the soft hair at her crotch and then permitted her to undress him.

Never had a woman meant so much to him. His wife had been picked out for him by his father and her father, but now he was with a woman who he had much affection for, and who made him feel twenty years younger.

She turned on the couch, went to her hands and knees and pushed her delightfully round bottom up at him. "Your favorite way," she told him.

For a moment the worry over his daughter was gone. He knelt behind her, probed for a moment and made the right connection. Then he eased into her and reached for her hanging breasts as he leaned down on her back.

"Yes, oh, yes!" Serilda said gripping and releasing him with her internal muscles which she knew set him on fire. He tried to hold back but quickly he knew the explosion was coming. He fought it off, then dissolved in a surging, roaring avalanche of pure, raw, animalistic satisfaction as his loins jetted the seeds of a new generation into her waiting vagina.

He panted and huffed and she settled down on her stomach taking him with her.

It was five minutes before he could breathe normally again. He came away from her and sat on the couch, looking at the clothes strewn around the room.

"You are a terrific lover," Serilda said kissing him gently on his lips. "I want the best of everything for you, perhaps even a son some day."

"A son!"

He had not even considered it as a possibility. But yes, it was possible. He was strong and fit, and Serilda was young and healthy. Yes, a son was possible. He kissed her gently, then leaned back to look at her. Large brown eyes, dark hair, brows curved and curious. A small nose over a tiny mouth that could do marvelous things to him and his staff of life.

"You make me so happy," he said.

The twist bell on the front door rang.

Serilda bounced from the couch, picked up a dressing gown from a chair and put it on, then went to the door. She came back a moment later with an envelope. She gave it to Hartley and watched him closely.

He tore it open and read the message.

"A report from my detectives in Laramie and Cheyenne. Seems there has been no sign of Herta in either town. The men will move on east along the railroad and keep up the search."

"She must have gone by train," Serilda said. "Any other way would not be practical."

"And Herta is a practical girl," he said. "I've taught her that."

Serilda took the message and put it on the table. "I'll get you a snack—a cold bottle of beer, some cheese and hard salami with some crackers. Then we'll make love again. The next few days will be good for me. I want you to save your strength and to make love to me at least once a day, every day, for as long as possible."

"Good for you?"

"Oh, Hartley, surely you know. A woman bleeds once a month. A few days after her bleeding stops and for a week or so she is at her best time to get pregnant. My darling, I'm in heat, like a bitch dog, and I want you inside of me every moment I can have you!"

"Yes, yes of course. But no more than once a day. I'm not a sprout of sixteen anymore, remember. We'll conserve my energy. Bring the snack, then I need to go see that new detective I'm to send on west. She must have been taken west somehow. But where am I to look? I still don't understand why I don't get any demands from the kidnappers."

Serilda looked away quickly. She would not meet his gaze when he spoke of Herta's going. She had promised, and nothing would make her break such a bond. If she did now, she would lose all hope of ever gaining the Minderhausen name. And to Serilda that meant everything.

Her brother had given her explicit instructions when he sent her here from Chicago a year ago. Somehow she had to get into the Minderhausen household. Anyway she could. If she could gain his confidence it would help. Her brother had been clear about that. She would offer him her womanly charms if it would help. Nothing must be left undone to pave the way for her family's ultimate revenge on the house of Minderhausen!

Serilda had done her part. They were so close, so near. If only the girl was not gone from the household. It made Hartley so nervous, so gruff and worried. Soon now, soon she would have the final weapon to use over the great master brewer. Soon she could tell her brother that she was pregnant.

Three

Buckskin Lee Morgan rode the big black gelding for three hours through the tepid darkness, working down the slopes of the Medicine Bow Mountains. What he thought was the Laramie Valley turned out to be little more than three miles wide and he had to bear hard left to go around a peak that spired into the night sky. He at last decided it must be Medicine Bow peak that rose to over 12,000 feet.

But north was the right direction. Sooner or later he'd run into the railroad and he could follow the tracks west along an easy grade right into Rawlins.

When the big dipper told him it was ten o'clock, he found a small stream and made camp. The black was a fine mount, deep, strong and not overly stupid. He'd do at least until Rawlins.

Buckskin didn't make a fire. He had a chaw on a big chunk of beef jerky, filled up on a drink of water and went to sleep. He didn't even think about the bounty hunter shivering in his underwear three hours behind him.

Morning brought a little stiffness and hunger. Buckskin boiled some coffee over a small nearly smokeless fire, then fried his last two eggs and the rest of his bacon.

With all of his immediate needs now attended to, he broke camp, mounted the black and continued on to Rawlins.

By noon he had spotted the smoky trail of a railroad locomotive dragging a short string of passenger and box cars along the tracks eight or ten miles across the valley.

"Well, Blackie, looks like we found ourselves the way to Rawlins after all."

He grinned. It wasn't often he talked to his horse, but this one seemed to listen. He pricked up his ears and they moved on toward the tracks.

The train he saw had been heading east, which meant there probably would be one going west sometime that day.

It was well after noon when he hit the tracks and turned west. For a while he rode in the shallow ditch they had formed when they graded the track bed, then he moved out 100 yards to the natural roll of the Wyoming land and found the going easier.

About three that afternoon Buckskin picked up the pace a little. He could see a town ahead and tried to remember if there was another community on the tracks this side of Rawlins. He couldn't remember.

As he rode into the outskirts of the village he could see that it wasn't much of a town. There were 30 or 40 buildings, one main street next to the tracks, and a small train station. Main Street held maybe fifteen stores and a small bank.

He was walking the big black toward the closest bar when he heard shooting down the street. Two men surged out of the bank shooting back into the building. They grabbed horses at the tie rail, and covered two more gunmen who came out with bags over their shoulders. The four mounted, fired a half dozen more shots, and rode hard down a side street.

Buckskin was almost at the saloon when three mounted men stormed down the street toward him, their guns out. They saw Buckskin and all turned sharply and headed for him, their weapons up and firing. Buckskin jerked the big black to the side and rode hell bent for breakfast down the alley beside the saloon, turned back the way he had come and pounded hard down the street and into the flatness of the Wyoming prairie.

For a moment the three riders from town lost him, then they came out from behind some builidngs, saw him and fired two rifle shots at him.

Buckskin was not willing to slow down and explain to the men that he was just riding into town. He couldn't have possibly done anything to deserve such a greeting. He knew that innocent victims with four or five rifle slugs in them find it hard to convince anyone of their innocence.

The big black resopnded to the chase for nearly a mile, then the all day ride began to tell and the three men on fresh horses gained on him. Buckskin hunted for a spot to make a stand. A quarter of a mile over to the left he saw a small outcropping of boulders and half a dozen stunted trees. He angled for them. Halfway there he knew he wouldn't make it. His big black was on his reserve supply of energy, and about to run out.

A rifle cracked and Buckskin waited for the slug to find his flesh. The three riders were less than 50 yards behind him, and even with the uneven platform of a galloping horse, a shooter should be able to hit him one time out of a dozen.

The next three or four rounds sounded strange. They almost seemed to be going in the wrong direction. He looked up at the rocks ahead and saw sun glints from at least two rifles firing over the rocks.

Great, a crossfire. How did he get into this mess? He spurred the big black to try one last surge to the rocks. At least he could confront some of the gunmen.

He looked behind him at the three chasers and saw one of the riders there take a round in the shoulder and pivot off his mount. That's when he realized the guns behind the rocks were not firing at him. They had targeted the three men chasing him.

He slowed so the black would last and rode to the rocks and around them. A smallish man with a hat pulled down low grabbed his horse as he pulled up. Buckskin didn't waste time talking.

He caught his Spencer out of his saddle boot and crawled up beside the other two men firing over the rocks.

The two remaining men on horseback sat 300 yards away looking at the rocks. Buckskin sighted in and punched a hole in one of the two riders with his second shot. That was enough. The men turned and picked up their wounded man and rode back toward town.

Buckskin rolled over on the rock and looked at the men beside him. Both seemed to be small, but they could use their weapons. One looked over at him and Buckskin grinned. The gunman didn't look more than fifteen.

"Thanks for the help," Buckskin said. "Another ten minutes and they would have nailed my hide to the ground."

"You're welcome," the young looking shooter said with a voice that wasn't quite right for the face. Someone laughed behind him. He turned around to see what kind of a man would laugh that way.

The person walked up leading four horses and laughed again. Then the hat came off and a tousle of black stringy hair spilled out. She was a woman in men's clothes.

"I bet Dutch $50 we could save your ass, you peckerhead. She figured they was too close to you. What the hell was them three lawmen chasing you for?"

Buckskin looked at the others now. They took off their men's low crowned black cowboy hats and it was plain that all four were women. One looked Mexican, and one was tall and rangy when she stood up. Two had short hair.

The tall one who had been shooting over the rocks came down and held out her hand. "My name is Dutch Smith, and I run this outfit. What were those guys chasing you for?"

Buckskin looked at the four again. All four wore black hats, all four rode black horses. "I finally figured it out. You four are the ones who just knocked over the bank back in town. I rode up a half a minute later. The posse came charging around the corner, spotted my black hat and black horse, and decided I'm the fifth one in your gang and start shooting at me."

Dutch Smith laughed. "Figures. That sheriff is shit dumb in that little town. Wouldn't know his mouth from his ear if his ear had teeth."

Buckskin took off his hat and shook his head. "You four women held up that bank in town?"

"Shit yes, sonny, best place to get money," the older woman with the long black hair snapped. She held out her hand. "I'm Maud Lowden. This little outfit was my idea, but Dutch there is our boss lady. You got a handle or do we just call you Peckerhead all the time?"

"Buckskin Lee Morgan, ma'am. Pleased to meet you."

Maud held out her hand. She wore men's pants, a worn leather jacket and the black hat like the rest. He guessed she was under twenty-five, could be pretty if she'd wash her face. Then quickly he saw she had used some dirt or something on her face to make her look different, more manly. But the leather jacket didn't quite conceal her breasts.

"Like Maud told you," Dutch said, "we didn't know who you were, but we figured if the law was chasing you, you couldn't be all good. Welcome aboard. Whether you like it or not you just bought in on a bank robbery, and you wounded a deputy sheriff."

"Hey, I've got business in Rawlins. I'd be proud to join you, but come dark, I'll be moving on down track."

"Not so," a voice said behind him and he heard the deadly click as a six-gun cocked. Buckskin turned slowly.

"This is Pris Johnson, Mr. Morgan," Dutch said making the introductions. "Pris likes to use that .45 and she isn't too particular who gets in the way of the hot lead. But she's right. You turn up in Rawlins and the law spots you, they know the rest of the gang will be there, too. We can't let that happen."

Dutch pointed to the other woman standing nearby. She took off her hat and shook out long black hair that was clean and shining.

"Buckskin, meet Navaro. She speaks little English, but communicates extremely well with six-gun or rifle. I'm afraid you'll be much safer with us for a few days than out on your own. Fact is, we'll be safer as well. You see, we're going to Rawlins ourselves."

"We can talk about that later," Morgan said. "Isn't it dangerous to stay here? Seems like you're just begging for another posse to come after you."

"It'll take Sheriff Carson at least three or four hours to put together a posse. Townfolk in Sinclair aren't enthused about going on a shooting ride. We've robbed this bank before, two months ago. That time we got away without a shot being fired on either side."

Buckskin grinned and laughed. "I'm not laughing at you ladies. It's just that I've never even heard of an all woman bank robbery gang before."

"That's the way we want it," Pris said. "You a cowboy or what?"

"Right now I'm running from a bounty hunter," Buckskin said.

All four of them looked at him.

"No shit?" Maud asked.

"True. From Arizona. It was a fair fight but they didn't think so."

"Stay with us, we'll ventilate any damned bounty hunter who tries to find you," Pris said.

"We better move," Dutch said. "We can talk as we ride. I figure we'll go south into the foothills and work west. That way we'll be able to see a posse from ten miles away. Not a good tracker in that little jerkwater town. We can confuse anyone they send after us."

They rode.

Buckskin moved up beside Dutch. "You really heading for Rawlins?"

"Yes, we all live there."

"How do you get away with it? You've hit banks before?"

"This is our seventh bank and one railroad express car. We don't like railroads. They send detectives who don't give up. We stick to banks, now."

"But how can four of you hide in a little place like Rawlins?"

"Hide? We don't hide. Maud and I are widows, we live together in a little frame house at the edge of town. We're scraping along on our savings. Pris lives alone. Navaro lives with a Mexican couple in town. We all just blend into the community. We don't even know each other in Rawlins."

"I won't know you either. All I have to do is buy a new hat and nobody will even think that I'm one of the bank robbers."

"Maybe. Trouble is, you owe us?"

"Beg your pardon, ma'am?"

"Call me Dutch. I said you owe us. You would have had your ass shot off back there if Navaro and I hadn't stopped that three man posse of deputies. Your black near give out on you, right?"

"True."

"So you pay us back. We stop at Rawlins for two days to rest up and get set up again, then we take the train to Rock Springs, rent horses, rob the Rock Springs Territorial Savings Bank and ride into the Great Divide Basin and back to Rawlins."

"That's eighty, ninety miles."

"So, you got saddle sores?"

"You want me to help you rob the bank."

"Right. You owe us."

"I've got a job waiting for me in Rawlins."

"Who with?"

"Hartley Minderhausen."

"The big beer man? Richest guy in town? We should rob him sometime, but we never hit anything in Rawlins."

"Smart."

"So you're a few days late for the job. You owe us." She looked at him with a· slight frown marring her pretty face. "You really wanted somewhere, with posters and everything?"

"Arizona and Idaho, both complete frauds and miscarriages of justice."

"Yeah, ain't it always. Tell me about yours."

He told her.

"Yeah, tough. Mine is a little different. Maud's old man and my husband both rode with a group of gentlemen who were going to be more famous than the James boys. They went out on their second robbery, a small bank, and my man and Maud's got their heads blown off with a sawed off shotgun, and the other three were captured. Ain't that a kick in the rear end?"

"You took over your husband's business?" Buckskin asked.

Dutch grinned. "Kind of. Phil would tell me by the hour exactly how he planned on robbing this bank. He had it all worked out. But there's always a chance for something to go wrong. Like today. Our plan is never to use our guns, never to be seen leaving a bank, never to let a witness be able to identify any of us. It doesn't always work. But it will in Rock Springs, because we have a fifth person."

Buckskin let it pass. He would change their minds later. Sinclair, the little town he was just chased from, lay 20 miles from Rawlins. He had to go there anyway. The female bandit gang fascinated him. He had never even heard of such an idea. Now and then a single woman "badman" showed up, but not a whole gang of them.

Dutch and Buckskin rode a little ahead of the others and now Buckskin asked a question he had been pondering. "I see why you and Maud joined the group. What about the other two?"

"Pris is a special case. She was violated by her uncle when she was twelve, thrown out of the house by her father when she was thirteen, became a beggar to live. Learned how to steal and was arrested and escaped twice. She's been run out of two towns and generally hates every man she sees, including you, Buckskin Morgan. Oh, she's just 19 years old."

"I'll watch my back. What about Navaro?"

"She came up from New Mexico Territory where a sheriff ran her family out of a squatter's shack on a small ranch. The sheriff killed her father and mother and thought he'd killed her. She lost one eye and has all those scars on her face. I found her one day eating out of a garbage can behind a cafe. I took her home and got her healthy as she'll ever be, then found a Mexican couple in Rawlins who let her live with them for helping around the house. Not ideal but it works so far.

"In a few more months, Navaro will have enough money so she can go back to New Mexico and open a little cafe of her own. She does not like lawmen—any kind of lawmen."

Dutch looked over at him.

"Don't do it, Pris would kill you."

Buckskin looked at her. "I'm not thinking of trying to ride away from your little ladies sewing club here. Happens that I do agree with you. I owe you women something." He rode closer to Dutch. "Besides that, I'm fascinated. I want to find out what's doing all the jiggling and shaking under that shirt of yours."

Dutch looked up, fire in her eyes for a moment, then she grinned. "Good. I was beginning to wonder if I would have to be the one to do the seducing of you tonight."

Four

Dutch Smith and her gang, and Buckskin Morgan, rode for six hours southwest into the foothills of the Medicine Bow Mountains, found a small creek and made camp. There wasn't a whine, not a whimper, not a pout or a complaint from the four women as they rode or as they set up their small overnight.

They were as disciplined and trail hardened as most cavalry outfits, and Dutch was definitely the boss lady. She picked out the camp and the women went about their duties of gathering wood, making a small cooking fire and standing lookout for as long as the light lasted watching the country to the north from where a posse would have to come. They saw no riders.

Supper that night was reheated baked beans, country fried potatoes made from previously boiled ones, hard biscuits and jam, and all the coffee they could drink. There was plenty of food.

"Isn't this better than working for some old brewer?" Dutch asked. She had taken off the leather jacket and now Buckskin knew for sure what was doing all the jiggling under her crisp white blouse.

"Brewer?" he asked.

"Sure, in Rawlins, Minderhausen runs the biggest brewery this side of Omaha. Makes good beer. He's run a lot of small brewers out of business along the Union Pacific line."

"He didn't say what his business was, or what the job was. Just the fee."

"So you're a hired gun," Dutch said, a note of awe in her voice. "Never met a real gunslinger before."

"Not a real gunslinger, more a regulator for hire. A kind of private sheriff."

"For those who can afford it," she said.

"Man has to be paid for his labor, only common decency."

"Woman has to be paid, too. That's why I took up a good paying profession. So far, so good."

Buckskin noticed that from the very first, the other three women had stayed away from him. Either they didn't like him or left him to their leader. Now, one by one the three came up and said goodnight, took their blankets, and vanished into the darkness up or down stream.

"We never sleep around our fire," Dutch said.

She had combed out her hair and it was longer than he first thought, almost to her shoulders.

She had kept it pinned up and controlled with a bandana under her big hat. Now the soft brown locks flowed around her face.

"Sleeping near a campfire is like inviting somebody to sneak up and kill or capture you. It's worked out so far."

"How many banks?" he asked.

"I told you before, seven, counting today. It really isn't that hard once you work out the procedures. We know who does what and what to do if something goes wrong."

"Like you say, so far, so good." He stood, went to his black and took his blanket roll off and came back.

"You have a good spot picked out to sleep?" he asked.

"No, but we can find one. I always stay closest to the fire."

She picked up her blanket and moved into the brush. Dutch picked out a level spot and tramped the ground to make sure there were no snakes there, then kicked away some branches and sticks and spread out her blanket.

Buckskin unfurled his and sat down on the edge.

She dropped down beside him. "Do you know I haven't had a man since my husband died. Nearly two years now."

He tried to see her expression but the moon wasn't that bright tonight and the trees blocked out most of the light.

"Some women don't seem to need it. They tell me they get by nicely without a man pawing them.

"True. Some do, but not me. I miss it ever so much."

Buckskin put his hand on her shoulder and she brushed it away.

At once she turned. "I'm sorry. I didn't mean to do that. It's just that I've been doing the leading, making the decisions for so long."

Buckskin reached over and kissed her. She clung to his lips, her hands on his shoulders as she came closer to him. When the kiss broke off she sighed gently and he could see her face. She was smiling.

"Oh, yes!" Dutch whispered.

"Pretty lady, you make as many decisions as you like, be as fast or as slow as you want to be. This is your party. Anything you want to do is perfectly fine with me."

She leaned forward, pushed her breasts against his chest and kissed his lips hard and demanding. Her arms went around him and she kissed him so hard his lips stung. Then he opened his mouth and her tongue darted inside, probing, licking, touching him everywhere she could.

When she stopped the kiss she was breathing hard. She pushed her chin over his shoulder and kept her arms around him.

"This feels so damned good!" she said softly, yet the words brimmed with feeling.

He kissed her ear and she wiggled against him.

"That's nice. Nobody ever did that to me before."

He moved slightly and licked the inside of her ear and she giggled quietly. When she recovered she pulled away just a little. "I don't want to make too much noise or Pris and Maud will tease us tomorrow."

"Let them tease, we're the ones enjoying it."

"I'm enjoying it. I thought I might be a little . . . shy."

He kissed her again and this time his hand eased around one of her breasts. He was pleased how large it was. She moaned in her throat as he fondled her and when the kiss broke off he had his hand under her blouse. She wore no undergarment. Her breast was warm and he tweaked her nipple and could feel it enlarge. He kissed her again, then unbuttoned the fasteners on her blouse and spread it back.

"Marvelous!" Buckskin whispered. "The most beautiful part of a woman is not her face, it's her breasts. Totally delightful."

He caressed both globes now, building her fires, making her shiver. He bent at last and kissed one glowing breast. She climaxed, pushing aginst him, then dropping backward on the blanket as her hips pounded forward and her whole body shivered and jolted and spasmed until he thought she was having a seizure. He lay partly on top of her and kept kissing and licking her breasts as she climaxed again and again.

He lifted away from her mounds and she gave one more tremor and sighed long and deeply.

"Oh, my god! That was so beautiful. I'd forgotten how thrilling, how satisfying it is." She pushed up and shucked out of her blouse. "There's only one thing that's better than climaxing that way."

She had been whispering. Now she leaned close to him. "The only thing better is to have you hard and stiff and pushed up inside my hole."

"Lots of time," Buckskin said.

She shook her head and reached for his crotch. Urgently, she opened the buttons on his pants, then unbuckled his belt and pulled his pants apart. She dug through the underwear until her hand closed around his rigid penis.

"Good Lord, I almost climaxed again when I touched you. It has been a long time, much too long."

Then she was taking down her own trousers, forgetting to pull her boots off first and swearing softly as she finally got off boots and pants. She was now sitting beside him with only soft cotton underpants on.

She caught his hand and pushed it between her legs. He caressed her inner thighs, working higher and higher. When she trembled, he moved down and worked up again. At last his finger brushed across her crotch and he felt a wet spot on the material. He touched it gently again and again, found the soft node and rubbed it through the cloth. She looked up at him in surprise, then rumbled into another climax that brought tears to her eyes. When the surge of emotion sped through her she sat up and kissed him.

"I didn't even know, that you knew . . . I mean, my husband of three years, never did . . . oh God, but that was fantastic!"

She pulled down the panties and then naked in the filtered moonlight, she took off his boots and pulled down his pants.

She kissed his flat belly over his short underwear and moved them down a half inch, then kissed again into the black hair that showed. Like a small girl unwrapping a present, she edged down his underwear until his little belly showed and more black hair.

As she worked his clothes down, he caught her hanging breasts and caressed them. She shuddered and nodded at him and then pulled his drawers down so his stiff penis popped up.

"Oh, Lord!" She said softly. She bent and kissed the shaft, then held it with both hands.

"Inside me, Buckskin Lee Morgan! I want that big pole jammed up my little cunnie right now! Only it's been two years, so I'm practically a virgin again."

He pushed her down on her back, spread her legs and lifted her knees. Then he knelt between her thighs. Gently he rubbed up them to the moist spot. He bent and applied saliva to his member and dropped down and probed gently.

She was ready. She accepted him with a pre-lubricated entryway and he plunged into her depths with no restrictions.

"Oh God!" Dutch cried out loud.

From somewhere in the dark they heard a laugh.

"Damn! Took the cowboy long enough," Maud's irreverent voice bellowed.

"He done her, now maybe I can get to sleep," Pris said.

Dutch grinned through tears of joy. "Told you they would be listening."

"Who cares?" Buckskin said. "Loving is more

fun than listening."

He pumped hard into her twice, then again, and the smile on her face turned into ecstasy as she closed her eyes and moaned each time he stroked.

"Feet up," she said, and at once lifted her legs over his back and twined them together around his torso. It put more pressure on him and he pumped harder.

"Oh God!" Dutch screeched. Then she let out a long, high yell of triumph and gloating as she climaxed again. Buckskin couldn't hold back a second longer and jolted into her a dozen times so hard he drove her up on the blanket. They both collapsed in each other's arms and didn't move for ten minutes.

"Beautiful!" Dutch whispered in his ear. "So wonderful, so marvelous. It brings back so many memories of good times in bed with my husband."

Bucksin could talk again. His mini death had been defeated and he grinned at her in the moonlight.

She kissed his nose. "I don't kow about you, but I figure that I can sleep while we're riding tomorrow. Tonight, I'm going to pump you all night, or until I wear you down to a limp worm. I'd say you're good for six or seven times."

"Been known to happen," he said. "The only problem is you have to stay awake to enjoy it."

"I'll stay awake. I may not sleep for three days. So much to remember and relive already. How about staying in town with me? You don't even have to marry me, just poke into me every two or three days. We could open a store! I've got plenty of money. It's all stashed away in a safe place . . . not in a bank. Last count I had a little over $16,000. We don't get much out of these small banks."

"How much today?"

"Nobody counted, but I'd guess maybe $4,000. We got every bill and every gold coin in the place."

"Times are hard all over," Buckskin said.

It was a short night. They never did finish the fifth try, went to sleep in each other's arms and woke cold and sore, but so extremely satisfied that they didn't notice anything else.

The other three were already at the campfire when Buckskin and Dutch came up. Coffee was ready, and they had bacon and flapjacks.

"You brought milk along to make hot cakes?" Buckskin asked.

"Damn right!" Maud said. "We're gonna eat good no matter where we are. Two eggs broke in a little jar for hotcakes, another jar for milk. Hell, no big deal. Speaking of big deals. . . ."

Dutch shot an angry glance at Maud who grinned.

"Hey, Dutch, I was just funnin' you. Bet you a one legged sailor it was worth it."

"Yes, it was worth it," Dutch said with a smile, and everyone laughed. It wasn't mentioned again.

After breakfast they rode. Pris had been on lookout, and when she came back to camp she said there was no sign of any posse out as far as she could see, about eight miles in the morning haze.

They rode northwest out of the foothills and down into an extension of the Great Divide Basin toward Rawlins.

Buckskin wasn't sure just what he would do when he got to the town. He had a job to go to, but he owed the women something, too. And Dutch Smith was not the kind of a woman that he would walk away from without regrets. He'd just have to see what happened and play it by ear.

He watched Dutch ride the roan beside him. What a fantastic woman—and a bank robber. It was the first time he had made love to a bank robber. This morning she didn't wear the leather jacket and her breasts surged forward struggling to get out of the white blouse but not quite making it.

Buckskin sighed. Yes, she was the kind of a woman he would have a lot of trouble just walking away from.

Five

Alonzo Warnick had shivered around his small fire for an hour after Buckskin Lee Morgan left him. For a while he was so angry that he couldn't think straight. Then he realized he was lucky to be alive. Morgan was tougher than he had imagined. He wouldn't make that mistake again.

He got up and used a sharp rock to rip up half of the blanket. He made himself a skirt that would cover him. He used folded pads of the blanket material for his feet and tied them on with long strips of the same blanket. Then he broke off low hanging branches to make a soft bed and pulled more of the branches of the pine trees over him as a blanket. He would sleep warm enough. He was glad it was not the middle of winter!

With morning he awoke cold, sore and stiff. He

had a long drink of water for breakfast since Morgan had taken all of his food and utensils. All he had was the blanket and his underwear. He used one strip of the blanket to make a covering for his head, tieing it under his chin so his balding head would not sunburn in the midday heat.

Warnick knew he must look strange, but he would survive. Now, all he had to do was walk 40 miles to town. Two days, if he didn't get lost. He started out strongly, stopped to retie his blanket pads on his feet. They would work well and protect him. All he had to do was walk.

Warnick took his direction from the rising sun, turned north and headed for the railroad tracks. He couldn't afford to get lost without any food or weapons. Hit the tracks, turn east and hope for a ride from somebody before he had to walk all the way to Laramie.

The second day he got a ride and a pair of pants from a cowboy heading to Laramie looking for work. Once in Laramie he went to the sheriff and explained his situation.

"Sorry, Warnick. I understand your problem, but even if this Lee Morgan is wanted, he's out of my county. We don't have money to set up bounty hunters. I will loan you a dollar for some food. Can't you send a collect telegram to somebody and get some money?"

"Not a chance. Isn't this Saturday?"

The sheriff agreed with Warnick that it was Saturday afternoon. Outside it was getting dark. Warnick stood near a saloon until a man came out weaving and barely able to stand up.

Warnick offered to help him walk home.

A half hour later the man was minus his boots, his shirt and a light jacket, as well as his purse which contained $12 cash money. Warnick had rolled him into an alley six blocks down where he would sleep off his drunk and awaken sometime tomorrow morning.

Warnick stepped into the Lonesome Lady Saloon and began playing poker. When the game was over just after midnight, Warnick had $180. He got a room at the hotel and pushed a chair under the door.

The next day he rested in his hotel room. No stores were open so he would lose a day.

Monday morning he bought a new shirt, a new pair of boots and a hat and caught the 8:12 train heading for Rawlins. There was a chance that Morgan could be there. That was the next town, and Warnick knew that he could identify that big black stallion if he found it.

The first thing Warnick did when he got to Rawlins was take a hotel room, have a long hot bath, then telegraph to his bank in Omaha a secret code built into the ten word limit. The charge for the telegram with six dollars. The code instructed the bank to withdrawn $300 from Warnick's account and send it in cash by registered mail to him at Rawlins, in care of General Delivery.

That done, he made a few discreet inquiries with bartenders in the first three saloons he came to. Two of them recommended the same man, the third a second man. He found the first man in a saloon down the street.

Scar Phillips was not an attractive man. He was large, well over six-feet tall, with arms that hung too long on his square body and hands that looked like dinner plates. The scar on his left cheek came from his eye down across his cheek and halfway down his neck. Most people wondered how the man could stay alive with a slash like that.

He only grunted when Warnick bought him a beer and said he wanted to talk. They sat at a table against the wall, and Scar's back was pressed there as well.

"My name is Alonzo Warnick and I want you to work for me. I'm not sure when I'll need you, but the price is two dollars a day and fifty dollars if you capture the man I want. Fair enough?"

"Want him alive or dead?" Scar asked. He didn't wait for an answer, tipped up the mug of beer and drained it without a breath, then looked at Warnick.

"Either way that works, but I'd prefer to have him alive, for a while at least."

What Scar called a smile slanted across his face. But with the scar tissue on his left cheek, only the right side of his face smiled.

"Do you know Lonnie Gunther?" Warnick asked.

Scar looked up, anger twisted his face. "Yeah, I know the dirty little son of a bitch. A mean bastard. Likes to use a knife."

"Can you work with him?"

"Hell, yes. We get along fine. What's the job?"

"I'll let you know soon as it starts. First I need to do some tracking."

He made arrangements to contact the big man through the bartender and went to find Lonnie Gunther. He was a small man, not over five-four. He took out a knife and cleaned his fingernails as they talked.

Lonnie wore a bill cap pulled low. His skin was pocked and his eyes wary. As soon as he knew it was a job, he relaxed and drank another beer.

"Can you work with Scar Phillips?"

Lonnie laughed, pulled at the beer. "Scar? Hell, why not. He's half ape and buffalo dumb, but you hire him, I can work with him. For the rough stuff and breaking people in half, he's handy to have around."

"You can use a six-gun as well as that knife?"

"Yep."

"I'll contact you here when I need you." They had already talked about payment.

His next step was the livery stable. The stableboy was on the simple side and didn't understand Warnick's question. He found the manager reading a book.

"Hell, I don't know if a big black stallion came in last couple of days. You got eyeballs, go take a look for yourself. Or I'll do it for you for a dollar."

Warnick went out into the barns and checked the stalls. He didn't find the big black stallion.

At the hotel, he looked down the register. Morgan's name wasn't there. He asked the room clerk, but she said she hadn't seen anybody like Morgan come in the last two or three days.

"Sweetie, a handsome chunk of man like you describe wouldn't slip past Wanda, I can guarantee that. He ain't in this fleabag hotel."

Outside he saw another small hotel, but had the same results.

Warnick was a man with a lot of patience. He had a big personal debt to pay back to Morgan before he killed him. There was a lot of satisfaction owed for taking his gun and pants and his boots. He'd find the big bastard and take him apart, kneecap by kneecap—and he'd laugh all the time.

Less than a quarter of a mile away on the west side of Rawlins, Buckskin Lee Morgan settled down in a rocking chair and stroked a short haired tabby cat.

"Nice place," Buckskin said. "Looks like you're careful not to spend too much money."

"You noticed," Dutch Smith said. "We planned out everything before we started. We don't aim to do any time or to decorate a hangman's party."

The blinds were drawn in the bedroom where they sat. On a small table lay the three bank bags they had taken from Rocky Center Bank.

"Time to count up," Dutch said.

The other three women were there. They pulled up chairs and opened the bags, separating the money by denominations of bills and the gold coins by size.

When it was separated, Maud counted the cash.

"Used to work in a bank once, years ago," she said. "Got the knack for cash."

She counted it out loud, the singles in stacks of fifty, the larger bills in hundred dollar lots, laying the stacks out crossing each other like a rail fence.

The total on the cash was $3,756.

"Not a bad couple of day's work," Maud said.

Pris nodded and licked her lips. Navaro sat and watched. Buckskin was sure that she couldn't follow the counting. Her black eyes took in everything and Buckskin knew she was relying on Dutch to be fair with her.

Dutch took out a book and entered the amount. Then Maud did some figuring with a pencil and piece of paper. She divided the figure by four and then proved it by multiplying the divided figure by four.

"Nine hundred and thirty-nine bucks per woman," Maud said. "Lordy, that's as much as I made in four years working at that bank in North Carolina."

Dutch passed the book around and let each woman write in the amount on the page with her account. Dutch spoke slowly with Navaro in Spanish. The girl nodded. Then Dutch multiplied the total dollar amount in the account book times six, which was the value of the dollar in pesos.

Navaro's eyes glowed when she saw the figure. "Si, si!" she said.

Dutch took out $30 and gave it to Navaro, then subtracted the amount from her account.

Pris motioned for Maud to count, and she measured out enough of the bills to equal $939. Pris put rubber bands around it and without a word to anyone hurried out the door.

Navaro came to the others and chattered something in Spanish that was too fast for Buckskin to catch, then she walked out the darkened back door.

"Yes, I'm the banker," Dutch said looking at Buckskin. "I don't kow what Pris does with her share, but she made it clear from the start she wanted her split every time. I knew that Navaro and her adopted family couldn't handle all that money. I suggested that she let me keep it for her. She trusts me. Maud here don't trust nobody."

"Like hell!" Maud flared before she saw the teasing in Dutch's face. "Yeah, well, these days a body's got to trust somebody."

"You want some cash?" Dutch asked Maud.

"Hell no, I got piles!" She roared at the double meaning of the word.

Buckskin still hadn't decided what to do next. He should report to Minderhausen, but he felt an unusual debt to the four women for protecting him back there in the wilds. They might have even saved his life.

"You've decided to go to Rock Springs?" Buckskin asked the women.

"Yes. We'll take the morning train when it pulls out of here at ten-fifteen. The others will be there. We get on separately, each with one small, cheap suitcase or sack which we will discard in Rock Springs."

"You still plan on riding back here?"

"We always do. It seems to throw them off the track since they assume we'll take the train."

"And you want me along on the hit on the bank?"

"Damn right!" Maud said.

"Yes, we'd like to have you with us," Dutch

said. "We voted. I have a rather special interest, of course."

Maud grinned. "Hell, woman, nothing wrong with wanting to get your pussy poked a few times more. We got to grab a good man when we get the chance."

Buckskin watched Dutch. She started to blush, then swung her fist at Maud and hit her in the shoulder. The action killed the blush but not the embarrassment.

"Hey, I call a spade a spade, always have. Embarrassed my man half to death time or two. Then when he figured I was gonna say something kind of strange, he'd reach down and grab my crotch and shut me up quick."

Buckskin and Dutch both laughed this time.

Dutch put her arm around Maud. "Now will you get your butt out of here. This is my bedroom as you may remember, and just looking at all of that money gets me to feeling just horny as hell."

"About time, he should be rested now." Maud turned and stared at Buckskin, then her glance went down to his crotch and stopped. "Christ, but I bet he's hung like a stud horse." She laughed and hurried out the door before Dutch could hit her.

Dutch closed the door and leaned against it. She looked at Buckskin and shrugged. "Did that bother you? Maud gets sort of bawdy sometimes. I've got to find her a man. But not you. I want you as long as you're here. Will you do me a small favor?"

Buckskin came up beside her and put his arms around her. "Pretty lady, you can ask me to do just about anything you want to and I'll oblige."

"Will you seduce me nice and gentle and slow, and not say a bad word, and let me think back to when I was sixteen and a nice boy next door and I got curious and started feeling of each other? It was four feeling sessions before we finally went all the way. Such a beautiful, innocent time. I'd just kind of like to remember that."

"Tell me about it as we go along," Buckskin said. He reached up and kissed her cheek, and she smiled.

"That's how it started. We lived next door and sometimes we'd play in the back yard. There was a little woods and he climbed a tree and put up a swing. I'd tell mother I was going out and swing and Jimmy, that was his name, would slip out and meet me in the woods."

"You tell me all about it and we'll try to re-enact the scene, bit by bit." Buckskin frowned. "But it's not going to take us four sessions."

"Good," Dutch said and leaned in and kissed his lips gently, her eyes bright.

Buckskin grinned. It was going to be an interesting afternoon.

Six

The four ladies of the shooting club boarded the westbound train as soon as it stopped at Rawlins the next morning a few minutes after ten o'clock. Buckskin Lee Morgan stayed in the station until just before the train was ready to go, then walked out and stepped on board just before the conductor picked up the small step.

Buckskin Lee Morgan went to the first coach and sat a seat behind Dutch. He didn't think he would have known her in her woman's dress if he hadn't watched her put it on that morning.

He saw Maud and knew her at once, but he hadn't picked out the other two yet. Clothes certainly made a difference.

He had changed to a clean shirt and a leather vest, polished his boots and brushed off his low crowned black hat.

There was no one in town who knew him, still he didn't want to take a chance of standing around for public inspection too long. Buckskin had been on dozens of train rides, but he was still thrilled by the grace and ease, the feeling of surging power when that steam engine a hundred feet away huffed and puffed and the whole string of cars moved at its command.

Besides the train was so fast! It would slam along daylight or dark at an average speed of about 35 miles in an hour. The 80 miles to Rock Springs would take them a little over two hours on the train, depending on how many stops they made along the way. The ride back on horses would take three days—if nobody was chasing them.

Buckskin wished he had talked Dutch into letting him sit with her on the trip. It would be a long two hours without anyone to talk to. At last he dozed and had a small nap. The seats were much better than a stage coach, the trip a lot quicker and smoother.

He awoke with a jolt as the train braked to come into some town.

"Rock Springs," the conductor called. "Rock Springs, Wyoming Territory. We'll be here for a meal stop. Twenty minutes and we don't wait for anyone. Twenty minute stop here at Rock Springs."

Buckskin sat up and looked at Dutch. She had turned to see if he was awake. She smiled, winked and then turned around and ignored him until they were off the train and walking down the street.

Maud went ahead and rented a room in the Shelton Hotel on the ground floor. Within the next hour, the other three women wandered into the room, changed clothes and came out dressed as men using the clothes they brought with them in their suitcases. They wore their hats pulled low to help in the disguise.

Buckskin rented the horses. He told the livery man he had some business men coming into town who wanted to see the Wild West and needed horses. He paid the rental fee for them from money Dutch had provided. He picked out the best looking horses available, put saddles on them and put them on a lead line and took them out to the edge of town.

Maud was already there. She mounted one horse and took two others back toward town to pick up Pris and Navaro. Buckskin took the last horse and spotted Dutch walking toward them. They all mounted and made sure of their timing.

"The bank closes at three o'clock," Dutch said. "We arrive singly at five minutes until three. Promptly at three o'clock the assistant manager should lock the front door. If he doesn't, I will. Then we go to work."

"There's an alley here with a back door to the bank," Maud said. "I'll have the horses there so we won't have to worry about the front door."

"Everyone have handkerchief masks?" Dutch asked. They all had them around their necks cowboy style. "Buck, I want you to do the talking. Your voice sounds better than ours. Make everyone inside the bank lay face down on the floor.

"Pris and I will clean out the tellers' cages and the vault. If there are only two or three customers and three or four bankers, we'll tie everyone and gag them before we leave. No gun play at all. Pris, do you hear me? No shooting."

"Yeah, right, right, unless we need to," Pris said, a scowl growing by the second.

"Easy, babe, easy," Dutch said. "It'll go just fine. No big problems, the way we like it. We'll be in and out and riding down the trail before they know what happened. If we get separated we move along the tracks east, just to the south of the tracks and out of sight."

Buckskin laughed dryly. "I really don't believe I'm doing this. I've never robbed anyone before."

"There was a first time for all of us. The law made you into an outlaw, this is just getting back at them a little. Remember, they can just hang you once."

Buckskin snorted. "It's that first hanging that I'm worried about."

"Hey, there's nothing to worry about," Dutch said frowning at them. "Five out of the seven banks we've done there was no gunfire, and we were in and out before the town knew we were there." She checked her pocket watch. "We have fifteen minutes. Let's split up and move into the target. You saw it when we got off the train. Middle of the block leading back to the alley. Let's go."

They split up but Buckskin trailed Dutch. She waited for him.

"You ain't getting religion on me, are you?" she asked.

"Not really. The law has battered me around more than once. One little bank isn't going to make any difference—long as we get away clean."

"We will. I know these small towns. They expect the best of everyone, and usually they're right. Now, we better split. Trail me aways."

Buckskin let her get ahead, then followed. She tied up in the alley and went around to the front of the building. They were the last ones at the alley hitch.

At the front of the bank Pris went in first, then Dutch. Buckskin followed her and then Maud and Navaro came in. They made motions like working on deposit slips or checks at the small counter at the side of the room. The clock in the bank struck three and the assistant manager went over and locked the door.

Buckskin pulled up his mask and walked up to the banker and eased the .45 out of its leather home. He pushed the weapon in the man's face and patted down the banker. He had no gun.

Buckskin pushed the bank man down on the floor. There were two men customers in the bank.

"Gentlemen, this is a stickup!" Buck bellowed. "You and you, lay on the floor now, face down. Tellers, down on the floor now!"

Navaro had pulled up her mask and taken out her revolver and covered the three men in front of the cages.

The rest of them had their masks up as soon as Buckskin shouted. Maud raced for the back door and made sure it opened to the alley. She propped it open with a chair.

In the teller area the women emptied the teller cages. Dutch was in the open vault stuffing paper money into a heavy bank bag. She came out and nodded. The women pulled rawhide strips from their pockets and tied the three tellers and the manager, then gagged them.

Navaro had tied up the three in front and gagged them.

Less than four minutes after they entered the bank, the five of them walked out the back door with the money and let the door close and lock.

They left the alley by twos, separating by a block as they walked their mounts to the east, heading for the tracks. Just outside of town they came together and rode hard for a quarter of a mile into the open valley away from the tracks southeast.

Navaro let out a Spanish yell, and Pris fired two shots in the air, then they settled down and rode steadily eastward.

"Like taking candy from a baby," Maud said, grinning and showing where she had two teeth missing.

"Easier," Buckskin said. "A baby always yells and screams and cries when you grab his candy."

They rode steadily for an hour. Pris angled up to a small rise and looked around, then came back.

"Nobody following us, not that I can see. Looks like we fooled them bastards again."

"Looks that way, Pris," Dutch said. "You all did your jobs exactly right."

"Easier when we have a good man's voice to

yell at the people," Maud said. "Maybe we can sign Buckskin up permanent with our bunch."

"Afraid not," Buckskin said. "This kind of work is too hard on the nerves."

Dutch lifted the gait into a trot and they moved out a little faster. She came up beside Buckskin.

"I figure two ten-hour days and we'll be back in Rawlins."

"That means we ride until one o'clock tonight," Buckskin said. "Doubt if the troops will take kindly to that. Seven hours today is about all we're going to make."

"I guess there's no big rush. Nobody will miss us back in town. We'll take another day."

"Good, we can stop when it gets dark, about eight," Maud said who had been listening. "Can't expect me to cook in the dark. Better make that about seven."

They stopped just a little after six because they found a good stream coming down from the far foothills. There were enough trees and brush to hide them and mingle their campfire smoke through the trees.

Maud had a pot of stew heating up ten minutes after they stopped and Buckskin wondered when she had cooked it. Evidently she cooked it in Rawlins and brought it on the train in a jar.

Pris ate her supper without saying a word. She sat by herself and two or three times Buckskin found she was looking at him.

"Pris is in one of her moods again, Buck," Dutch whispered to him. "Take it easy around her. She'll come out of it before long."

As Dutch said it they heard a weapon cock and

almost at the same time a revolver fired a round into the ground six-inches from Buckskin's boot.

"Buckskin has really fooled the rest of you. Especially you, Dutch. I know this bastard for what he is. He's going to turn us in. Going to get us all hung just because that one stupid bank guard pulled his gun and I had to shoot him.

"That's what he wants to do, but I won't let him. I'm going to kill him. But I'll do it slow, the way the Cheyenne do. I want to roast him head-first over a fire, but he's too heavy to string up that way. Kneecaps first, I think. Then the bastard can't run away. Yeah, kneecaps first!"

Dutch looked at Pris and frowned. "Pris, I don't understand all of this. I thought Buckskin Lee Morgan just helped us rob the Rock Springs Bank."

"Well, of course he did. Now he's going to shoot all of us and take the money. I figured him out quick first time I saw him. Then last night he pumped you, Dutch to get on your good side. He's clever. I've seen his kind before. Got me one in Fort Worth one night. Oh, I made him confess before I shot the bastard. He admitted to everything I told him he did."

Buckskin eased to his feet.

"Hold it! Don't move again, bastard. I know your tricks. Just stand still right there by the fire."

"Pris, glad you came over," Maud shrilled. "I was about ready to count the money. Wonder what your share will be?"

"Count? We count when we get back home."

"Usually we do that. Are you telling me I can't

count it now?"

"No, Maud, no, course not."

"Good gather round then, and we'll count."

"Just as soon as I shoot this bastard man here. We don't need him."

Maud looked at Buckskin, nodded slightly.

"Look, Pris. I figure this is more important. Here, you hold this bag of paper money. I'll get the other one." Maud tossed the money bag at Pris who grabbed it. She looked away from Buckskin to catch the bag.

Buckskin moved at the same time, slammed his hand down across her wrist and the weapon fired into the ground near the fire as it fell from her hand. Pris wailed in real pain as she looked down at the gun, then back up at Buckskin Lee Morgan.

Slowly she moved the few feet toward him. She grabbed him and reached up and kissed him. Then she stepped back.

"Why did you do it, Morgan? Why did you pick her and not me? I'm a person, too. I've got feelings." She unbuttoned her shirt and tore it off, then pulled off the blouse she wore underneath, exposing her breasts.

"Right now, right here, you have to poke me! Come on. Right now, Buckskin! If you don't, I'll wait my chance and put a bullet through your brains. I'm not bluffing. I mean it!" The last was shrilled into a scream.

Dutch caught Morgan's attention and nodded.

Morgan unstrapped his gunbelt and lay down the weapon. He took off his hat and walked toward her.

"First we'll have to get rid of some of those clothes, and find a blanket."

Pris darted to one side, caught up her own blanket and spread it on the grass near the fire. Then she sat down and began taking off her boots. Navaro moved away toward the trees.

"No, goddamnit! Dutch, make her stay. I want you all to stay. I'm not strange. I do like men. It's just that most of them are such bastards!"

Pris had stripped off her boots, then she unfastened the pants and pulled them off, taking with them her underdrawers. She sat on the blanket, naked in the twilight. She motioned to Buckskin.

"You can't get any nookie way up there, Buckskin Lee Morgan. Sit down here and let me take your pants off."

He sat beside her and touched her breasts. At first she pulled back, then she smiled.

"Yes, yes, do that. It feels good, it really does."

It was a first time for Buckskin Lee Morgan. Never before had he made love to a woman while three others watched. He wasn't sure he could.

Pris pulled down his pants and shorts and yelped in delight when she saw Morgan's erection.

"Oh, my, yes," Pris said in a little girl voice. "I remember the big whangers like that. They hurt me then, but this one won't hurt me. Do it now, Morgan!"

The other women tried to look away, but Pris caught them.

"Watch us!" she snapped. "I want you all to know that he poked me, too!"

He tried to warm her up, to get some honest desire from her, but there didn't seem to be any there.

"Right now, Morgan, spit on me and push it in."

He did. Pris had no reaction whatsoever. He stroked half a dozen times, pretending to have a climax, and came away from her.

She sat up and looked at him. "Damn, but you were a fast one. Cost you two dollars." She wailed with laughter. "I'm just fooling you, making a joke." She put her clothes back on slowly, then looked at the other women.

"See, I can do it, too. Just like you. So don't laugh at me. I can do anything you can do. But you can't do what I do. None of you little girls ever killed a man. Just remember that."

Pris stood up, carried her pants and her boots and blanket and walked off into the woods. She came back a minute later without her shoes or pants.

"Good night everyone," she said and even Buckskin could tell the change in her voice. She was like the old Pris he had heard and talked with before.

That night, Buckskin didn't sleep with Dutch. He took his blanket and walked a quarter of a mile upstream and bedded down in a thick brushy spot. He slept with his six-gun in his hand. If anyone came within 50 yards he would be awake instantly.

Seven

Hartley J. Minderhausen scowled at his secretary. "No damn word from this Buckskin Morgan yet? Where in hell is the man? He was supposed to be here three days ago."

"No messages from him, Mr. Minderhausen."

"The train gets in about nine o'clock. Get down there and check it, see if you can find anybody who looks like he does. Ask around."

"Yes, sir. And Karl is still waiting to see you."

"Send him in. At least that's something I have some control over."

Karl, one of the master brewers he had brought over from Germany, came in with his hat in his hand. Karl spoke only German and for the next two hours Karl and Minderhausen worked out a delicate problem in the brewing process that was a little awry. It was a subject well known to Minderhausen, and it gave him a great deal of satisfaction to be able to solve it.

Then he settled behind his desk and checked a folder. The detectives looking for Herta had found nothing. They had searched both east and west along the tracks and could report finding no traces of his daughter or anyone who knew anything about her. Herta was a striking girl, she would be noticed if she were traveling of her own accord. But if someone had disguised her, forced her into a carriage say. . . .

He shook his head and tried not to think about it. He had such plans! Such a future all planned out for his daughter. This was America, the land of opportunity. Where an immigrant German brewmaster could become the owner of his own brewery! When Herta was twenty he would find a good German boy who liked Herta and would agree to the marriage. He'd find a boy who wanted to learn the brewery trade, and who was smart and respectful. Someday the boy would take over the business and his daughter would be well provided for, as would his grandsons and granddaughters.

But now, no Herta. No dreams.

"Got Dammit!" he said shaking his head. There had been no sign of the Morgan man on the morning train. Now it was noontime, and as he had been doing lately, Minderhausen went up to his big house for his dinner.

Serilda would fix him a good German meal. She was an excellent cook and always surprised him. Today was no exception. Sauerbraten and a delightful salad. He ate his fill and motioned for

Serilda to come around the table. She knelt in front of him and he bent and kissed her, then fondled her breasts.

"We have time to create a son," she told him in German. Her hands moved to his crotch and rubbed and soon he was sitting on the floor beside her pulling at her dress.

Serilda smiled as she took off her clothes and looked up at him from where she lay on the polished hardwood floor.

"Yes, my darling, yes. Make me the mother of your son!"

Minderhausen tried as hard as he could.

When he got back to the office an hour later, Hans caught his attention and nodded toward a man who sat on the hard bench in the outer office.

"Mr. Morgan has arrived, Mr. Minderhausen."

The brewer went straight to Morgan who stood.

"Morgan, you're late. Come into my office, you have a lot of work to do."

Buckskin Lee Morgan grinned and followed the man. No introductions, no 'hello', no 'nice to meet you', just 'you have a lot of work to do.'

Buckskin was impressed by the brewer's office. It was twenty feet square with trophy heads on the walls of elk, moose and deer as well as a mountain goat. Expensive dark wood paneling on all four sides gave the room a dark look, but decorative lamps burning now in midday added light. Heavy drapes closed off half the windows across the front.

The man's desk was twice as big as most

Buckskin had seen with a rich curly maple top that had been polished and varnished to a high glossy sheen.

Minderhausen sat in his big leather chair and stared up at Buckskin.

"Sit, sit. You are three days late."

"I got involved with some problems on the way here, but I'm ready to go to work now."

"Goot! My daughter has been kidnapped. I want you to find her. She is eighteen years old and vanished almost two weeks ago now. I've had detectives out scouring the towns along the rail line both ways, but no one has seen her."

"Have you been sent a ransom note demanding payment for her?" Buckskin asked.

"No. That's part of what worries me. I expected a demand long before this."

"Sometimes a kidnapper will wait to build up the worry and sense of loss."

"Wait two weeks? I am going out of my mind. You must find her and bring her back."

"Picture?"

Minderhausen handed him a photograph of the girl, the one from his desk that an artist had colored with oil. Buckskin saw a beautiful blonde girl with a slender figure and a wonderful smile. Why had there been no ransom note?

He listened while Minderhausen told him what he had done to find her, where his detectives had looked, and the total lack of reports.

"These men have found no one who has even seen my Herta. A pretty girl like her would be noticed. That and no ransom note. I am fearful what has happened to her. You must find her."

"The local law?"

"They have done nothing. It's almost certain she isn't here in town. No one could hide my Herta here for two weeks without someone seeing her."

"Agreed. Could I look at her room in your home?"

"No, that's private, personal."

"You can come with me. I might find something that would give us a clue where she is. Did you search her room completely?"

"Of course not, that's private."

"It's also your home and could give us some leads. I'm going to insist that we look through the room."

Minderhausen scowled. "You sure it's needed that we do this thing?"

"Absolutely. Otherwise I'm on the next train and am going back to Denver."

"Very well. We go now to my house. Do not get so excited. We must find Herta. I will pay you five thousand dollars when you bring her safe back to me."

A short time later, in the big house on the small rise, Buckskin looked over Herta's bedroom. It was well furnished, with fancy pillows and a four poster bed with hand quilted bedspread and ruffles around the top to match.

Everywhere he looked he saw the result of the beer money making life easy and pleasant. Who would kidnap her? Why had there been no ransom note?

He sat down at a small dressing table and looked at the things on top.

"Nothing has been moved or changed since she left," Minderhausen said.

He stood stiffly in the door, showing that he thought this was not a polite thing to do. Buckskin ignored him. He hoped to find something in writing, a diary, some sheets of paper, a note perhaps that would give him some clue about what happened to the girl.

The more he saw of the situation, the more it seemed as if the girl might have left of her own free will. But why would she drop out of the lap of wealth to go out on her own? He wouldn't even mention the idea to Minderhausen. Bringing it up now would not help him find the girl.

He searched the small study desk across the room. Buckskin was surprised to find books on philosophy and French on the desk. There were papers, two pencils, a pad of paper. Nowhere did he find a diary or any letters. Two small drawers revealed only a few pencils and sheets of paper, but nothing to help.

"You want to look through her closet and her intimate clothes as well?" Minderhausen asked with a frown.

Buckskin shook his head and went out the door.

"You were getting along well with the girl?"

"Of course. She was my daughter, a good German girl. She did what her papa told her."

"She was happy, contented living here?"

"Yes. I told you twice. Yes. Now go find her and stop asking me stupid questions."

"One more thing. Mr. Minderhausen, I don't want you to use my name. I can work better if no one even knows I'm in town. Keep my name out of it, and I'll do the best I can to find Herta. I also need a two hundred dollar advance for expenses."

"Two hundred? That's more than my brewery workers make in six months."

"Your brewery workers are not hunting kidnappers or facing their guns."

"Yes. Dot is true. You get it."

A half hour later, Buckskin talked with the clerk at the Carbon County courthouse. He checked the list of marriage license applications. Over the past two months there had been no license issued to a Herta Minderhausen.

Maybe she had been kidnapped. But perhaps Minderhausen wasn't telling all he knew about how his daughter felt just before she disappeared.

Buckskin walked down the street searching for some kind of a lead. Minderhausen had sent detectives each way along the railroad. It was the logical move. But Morgn knew he couldn't find out anything the others hadn't.

Right here, he thought. There had to be an answer right here in town. Who else could he talk to about the girl? Did she have a best friend? He could ask the woman he saw at the house. What was she, an employee? Housekeeper? Cook? He'd find out.

Five minutes later he rang the bell at the front door of the brewer's big house. The panel opened and the same woman he saw before looked up.

"Yes? Oh, you're the detective. You were just here."

"Right. I'm trying to find out what happened to Herta. Could I talk to you a moment?"

"Yes. But don't tell Mr. Minderhausen. He's so strict."

"I won't say a word. May I come in?"

She showed him to the parlor and they sat down.

"You knew Herta, I would think?"

"Yes, we were . . . friends."

"Good. What I'm wondering is did she tell you anything about her plans recently?"

"We talked before she left. She confided in me sometimes."

"Did she have a man friend, a sweetheart?"

"Oh, yes. But how did you know? No one knew, not even her father."

Buckskin frowned. "How could that happen?"

"Her young man came when her father was at work. He worked a lot. The romance got quite serious."

"And her father doesn't know?"

"Oh, no. He never would have approved. The young man is a clerk in the general store. He is not rich like Mr. Minderhausen is."

"And you didn't tell her father?"

"Oh, no. Herta made me promise. And she gave me money, too, not to tell."

"So Herta and her man eloped? They ran off on the train somewhere and got married?"

"Yes. That was their plan. She took her jewelry and all the cash money she had."

"Where did they go?"

"She wouldn't tell me. I helped her fix a dark

wig and some spectacles to disguise herself. They took the train."

"What time of day did she go to the depot?"

"The morning."

"So they must have gone west. What's the young man's name?"

"I won't get into any trouble?"

"I won't even tell Mr. Minderhausen I talked to you. What's his name?"

"Joseph Radowitz. He works at the Wyoming General Store."

"Thanks. Anything else I need to know about this romance? Did she say if they would come back after they married?"

"She wanted to, but I think she'll be too afraid for a while, maybe a year."

"You're sure you don't know where they went?"

"No, I'm sorry."

He watched her large brown eyes and dark hair and decided that she was telling the truth. Buckskin thanked her and headed downtown to the general store.

A few minutes later he talked to the man who owned the store, Carlos Radowitz.

"I was looking for Joseph, is he around?" Buckskin asked.

"No, no. He is not here."

The middleaged man, with a pencil behind his ear and spectacles resting on his nose, looked over the glasses and shook his head.

"Joey didn't even say where he was going. He tells me he's grown up now, he's twenty-one years old, he says. He has to learn to stand on his own two feet. Two weeks ago he comes and says he's got to go away for a while, to do some thinking. I tell him to go fishing, don't use bait and he'll have all day to think.

"He says no, he's got to do some real thinking. Says he'll be home in a few weeks, and borrows two hundred dollars from me. I let him go. Then last week I got a telegram. Six dollars for a telegram when he could send a letter for two cents. On the train mail gets places so fast these days."

"Yes sir, the train certainly is a great development out here in the West. Oh, where did you get the wire from, a long way off?"

"Kids are strange these days. The telegram came from Rocky Center, about sixty miles west of here on the railroad."

"Strange. Yes, you're right. A letter would have arrived in about the same time."

"Children just don't have any concept of thrift or the value of a dollar. I'll never understand them."

"It's hard. Thanks, Mr. Radowitz. I'll try to see Joseph after he gets back."

Buckskin walked out the front door grinning. He was making progress. No wonder there hadn't been any ransom note. There hadn't been any kidnapping. The kids were probably trying to figure out how to go home and announce that they were married. Buckskin had an idea neither of the fathers would be overjoyed about such a marriage.

No matter, it was a job, and while not exactly gun work, the pay was good. Buckskin headed back toward the small white house at the edge of town where two prim widow ladies lived. He could slip up the alley and preserve their reputations.

He wouldn't be there long. Just until tomorrow morning when he'd catch the westbound train heading for Rocky Center.

Eight

Herta Minderhausen sat in a shabby room at the Granger Hotel in Rocky Center and cried. She had never felt so alone, so miserable, so . . . so . . . so . . . she didn't know what. Joey had even quarreled with her today. She had wanted to buy a scarf she saw in a store window but he had taken her hand and pulled her past the window.

"You know we agreed not to spend money on anything except food until we decide what to do. We don't want to run out of cash. I absolutely won't let you sell your jewelry."

He had walked her back to the hotel, kissed her and put her in her room. She had wanted, and expected, that they would be married the first night they arrived, but he said it wasn't quite that simple.

"I'm Jewish," he told her. "We never talked about it but I thought you knew by my name."

"What's Jewish?" she had asked. He explained to her about the Jewish religion, the Hebrew language and culture.

"We have to be married by a rabbi, but there isn't one way out here."

"We can be married by a preacher and then later get married by a rabbi," Herta had wailed. "I just want to be married! I want to be your wife right now."

"It won't hurt us to wait a few more days. I still have a lot of work to do to figure out what I'm going to say to my father and to your father. He'll probably have me arrested if we *aren't* married, so we will be somehow. We've got this far, now is the time to think things through."

"I don't care about all of that. I just want to get married."

"I know and we will, soon. First, I need to send a telegram to my former rabbi in Chicago. He'll make some good suggestions what we should do."

"He won't. You're making this all up so you won't have to marry me." Herta screeched the words, then looked away and pouted. It had always worked at home.

He didn't touch her.

She looked at him. "You're doing this to me, after I let you . . . touch me last night. Now you don't respect me any more."

"I do, I do. I just want to do everything right, for both of us. My father isn't going to be overjoyed you know, when I marry out of my faith."

They had quarreled about it for two hours last night and again after breakfast in his room. At least the rooms were side by side. After they quarreled they made up slowly and then kissed several times and he had reached in and touched her breasts. That quickly led to them both starting to breathing hard, so she had jumped up and rushed out the door and back to her room.

One of her friends in Rawlins had become pregnant before she was married. Herta heard that you had to "do it" three times in three days to get pregnant, but she wasn't going to take any chances. She would keep her skirt on and her knees primly together until she got that marriage certificate right there in her hand.

Herta cried again. She looked out the window and saw Joey running across the street. He had a sheet of paper in his hand. Perhaps his preacher . . . no, his rabbi in Chicago . . . had told him to go ahead and be married by a Lutheran Preacher. She hoped so! Oh, god she hoped so.

Joey was grim faced when he came into her room a few moments later.

"He didn't understand! Nobody but us understands. How can everyone be so stupid."

Joey stopped and looked at her. He sat on the bed beside Herta and kissed her sweet lips. She smiled and kissed him back.

"This rabbi man in Chicago, he said not to marry me?" Herta asked, her voice small and faint.

"He's an old man with six children, what does he know? He's in Chicago where there are lots of

Jews. What can he understand? Is there a preacher in town? Let's get married today, just as soon as we can, right now!"

"Do we still have the marriage license?"

"Yes, we rode on the train to Rock Springs, county seat of Sweetwater county, and got it last week, remember?"

"Yes! I'll see if there's a Lutheran church in town. I'd prefer to be married by a Lutheran." She looked at him. "We'll really be married now right here. Then later on we can be married in your church, too."

"Synagogue."

"Yes, right." Herta jumped up and started for the door. "Oh, dear! We can't get married today!"

"Why not?"

"I don't even have a wedding dress."

"You can wear that white one you wore two days ago."

"Oh, I couldn't do that. I have to have a proper wedding dress and all the rest of. . . ."

"Herta, I'm marrying *you*, not some white dress." He kissed her and pulled her toward the door. "First we'll find out if they have your church here, then we'll decide."

They were married that afternoon in the Rocky Center Community Church. It had financial support by the Methodists and Congregationalists, and now had a Baptist minister. The wedding went smoothly and at five minutes to five, the Rev. Dale B. Parmley signed their wedding certificate, pocketed his two dollars and had his wife and eldest daughter sign as the two witnesses.

Herta cried as they walked back to the hotel. They both had registered under assumed names when they arrived so their fathers couldn't find them. Now Herta tried to wipe her eyes.

"Do you always cry at weddings?" Joey asked.

"Only my own. I always thought I'd have a big church wedding with six or eight bridesmaids, and lots of flowers, and the organ playing, and hundreds of my closest friends there."

"Your one closest friend was there, your husband, according to the power granted by the Territory of Wyoming and the Rocky Center Community Church."

He paused at her door, then opened it and turned. He picked her up and carried her over the threshold. "Not much, but it's our first home, even for a few days." He gently stood her on her feet and looked at the door. "I'll be right back."

He scurried next door, opened his room, grabbed up his clothes and suitcase and hurriedly returned to her room.

"Now this is *our* room, Mrs. Radowitz. We're man and wife, legally married, and I still can't believe it!"

Herta looked at Joey and a smile broke out over her face. "Yes, yes! We are married. And for right now we're going to forget all about churches and rabbis and especially what our fathers want us to do."

She held out her arms. "Hello, husband of mine."

"Hello Mrs. Joseph Radowitz . . . my wife."

He stepped to her and her arms went around

him and they kissed gently. Then he kissed her again and they eased down to the bed, clinging to each other.

He rolled halfway on top of her, making sure he wasn't too heavy and kissed her waiting lips. It was a long kiss. At last he came away and his eyes sparkled.

"Mrs. Radowitz, this is going to work out just fine."

"Mr. Radowitz, I think it's going to be wonderful. Isn't it about time we started taking off some clothes? I want to do it, Joey. I've waited for so long. I never have. I wanted you to be the very first."

"Yes, yes!"

He sat up and adjusted the hardness at his crotch, then tenderly reached out and brushed her breasts with his hand.

She looked at him quickly, then smiled. "Yes, Joey. Please."

His hand covered one of her breasts and rubbed it with soft strokes. Then he unbuttoned the fasteners and pushed the cloth back. He lifted her chemise and put his hand under it on her bare breast.

"Oh, Joey! That feels so . . . so wonderful."

She pushed in and kissed him. His hand stayed between them, caressing her flesh. Herta whimpered softly, then took a deep breath as their lips parted. She let her blouse fall off her shoulders and lifted her chemise up and over her head.

Joey stared at her bare breasts. They were larger than he had imagined, with broad pink areolas and small pink nipples. He petted them with both his hands, then bent and kissed one. Herta's eyes went wide and she fell back on the bed shaking and vibrating, her hips pushing up a half dozen times as she gasped for breath. Slowly the trembling eased off and Herta gave a long sigh.

Her eyes came open wide. "Oh, Joey! I . . . I've never felt anything like that before. Marvelous, absolutely indescribable. Can I do that again sometime?"

Joey smiled. He'd been with two or three girls and now he was sure that Herta had never been with a man.

"I can help you do that just anytime you want to."

He caught her hands and lifted her until she was sitting beside him. He bent and kissed her breasts again, working around each globe and then up to her nipples where he licked them and bit them tenderly. Herta clung to him as she climaxed again, harder this time, longer, as her whole body surged in sexual response.

Tears seaped from her eyes and rolled down her cheeks. She brushed at them when she quieted and stared at him.

"Oh, Joey, so . . . so fine."

He took her hand and put it over his pants where his hardness was straining to break free.

She looked at him quickly. "Is that your. . . ."

He nodded. Slowly he unbuttoned his pants, pushed them down and let his erection come out of his short underwear.

"Oh . . . oh . . . oh my!" Herta said softly. She looked up at him. "So big."

"Don't worry, everything will be fine. Wait, you'll see." He slipped out of his pants, then his tie and his jacket and shirt and stood in front of her naked.

"My so . . . so beautiful. A man is really beautiful, so strong, so muscled."

He lifted her to her feet and helped her slip down her skirt and two petticoats. She stopped his hand when it reached for the new kind of silk panties she wore. Instead, she slid on the bed and patted the place beside her.

"We have lots of time, right?"

He sat beside her and caressed her breasts. "Yes, wife of mine. We have all afternoon and all night. Then we have all tomorrow and another week."

She smiled. "It won't take me that long. But for years and years I've been told not to do this and now suddenly, after a few words by a stranger, it's all right. This takes me a little time to get used to. But I do love you and I want to be with you always and always, forever and forever. In a few minutes we'll do everything I've always heard about."

It was nearly an hour later before Joey at last got her panties off. Then he slowly seduced her, inch by inch, as he kissed and petted her and worked his hand down her torso.

Then, when he thought he could stand the waiting no longer, she smiled and pulled him on top of her.

"Yes, Joey, now, I want that big thing deep inside me the way it's supposed to be. Please, Joey, make love to me right now!"

Once he got Herta started she didn't want to stop. He had to make her wait a half hour between times, and then after six lovemakings, he begged off and said they should go get something to eat. They had missed dinner and supper.

"Has it been that long?"

She lay on the mussed bed glowing from the last long climax she had experienced when he shot deep inside her.

"Well, why don't you go get us some sandwiches or something from the dining room and come back up here? Bring a bottle of wine, too. This is our wedding day!"

He dressed and was back quickly with two full roast beef dinners from the hotel's kitchen, and a bottle of wine.

"Hello Mrs. Radowitz."

"Hello husband of mine, Mr. Joseph Radowitz. That makes me Mrs. Joseph Radowitz and Daddy or anyone else is not going to change that."

It was the first time since they had made love that either of them had mentioned the tough road that lay ahead for them.

"Forget that. We won't worry about anything tonight. Tomorrow will be plenty of time to worry. Now, let's have our wedding dinner, and lots of wine, and then go back to bed and figure out a new position to make love in."

She looked up quickly. "You mean there are other ways?"

Joey grinned. "I once saw a sheet of paper that

showed thirty-one difference positions for making love."

Herta blushed and the redness came down all the way from her face and neck to her bare breasts.

"Goodness, I can't imagine." She lifted her brows. "Joseph Radowitz, you are teasing me. I think we better have our dinner so you can rest up."

"Are you going to eat that way, all naked and sexy?"

"Absolutely, and I want you to take off those silly clothes of yours."

He did. It was a perfect wedding day and wedding night. Neither one of them would have changed a thing. They would remember that day forever.

Nine

When Buckskin Lee Morgan got back to Dutch Smith's small house that afternoon, he found Dutch wearing a prim calico dress that fit tightly around wrists, neck and swept the floor.

"I know, unusual to find me dressed this way, but I had to go do some shopping. Interesting what we can buy now that the railroad's here. Fresh fruit, lots of canned goods, all sorts of good things to eat. Even some fresh fish packed in ice all the way from Chicago!"

Morgan caught one of her breasts with his hand. "Speaking of good things to eat . . ."

She laughed. "I don't think you ever get enough, do you, Buck? Later for that. It's my turn to cook supper. Maud is out shopping for some pieces of fabric for a quilt she's making."

"A quilt?"

"Right. Maud's second passion is quilting. She's had a rough life. I intend to help her be able to live in luxury for the rest of it."

"You've made a good start. How much does each of you have in your private bank?"

"A little over $16,000 apiece. Then I keep Navaro's money, too. But I do have another problem." She looked away. "Hell, I don't know how to say this. Don't really want to say it, but it's got to be said." She stared at her hands for a minute, then looked up.

"Truth is, Maud is getting just horny as hell. She's been a widow for two years now and ain't had herself a man in all that time. She's a woman who needs to get a man every once in a while. Hell, Buck, you're the best man we've seen in years around here. Maud and I share most everything . . ."

Buckskin grinned. "And so you want me to flip Maud on her back and poke her."

Dutch laughed. "Yeah, that's the idea, you mad at me for suggesting it?"

"Hell, no. But not tonight. I'm going to work on the morning train and I want one more good session with you in a real bed before I leave. When I get back I'll do Maud for you. Hell, Navaro too if you say so." Buckskin chuckled. "I've never been the gang stud to a bunch of women bandits before."

"Navaro doesn't need it, Maud does. How long you gonna be gone?"

Buck watched her, trying to match this sleek, pretty woman with long brown hair and flashing brown eyes with the rough, hard riding bank robber he'd first met.

"Gone? Might take a few days. You planning another bank for a while?"

"Not for a week or so. Casper is next on the list. We can get a stage from here to there. Then rent the horses in case we need them and double back into town and change clothes and ride the stage back."

"Sounds safe enough. Just so you get out of the bank without any shooting."

"Always plan to." She watched him. "Sure you're not mad about Maud?"

He caught her and led her to the sofa. They sat down and he bent and kissed her breasts through the thin fabric.

"No, I'm not mad." He sat up and put his arm around her and pulled her against him. She snuggled on his shoulder and sighed.

"But I do want you to tell me more about Maud. She's what, about 40, thick set and has a foul mouth. That's all I know about her."

"This part is easy. Maud picked up her language from her husband. He was a mule skinner for years, then the railroad came and he was out of a job. They were poor for a year before he and my man worked out the idea of hitting banks for pleasure and profit.

"Before that, Maud was just a wife. They never had any kids. Then the bank foreclosed on their little house and that set her husband Bull off on his drinking. He didn't have any money for whiskey so he caged drinks, begged for money, even finished up beers men left in saloons.

"Every time she'd go and drag him out of a

saloon he'd swear at her and she learned to give it right back to him as foul as he did.

"For three months our men did fine. Got a few banks, started to have a reputation. We were in Cheyenne then and they worked mostly down into Colorado. Then one day they tried their last robbery and both of them got killed.

"So that's our Maud. She's a good woman who's had a life full off shit and deserves better."

Dutch leaned over and kissed Buckskin hotly. "Sure you don't want to poke Maud tonight? Right about now she'd cut off a tit to get you in her bed."

"Maud sounds like a project. No time tonight because I plan on giving you a going away present—or two or three. So there won't be time for Maud. But when I come back, she's going to be my main concern."

"If we're here. If Maud and I haven't had our heads blown off by a bank shotgun guard."

Buck brought his hand up under her long skirt and eased it between her already parted legs.

"Then maybe we should make sure about you right now, before Maud gets home. You want to make love here, on the floor or the kitchen table?"

Dutch laughed. "In bed, I like to make love in bed best of all. You think you can get it up this early in the afternoon?"

"You begging for a mouth job?"

"I've been known to accommodate that way."

Buckskin grinned. "Shit on a shingle, let's give it a try."

They did and it worked.

* * *

When Buckskin stepped off the Union Pacific passenger car at Rocky Center the next morning about ten o'clock, he was surprised how small the town was. He'd never been here before that he could remember.

It looked a lot like other small western towns, with one main street and a few side streets and the houses stacked up in back of that. He had no baggage and watched other people getting off. Some were straight from Europe, he was certain. They would have a lot of adjustments to make in this wild country.

Now that he could check out the town better, it was evident that it had not been one of the railroad construction towns as most along the rails had been. It must have had a reason for cropping up at this place, but from a first look he had no idea what it was.

This was not the county seat, so he couldn't check for marriage licenses. Instead he would work the hotels. He looked down the street and found only one hotel, the Granger.

Five minutes with the desk clerk, and a crisp new dollar bill, and Buckskin knew that the couple had taken adjoining rooms but that now they were both in one room.

"I heard they got married yesterday afternoon," the clerk said. He was a slender man with an overbite and a nose that seemed to run all the time.

"I do know we served them supper in their room with a bottle of wine."

Buckskin headed for the steps to the second

floor. Rooms 204 and 205. They must be in one of them. He grinned. Being newlyweds they were probably still in bed.

He knocked on room 204 and received no answer. When he knocked on 205 there was an immediate response. He heard movement, then someone came to the door. The sound came through the wood.

"Yes? What do you want?"

"Message for room 205," Buckskin said. He could hear whispers beyond the door, then it opened a crack. Buckskin pushed it fully open and saw a woman on the bed pull a sheet up around her. The man had on only a pair of pants.

Buckskin grinned. "Sorry to break in folks, but your parents are worried about you. Especially your father, Herta. Oh, congratulations on your marriage."

"Who are you?" Joey asked trying to be stern.

"Name don't matter. Mr. Minderhausen asked me to find his daughter. He thinks you've been kidnapped, Herta. You better get a telegram off to him this morning assuring him that you are not kidnapped and safe and well. It's the decent thing to do."

Herta sighed. "Yes, you're right. I'll ask my husband what he thinks."

Joey nodded. "That's right, we're married, and our parents can't do a thing about it."

"Don't you think you should go back to Rawlins and talk to them about it like adults?"

Joey lifted his brows. "Yes, probably. But Herta's father is not exactly easy to get along with."

"That's undoubtedly an understatement."

"And Joey's father won't even think we're married because we didn't go to a rabbi."

"Only because there isn't one here, and maybe not in the whole Territory."

"You'll find several rabbis in Denver if that would be any help," Buckskin said.

"Yes, yes." Joey said. "Thank you. We'll have to go there just as soon as we can."

"Tomorrow we ride back to Rawlins on the afternoon train. Right?" Buckskin ordered.

"I'd rather not," Herta said. "We haven't even figured out what to say to Daddy."

"Just tell him the truth . . . for a change."

"Oh, my. He would get extremely angry."

"You've caused him a lot of worry, anguish."

"He doesn't have the right to tell us how to live our lives. I'll be glad to tell him that." Joey said it with a glint in his eye.

"Good for you, Joey. But we'll have to be back in Rawlins to do that. The train leaves here at four tomorrow afternoon. Let's all plan on being on it."

"We'll see," Joey said.

"The time for confronting your parents is now, before any more damage has been done. Don't try to sneak away. I'll be watching you until train time."

Buckskin stared at them a minute, adjusted his six gun in the holster and made sure they saw him do it. Then he stepped out and closed the door.

Buckskin left the hotel and went across the street to a small cafe and ordered some dinner.

He missed Maud's breakfast and was starved. He had no plans on watching the young couple. Joey looked bright enough to realize they couldn't run away any farther. The game was over, they were married, now it was time to go home and face the music.

Minderhausen would steam and sputter, but there wasn't much he could do about it. His daughter was legal age once married and he had no control of her life. Joey was twenty-one. Within a few weeks, Buckskin figured that the old man would welcome Joey into the family, bring him into the company and teach him the brewery business. He could always hire a brewmaster.

After dinner, Buckskin walked past the bank, found it open and went in and changed a five dollar bill into five singles.

He had worn a new soft gray hat on this trip, hoping it would remove him from the black hat Bank Robbery gang. He saw four rough looking men walking their horses down Main Street and for a moment one of the men seemed familiar, but he couldn't place the face.

Buckskin went on to a saloon across from the hotel and found a small stakes poker game for some amusement. He soon found that the largest of the men was cheating. Buckskin palmed an ace on the next deal and two hands later a second ace. On the next hand he ran the bid up on the cheater, delivered three aces over kings and won over $50. It put him back even and nearly wiped out the cheat.

Buckskin stood up after pocketing the cash.

"Can't win a big pot and leave the game," the large man said.

"You making the new rules of poker, asshole?" Buck shot back at him.

The other man lunged to his feet, his hand hovering over his six-gun.

"You, asshole, you trying to get yourself killed? I saw you cheating in the game, that's how you won. You made the mistake of winning too often. Now you lost your cheated winnings. Be glad you're alive."

"I don't have to take talk like that." The man stared at Buckskin.

As he watched, Buckskin drew his six-gun so fast the other man hadn't even touched the butt of his own weapon before the gaping muzzle hole of the .45 was aimed at his heart.

"Like I said, asshole, just pick up your money, keep your hands shoulder high and walk out of here before you wind up eating worms in boot hill."

There had been a gasp around the poker table as Buckskin drew. Now when he didn't fire, the looks were more of admiration than mere awe. He could have killed the other man.

"Go on," Buckskin told the cheater. "Get out of here. The next time you try cheating, remember the guy across the table just might be able to cheat better than you can . . . and be able to draw twice as fast as you can."

When the cheater was out the front door, Buckskin holstered his weapon and faded out the back door into the alley. He wandered down the trash strewn alley, past the outhouses for the saloons, and to the next street.

Back on Main, he went to the hotel and up to room 205. His knock on the door brought no response. He tried the knob. The panel was not locked. Buckskin jumped to the wall side and reached out and turned the knob, then pushed the door open.

There was no challenge of gunshots. He peered around the door jamb and saw that the room was empty. The suitcases he had seen before were gone.

Buckskin charged to the room beside that one but it too was empty. He raced down the stairs three steps at a time and grabbed the desk clerk.

"Did anyone come in here looking for the newlyweds?"

"Yeah, some gent said he had a wedding gift to deliver. I told him where they were." Colt slapped the man.

"Idiot! You probably just got them killed."

Colt rushed out the back door and spotted fresh hoof prints in the alley. Four horses, all shod, no distinctive hoof prints. It would be a miracle if he could track them, but he had to try.

He should have watched the kids closer.

Buckskin followed the four horses to the end of the alley, then saw them point across the street. He lost the prints in the highly traveled street, but on the other side picked them up. The four men did not want to parade their catch down busy streets, which might be their undoing.

He followed the tracks down two more alleys,

then they turned onto a little used street between houses. He lost them for a while at the first intersection, then figured out that they had turned south heading out of town toward the tree-lined banks of Bitter Creek.

The tracks were plain now. He turned and jogged back toward town and the livery stable. The time had come to get a horse.

Ten

Buckskin rode half the afternoon. The kidnappers were moving out far from town. He had stopped at a moist place where the horses had crossed and could tell that two of the mounts were double loaded. The hoof prints sank deeper into the soil than those of the other two horses.

Yes, they were the kidnappers. He had picked up a rented Spencer carbine at the livery and fifty shells, as well as a new box of rounds for his six-gun. He was ready, but where in hell were these people going?

He guessed the kidnappers were the same four rough looking men he had seen riding down the street earlier that day. Now he took time to recall the one man's face among the four he thought he should know.

As Buckskin concentrated on the face a fragmented clue or two came back, but then slipped away. He wasn't sure who the man was but now he was certain he had met him before.

He rounded a bend in the creek which had reduced in size to little more than six feet across and no more than half a foot deep, and saw the maze of smoke far ahead. In another two miles Bitter Creek would be nothing but a spring seeping out of a hillside somewhere.

The railroad had swung south with the Bitter Creek watercourse, but now it angled due east with the stream which had picked up more fresh spring water now and kept going at about the same size as it wandered through the high plateau.

The horse tracks angled on south toward the rise of Black Buttes, a string of barren ridges on the skyline. Once the tracks left the stream there was almost no cover. Buckskin pulled to a stop in a slight dip in the terrain and stared ahead.

The smoke he had seen was gone now, but perhaps a mile on up the draw he could see what looked like a half fallen-in building. Back a few miles he had seen the unmistakable signs of an old stagecoach road that was rapidly returning to its natural state now that the railroad was finished.

The building ahead might be an old stage station. It would be impossible to ride up anywhere near the place in the daylight and not be seen. There was a small creek angling down from the ruins, but it didn't look like it had enough cover for a man on horseback. He had to wait for darkness. He wished that he knew how the two young people were faring.

Now it was a real kidnapping. Now it would be a little tougher to earn his $5,000. Somehow, he knew the other way had been much too easy.

An hour after Buckskin had left the two honeymooners with a veiled threat that he would be watching them, someone knocked on their door. Joey had started to open it when someone kicked the panel inward and the force knocked him to the floor. Before he could get up, four men rushed into the room, all with six-guns out.

"Don't say a word," one man, evidently the leader, said quietly.

He was of medium height, heavily bearded, and his eyes glittered with a strange delight. He had only two fingers and a thumb on his left hand. The lower two had been cut off leaving short stumps. His name was Poncho Saterlee, and he had been an outlaw for six years.

"You, on the floor," Poncho snarled, "get up and sit on the bed."

Joey crawled backwards and lifted to the bed beside Herta. He put his arm around her.

"What do you want?" he asked.

"You no ask any questions, stupid. Now, both pack everything in your suitcase. Now, pronto! Hurry."

Joey nodded at Herta who stood and while watching the four armed men, put her clothing in the suitcase without folding it.

"Hurry, hurry. This not a damned picnic." Poncho urged them on.

Joey took a quick glance at the men. All looked

hard, tough, dirty and desperate. They were outlaws, he knew at once. He had seen a group such as this ride into Rawlins one day and half the stores slammed their doors closed and rifles came through firing slots up and down Main Street.

The four men had continued on out of town without a shot being fired.

"Now, fasten the cases, we're going for a ride. Didn't know you'd have a boyfriend here, Herta. Figured just on you."

"My name is Joseph Radowitz and the lady is my wife," Joey said with dignity.

"Well, now, ain't that sweet. The two of you gonna extend your honeymoon a little. Going for a short trip and the bride will ride in back of me. Joe, you try anything and she gets her throat slit, you understand?"

"Yes sir," Joey said.

He swallowed his anger, his rage. He knew now was not the time. Later he would deal with these men. Now they were armed and would shoot him down without a second thought. He must wait. He nodded and the men led them out the door, down the back stairs to the alley.

Poncho, the leader, mounted and two men lifted Herta on the horse astride behind him. Her skirt rode up to her waist and the men laughed and made lewd remarks.

Joey stiffened but mounted behind another man when told to, and they rode out of the alley, across the street and along another alley. The other two men not riding double carried the suitcases.

When they were well out of town heading south along a small stream, the suitcases were tossed into some brush.

"You be good and we'll come back this way and get them," Poncho said. "Now we ride. We have several miles to go before we will get to our camp."

Herta clung to the man in front of her so she wouldn't fall off. She had never ridden a horse and now she felt her legs beginning to chafe against the rough hair of the animal. She had on no proper hose. She and Joey had made love only a few minutes before the men came. She had simply thrown on a dress and some shoes to be somewhat dressed in case the detective from her father returned. The sun beat down on them cruelly. Soon she was so hot she could hardly stand it.

"I need a drink of cool water," she said to Poncho.

He laughed. "You'll get to drink when the rest of us do when we get to the camp. Now shut up or I'll make you walk."

They got to a partly fallen-in, old stagecoach stopover about four o'clock.

"This is where we're going to stay?" Joey asked.

"If it ain't good enough for you, I'll tie you hand and foot around a tree and you can stand up all night," Poncho said. The other three men laughed and pushed inside the falling down building.

"Used to be a stage overnight stop," Poncho said. "We found it a couple of years ago and fixed it up some. Looks worse on the outside than it does inside."

He was right. Herta glanced around the four rooms that still had walls. They were clean, had furniture and beds with blankets. The kitchen was intact with a wood range, a fireplace, a kitchen table and some cupboards.

One of the men took off his gunbelt, put on an apron and began the fire. Then he started to cook. He boiled potatoes, onions and carrots in a pot, then fried some kind of meat and cut it up into squares and put it in the pot with the vegetables. An hour later he had created a passable beef stew.

At the table they ate the stew, drank coffee and ate slabs of fresh bread and butter. The bread came from the Rocky Center bakery in town.

Herta finished her stew and sipped at the coffee. "So now that you have kidnapped us, you expect to get some money for our safe return?"

"Damn right, little girl," Poncho said quickly. "We sent your papa a letter on the afternoon train telling him what we want. $30,000 for your pretty little ass delivered safe and unharmed at the flag stop station at Bitter Creek. If anything goes wrong he finds a corpse, you."

"My father won't pay it, he's a most stubborn man."

"Pray that he does, little girl. Otherwise, you ain't got long to live."

Poncho looked at Joey, took away a pocket knife he carried, and then put him and Herta into a room with no windows. The stage station had been made out of mortar and native rock, and the walls were two feet thick. There was no chance that the pair could get out of their room.

The door was three-inch oak held in place with six-inch strap hinges on the side facing the kitchen. An iron bar an inch thick and three-inches wide clanged in place against tough iron holders barring the door from opening.

Poncho looked at the smallest man in the group. "Shrimp, you sent the letter on the train like I told you, express delivery today for sure."

"Right, right, think I'm stupid?"

"You are stupid, Shrimp, now shut up. Kelly, you go outside and stand guard. I don't want nobody slipping up on us just 'cause we ain't watching. Soon as it gets dark, you be special careful. I'll come out and take over at ten o'clock. Get out there."

A half mile below the old stagecoach station, Buckskin had ridden to the thin line of brush on the small creek that wound up grade and within 50 yards of the station. It must have been the water supply when the place was operating. The brush was high enough here to hide his horse, and to cover him as he worked uphill.

He tied his horse and worked his way silently up the far side of the brush as it grew darker from the dusk.

Smoke had been coming from the chimney again. The horses were not in sight. He guessed they had been taken in back of the half fallen-in coach stop. There must be a barn or corral on the far side he couldn't see. He rested the Spencer rifle over his shoulder. He wished he had a Blakeslee Quickloader like the army used to use. As it was, he had the eight .52 caliber shots in the Spencer repeating carbine and a pocket full of extra rounds. He would load them single shot if he had to.

Buckskin stepped across the small creek on rocks and bellied down to look out through the fringe of brush at the stage stop. At first he saw nothing new, then a figure moved out from the fallen down porch and leaned against the building. The man carried a rifle and had a revolver on his belt.

At least he knew there were still people inside, and it wasn't an old fire burning out in the stove or fireplace. The guard meant they were on the alert for anyone giving chase.

How does one gun attack four men in a fallen down stage stop? Cleverly. One at a time. First he had to dispatch the kidnapper outside, the guard. He moved quickly now up the line of brush to where the guard couldn't see him. It wasn't quite dark when he came even with the buildings. There were two structures, a barn and a shed probably for tack and equipment.

It was just dark as he made certain the guard was in the same position. Then he used the darkness and walked cautiously from the brush the 50 yards to the barn. Inside he found their horses, still saddled. That gave him the idea the men wouldn't be staying there for long.

He slid silently through the darkness to the equipment shed, then on to the edge of the stagehouse. To his left a screen door spring stretched loudly as a door opened, then slammed shut. He saw a figure moving toward the outhouse.

Buckskin waited for the man to get inside the small convenience, then hurried up and waited behind the door. As soon as the man opened the outhouse door coming out, Buckskin slammed the butt of his .45 down hard on the man's head.

The kidnapper slumped to the ground, unconscious and maybe dead. Buckskin didn't take time to find out. He ran back to the stage station and eased up to the corner where he could see the guard.

Buckskin knew he had to cut down the odds, get rid of more of the kidnappers. But he wanted to do it silently. Pick them off one at a time until there was only one left. Then he could deal with him.

The guard wasn't moving. He leaned against the porch support and watched and waited.

Buckskin found a hand sized rock and threw it a dozen feet ahead of him.

The guard came alert, looked in the direction of the sound the rock made hitting the ground, but didn't move. He had stopped humming and through the filtered moonlight, Buckskin saw him draw his six-gun.

Buckskin threw another rock. This one hit a rock on the ground and sounded louder. The guard moved again, then tapped on a window that evidently led into the main building. A moment later a second man joined the first.

"Heard something damn strange out there, Poncho," Kelly whispered. "Like somebody kicking a rock."

"Yeah, and maybe you just got rocks rattling around in your head. Shrimp, come out here?"

"Ain't seen him."

"He went to take a leak long time ago and ain't come back."

"Told you something is out there!"

"You're seeing things, stupid."

"Poncho, I swear to god—"

"Kelly, shut up and keep your eyes open. I'll go find Shrimp. Maybe he fell in."

The one called Poncho vanished back into the shadows and a door closed.

If the light had been better, Buckskin would have cut down the two men right where they stood. But he risked the chance of giving himself away and maybe not killing either of them. Now he still had three to worry about.

The old stage station was built like a fort. The walls must be two feet thick and made of native stone, he thought. Only the wooden porch had fallen down on this side. No chance to burn them out and anyway, Herta and Joey were inside.

What the hell could he do now, Buckskin wondered.

Eleven

Poncho eased out of the side door of the abandoned stage station and looked toward the outhouse through the faint moonlight. The door hung open. Damn well certain Shrimp wasn't inside now. He could see nothing else and no one was moving.

Poncho drew his six-gun and walked cautiously toward the shadows of the convenience. He saw the man sprawled on the ground six feet in front of the door. Shrimp wasn't moving. Poncho knelt and felt of his chest, then saw the gout of blood on his head.

"Damn!" Poncho said and looked around quickly. No one could be near him. He listened for a breath from Shrimp, then felt for a pulse in the big artery in his neck. Nothing.

He lifted up running and sprinted for the back

door of the stage station, slammed the thick panel, and threw the heavy iron bar across it. At the front of the rock station, he whispered for Kelly to get his ass inside. When the Irishman was safely inside, Poncho threw the bar across the front door and breathed easier.

"Shrimp is dead, skull bashed in."

"Christ, there is somebody out there," Kelly blurted. "I told you. You wouldn't believe me. I could have been slaughtered."

"This is a cautious bastard. We wait him out until morning. Two windows without bars, that's all we have to watch. When it's daylight he won't have any advantage."

"Yeah, if he didn't slit the horse's throats. If he did that what we gonna do?"

"We wait, Kelly, and figure out what we have to do when it happens. You're on first watch. You go to sleep and I'll kill you myself. Owen will go next. Keep the lights out and watch everything."

The next morning the five people left inside the stage station were undisturbed. Poncho showed himself at the front porch and then jolted back just in time as a rifle shot slammed past him into the stone building.

Inside he yelled at Owen. "See where he is?"

Owen, a tall rangy man with one eye, had been watching out the front window. "Yeah. Down about 50 yards, just across that little gully. Got good protection, but he's also pinned himself down. No way out of there."

"Good, keep him pinned. We're getting out the back way and riding for the next old stage station to the east. You know the one. You keep him bottled up in there all day if you can, then follow us, making damn sure he don't follow you."

"Right, boss. I can do that." Owen patted his Sharps 50, one of the buffalo guns that could pick the eye out of a fly at half a mile. "Me and Beauty here can do that."

The lean tall man broke an eight-inch square of glass out of the window and waited a moment, then he pushed the Sharps 1874 Big Fifty with the special buffalo rounds out the window. The Big Fifty used the longer .50-90 round that could stop the biggest buffalo with one vital shot.

Owen sighted out the window at the spot from where he had seen the rifleman fire. He cut the sight close and aimed one of the big rounds into the top of the small ridge of dirt over the spot where he figured the man had to be. Owen fired. The round kicked dirt and rocks into the gully and Owen grinned.

"Ain't no way he's getting out of there alive, I got anything to say about it," Owen said.

"Keep him in that hole least until noon time," Poncho said. "Then you get a chance, you come by the long way to that next old stage stop. We'll be waiting for you."

Owen grinned and watched the dead-end gully where the sniper had positioned himself. He saw a head lift up a moment, then vanish. Owen sighted in and blasted an inch of dirt and rocks off the top of the protective bank. The big round hit exactly where the man's head had showed.

"Give the bastard something to think about," Owen said as he pushed another round into the breechloading single shot weapon to be ready.

* * *

After Buckskin saw the front porch guard slip into the old stage station, he knew he had made a mistake. He should have tried to gun down the two when they had been in range. Pick them off one by one if he had to. Now they would button up and wait until morning.

There was nothing he could do now. He took the Spencer carbine .52 caliber and backed off to a spot about 200 yards away that should be perfect for daylight shooting. It was a gully about twenty yards long that started slow and then stopped with no real outlet. He had a good view of the fallen-in porch and the windows on one side. If the kidnappers didn't take off during the night, he would have a good field of fire on them in the morning.

Buckskin knew he would need some sleep. He stretched out on the sandy, rocky soil, dug a small hole for his hips so his back could lay flat and promptly went to sleep.

A raucous bluejay woke him in the morning just at dawn. He checked the old stage house but no smoke came from the chimney. Were they still there? He realized now that he had a good firing position on the old rock building, but he was in a poor spot if they returned fire.

An hour later he had heard no sounds from the stage house. A short time after that Buckskin saw a man show himself behind the fallen down porch. Buckskin lifted the Spencer and fired, but the man pulled back behind the rock wall before the slug could reach him. Had it been done on purpose?

Buckskin looked up at the blue pall of smoke around his position and swore at gunpowder.

A few minutes later he heard glass breaking on one of the front windows and a long gun poked out. Before he could get a shot off, a round ripped through the lip of the gully and splattered sand and rocks all over him.

Buckskin hunkered down below the top of the gully and swore. The booming roar of the rifle meant only one thing: the gunman up there had a Big Fifty, a buffalo gun with great range and accuracy. If the man could fire the weapon with any skill at all, he could keep him pinned in his gully until dark. Unless Buckskin could discourage him.

He moved down the ditch from his previous position, lifted up and fired all in one quick motion, then dropped down. His round broke glass but he didn't see which pane. There was an answering round, which is what Buckskin wanted. He had levered in a new round and as soon as the dirt sprayed he was up and aimed at the empty pane and put a round directly through it.

He knew the man with the Sharps 1874 had to hand load a new cartridge, and he couldn't do it that fast. Immediately after the Sharps fired was the best time to shoot back.

This time there was no counterfire, and Buckskin pulled the magazine tube from the butt of his Spencer and replaced the three fired rounds, then put the tube back in its position. Now he had eight rounds ready to fire again, if he needed them.

Sounds came from the building now, or behind it. He heard the horses and berated himself for not killing the animals last night. At least he could have unsaddled them and turned them loose to prevent his quarry from using them again. It was a mistake he wouldn't make again. Live and learn. But that was true only if you lived long enough.

He moved again, as far from the building as he could get along the gully and lifted up and looked past the side of the old Ben Holiday Overland Stage Station. He stared along the far side. The horsemen could go straight behind the concealment of the station house for a quarter of a mile, then swing left. By that time he would have no idea which rider was which. He couldn't fire on them because he might hit Herta or Joseph.

"Damnit!" Buckskin exploded. "Outmaneuvered by a shit-faced kidnapper."

He put his hat on a stick and edged it up over the top of the ridge, pulled it down quickly, then raised it again three feet farther on.

The gunman was good in the stage stop. He had guessed the direction of movement and blasted a round through the top of Buckskin's hat, knocking it off the stick and to the far side of the depression.

So much for trying some fancy footwork to get out of there. It was a good move to draw his fire, find out where he was positioned.

He heard more glass break and moved down the ditch, lifted up and checked the window. What he feared had happened, had. The gunman in the stage stop had broke out another small square pane of glass in the same window only on the far side. There were still four panes of unbroken squares between the smashed ones. Now Buckskin wouldn't know which spot to aim at with quick counterfire after the Big Fifty had fired.

He heard more talk behind the rock building now, and could make out a woman's voice raised in anger. A short time later he saw the little caravan of three horses move away from the protection of the building far up the side of the ridge and ride eastward. Two of the horses held one rider and the third was double ridden. He couldn't risk a shot.

Just as the riders came in view the Big Fifty coughed again, then again and again. Each shot showered rocks and dirt from the top of the gully. The man behind the weapon was a marksman.

After the last shot Buckskin lifted up and fired through the left hand side broken window. The round went through cleanly without breaking any glass, but he had no idea if it hit anything.

He slid down in the ditch and waited. What in hell could he do? How had he gotten himself into this dead end? Damn the darkness. Sometimes it played tricks on a guy.

Buckskin took an occasional look at the building and around the sides so he wouldn't let the guy slip up on him. But for all counts, it was a stalemate. The man in the house had to stay in place to keep Buckskin pinned down. The difference was the Big Fifty man could move at any time.

"Hell no!" Buckskin muttered. He wasn't going to sit there and be pinned down for 14 hours. Now he looked at his problem with a more critical eye. The gully ended abruptly against a rock face. Evidently there was an underground waterway where the runoff water went.

Strike one.

To the front of the nearly 100-foot long ravine it was open toward the gunman without the slightest bit of cover. That was strike two. The ravine was only deep enough to cover him even crawling for about 50 feet. What was just behind the gully? The land here was half desert, a southward extension of the Red Desert.

As he remembered a map he had seen, the Continental Divide was just to the north of his current position. But this was that unusual spot where the Continental Divide formed a rough oval splitting on each side and coming together again, leaving a spot in the middle called the Great Divide Basin. It was a huge water sink with water from it having no real outlet. There were alkali flats in the center of the basin and sand dunes.

Now the only rivers in the basin, Sand Creek, Bear Creek and North Fork all ran into a small unnamed lake in the middle of the basin.

The dry, treeless hills didn't help his escape plan any. And then remembering the murderous thunder of the Big Fifty, he wanted to be damn certain that any escape attempt would work.

The area slanted generally upward from the

draw, which made it all the harder. Rocks? He looked toward the back and saw a mass of rocks that he first thought were too small for protection.

But the more he checked them, the better they looked. They were 30 feet from the edge of the ravine. He bobbed up once and looked farther along the rocky outcropping. Yes, there was enough cover to get him to the small brushy creek he had worked his way up before. From there he could get away safely.

He felt better. There was a chance of getting away. A chance. How good? If he had some kind of a diversion, something to pull the sniper's attention elsewhere, his chances would be better.

A fire. Was there enough dead, dry grass to start a fire? He moved down to the deepest end of the ravine where he could stand and bobbed up and checked the area just over the edge forward.

Yes! The overflow from the gully during a hard thunderstorm must have left enough residue wetness to grow a lush area of grass. It was no more than 20 feet square, but would make a fine diversion. Now the grass was dead brown and dry as tinder.

He went back to the middle of his grave like ravine and checked the way to the rocks. Yes. He would have to roll over the lip of the back of the ravine, surge up in a running start and take about ten running, charging strides to the first cover.

Ten second. Too long.

There was no way he could cut down the time.

The diversion would have to work . . . or he could be dead. He worked a second diversion idea around in his head. First his hat with a big rock in it peeping over the top. Then the fire, then the run back to his point of departure and roll over the lip.

Yeah. It should work.

If it didn't, he was dead. That guy with the rifle was good.

Wind? Which way was the wind blowing? Back toward him. Good, the smoke would help hide him. He went to where he would start the fire and dug out his matches. The wind wasn't so strong that the flames wouldn't burn against them through the thick dry grass. He found some dry weeds and grass and built a small torch, then he put it down and reversed the order.

First the fire, then the hat, then the dash for freedom. More time for the smoke to help hide him.

Buckskin lit the match and started the torch on fire. Then he pushed it over the top of the gully and saw it land in the grass.

Twenty feet up the gully he put the big rock in his hat and edged it up so it stuck over the top. Then he ran for the jump out of the gully spot.

Half a minute and there had been no shots. The smoke began to drift back toward him. He stifled a cough, then saw that it was blowing over the gap between him and the rocks.

Now! Buckskin surged up and over the back side of the gully, rolled twice, then came to his feet in the smoke. For a moment he was afraid it was too dense to see his way. He heard the rifle crack as he came to his feet. One hard running stride, two, three. He was up to nine strides and about ready to dive behind the rock when the booming blast of the Big Fifty echoed down the hills again.

At the same time he felt something slam him in the upper arm and spin him around. He dove and skidded on his left shoulder as he rolled again behind the rocks.

The pain came in gushing waves. He'd been hit high on his left arm with that big, ugly, .50-90 slug. Enough to tear a man's head off. He couldn't even look at it now. He crawled. Now and then his rump showed over the rocks, but enough smoke drifted past to cover him.

Two minutes later he cradled the long gun against his chest as he sat up behind a big rock. His left sleeve was soaked with blood. He took off his bandanna and tried to wrap it around the bloody spot. He didn't want to look at the wound. He knew it was bad. Now he had trouble lifting his arm.

He got the bandana wrapped around his arm, but had no way to tie it. He took it off and with his teeth and his right hand ripped one end of the cloth down six inches.

This time when he wrapped it, he could tear the end some more and tie by holding one end in his teeth. He fastened it tightly around his biceps. It was sturdy enough that the blood flow slowed and then stopped.

He crawled downhill toward the brush line. Soon the protection was high enough so he could walk. Now he had to get to his horse and get into some town where a doctor could look at his arm. He didn't want to lose it. No job was worth that. He blinked back the pain and pushed his left arm through the buttons on his shirt to hold it in an improvised sling.

Now he had to get to his horse and ride north to the tracks. Then a few miles east to the flag stop on the U.P. tracks called Bitter Creek.

Twelve

Buckskin Lee Morgan found his horse exactly where he had left the mare, contentedly chomping on some sparse grass near the small creek that was going to wind up eventually evaporating out in the alkali flats somewhere.

It seemed like two miles until he found the mare. Actually it was a little less than a quarter of a mile. He mounted with some difficulty, bleating in pain when he had to use his left arm to steady himself. Then he rode as fast as he thought prudent. He didn't want to lose his horse, but neither did he want to have his arm cut off.

He came to the railroad tracks after about two miles and tried to think through his reasoning to go to Bitter Creek. It was closer, but it was even smaller than Rocky Center. He tried to remember more about it from when they had stopped there on the train. A flag stop. Maybe ten buildings. There would be no doctor.

Reluctantly, he turned toward Rocky Center. He knew there was a doctor there, had seen his shingle. What was it, eight or nine miles. Two hours. He could stay alive for two hours. He urged the mare along the right of way and headed for Rocky Center.

The tracks took a fairly straight shot northwest, heading for the small town along the easiest grade level available. It went around a dry, barren ridge, then curved to the west.

It took him more than two hours to get there. His arm began to bleed again, and one time he caught himself just before he fell off the horse. The mount had stopped. He had dozed in the saddle and the mare reached down for dry grass.

Now he sang a little song out loud as he rode to keep himself awake.

The sight of the town brightened his interest and he was feeling better by the time he came to the doctor's neat white house near the middle of the small town. He slid off the saddle and yelped in pain when he hit the ground. His arm had come out of his shirt front and hung at his side. It hurt too much to move it.

He pushed into the doctor's office and saw two women waiting. One was pregnant. She turned away. He saw a door open and a woman looked out.

"Yes?"

"Got an arm with a big hole in it. Be obliged if you could have the doctor take a look." The woman looked at the blood soaked sleeve, then at his fingers, and he saw blood dripping from them. He caught his hand and held the blood.

"Sorry about the mess."

She took hold of his right arm to steady him and walked him through the door and to a small room where a man had just washed his hands. He looked up.

"Gunshot?" he asked.

"Big Fifty," Buckskin said and sat down heavily on the chair the woman aimed him at. He barely made it.

The doctor cut off the kerchief and then scissored a hole in his shirt sleeve and looked at the wound.

"Don't think I've ever seen anybody alive before who got hit by a Big Fifty. Sure didn't do your arm any good. You looked at the hole?"

"No."

"Good. Missed the bone, tore a chunk out the top of your arm. Missed most of the big muscles in there. You'll live. This gonna hurt considerable, and we got no time to get you drunk. Want to try some of this new stuff I got? Its called ether. Knocks you out like a club to the head and you won't feel a thing."

A new wave of pain swept through Buckskin. "Heard about it. Give it a try."

The medical man took out a bottle, sent his wife out of the room and wet a small rag.

"Gonna put this over your nose, you just breathe natural. Breathe deeply and it'll be done in a minute."

Buckskin thought he tasted something foul.

When the cloth came over his nose he struggled a moment, then relaxed and breathed in the strange smell. Three times he breathed and then blue lights came on and reds and greens and the whole world turned upside down and then suddenly, everything was black.

It took Doctor Wilburforce ten minutes to repair the damage on the wounded arm. He washed it out well, cut away some of the torn flesh and then stitched the wound together with waxed sewing thread. He put some salve on the wound. It was half an inch deep and had gouged out flesh and tissue.

Then he bandaged it well and waited for the big man to come back to consciousness.

Buckskin felt like a horse had kicked him in the head. His head pounded and his mouth tasted terrible and then he felt the pain knifing him in the arm and he groaned.

When he tried to sit up he fell back hard on a high bed. The woman was at his side in a moment.

"There, now, you're coming out of it. Just relax and rest easy for a minute. Won't be so bad. Now, can you open your eyes? That always seems to help."

"Enough of the talking, fix my arm. Hurts like thunder!"

The woman laughed softly. "It's all fixed and you've been having a nap for almost a half hour. You got a little too much of the ether. But you'll be fine in a few minutes."

"He fixed my arm?"

"Look at the bandage. You didn't scream once.

Lots easier than getting six big men to hold you down."

"Yeah, lots easier on me too, and quieter."

An hour later, Buckskin was ready to leave the office. He had a small bottle of laudanum the medic had given him.

"Now don't take too much of that at a time. It'll dull the pain if it gets too bad. But this stuff can be terrible. You take very much of it over several weeks and it gets addictive so you can't live without it. You best get a hotel room and rest easy the remainder of the day and tonight. Then you get at least three days bed time. Next, you take it easy with that arm for at least a month. No horseback riding, no chopping wood. Nothing to get that wing above your shoulder, or you could hurt something up in there permanent.

"The laudanum will help you ease down a little. Just do like I say. Hotel isn't too bad for a few days rest."

Buckskin walked out of the office an hour later. He hadn't tested any of the medicine. He was tempted. His arm hurt like a red hot branding iron was pushed into it.

At the small railroad station he wrote out a message to Hartley J. Minderhausen:

"DAUGHTER ELOPED, NOW MARRIED. THEN WAS KIDNAPPED FROM ROCKY CENTER BY 4 MEN. GIVING CHASE. REPORT MORE LATER." He signed it Morgan.

During the past two days, Alonzo Warnick had been busy. He had tracked his quarry and now was only a day behind him. He knew Buckskin had come to Rocky Center, knew he had left town hurriedly.

Warnick had three men with him now, all working for a dollar a day and a $100 bonus if they captured or killed Buckskin Lee Morgan. It was pure chance that he learned Morgan had come back to town. The hotel clerk who had rented Warnick two rooms the day before had earned two dollars showing Warnick when Morgan had checked into the hotel and then left. Now he signalled to the bounty hunter as soon as he came back in the establishment after his midday meal.

"We have the pleasure of serving the gentleman you were inquiring about again," the clerk said. He held out his hand.

"Now, he's in the hotel now?"

The clerk's face remained impassive. Warnick put a dollar bill on his hand, and when the hand didn't move, Warnick put another one on it.

"Yes, he checked in just before noon. Seemed to have something wrong with one arm or shoulder from the way he walked. Room 114, end one on first floor near the alley."

"Is he there now?"

The clerk held out his hand again but Warnick punched him hard in the belly and he doubled over. Warnick pulled the clerk up by his ears and stared into his face.

"Is Morgan here now?"

The clerk, who couldn't have said a word to save his life due to lack of air in his lungs, nodded. Warnick dropped him and he crumpled to the floor.

Warnick hurried outside where he had left his three men and sent one around to the alley to watch for any movement there. He and another man went down the hallway. The fourth man was put at the other end off the alley so Morgan couldn't escape in that direction.

"Damn, we've got him!" Warnick said softly as he pulled out his new fangled .38 short barreled revolver and thumbed the hammer back. They walked silently to room 114 and Warnick tried the handle. The door was locked.

Inside the room Buckskin had lifted the window of the room for some fresh air. He was about to lay down for some of the bed rest the sawbones had recommended, when he heard the footsteps in the hall. He glanced at the door. When he saw the door knob turn he grabbed his Spencer and his six-gun and sat on the window sill. He eased out of the window just as the door flew open and a man stumbled into the room.

Buckskin shot him, then dropped to the ground and ran toward the alley mouth. A man stepped out and fired once with a revolver. Buckskin didn't stop running. The Colt in his right hand barked twice and the man slammed backward three feet and crumpled in the dirt.

Buckskin hadn't stayed alive all these years by chance. He had tied his horse in a little used stall halfway down the alley. Now he ran to the horse, put his left foot in the stirrup and heaved himself into the saddle. He was almost to Main Street before he thought about his arm.

It would hurt later, he knew. He would pay for using it now. But the sudden surge of danger had shot power into his bloodstream and he used the arm as if it didn't hurt at all. The Spencer nestled into the boot and he charged down the alley to Main Street, barely missed a team pulling a wagon and darted past two women in fresh gingham dresses.

Five minutes later he was well out of town. He had seen one horseman behind him, then one more joined in the chase. Only two of them. It had to be Warnick again. Maybe this time he could take care of the bounty hunter once and for all.

Buckskin did not worry about the two men he had shot. He probably killed both, but they were working for a bounty hunter and fair game. The law wouldn't be concerned. Most bounty hunters did not work with or go to the law, since then the hunter would have to split the reward with the lawman.

This happened more often than not, even though lawmen were not supposed to accept reward money for working within the bounds of their duty.

He checked behind him. Two men riding, not gaining, but there, within sight. This time he had struck out to the west. It was unknown territory for him, except for a quick ride through it after the bank robbery.

The land here was a little more forgiving and ahead he saw a small canyon and some trees. In the barren land they were a relief. How could he use them to his advantage? This whole area was over a mile in the air slanting up into really tall mountains seemingly on all sides.

He rode for the shimmering green in the distance, maybe three miles away. His arm throbbed now with a constant pain. How could it hurt so much? The jolting ride of the horse slammed the pain deeper and deeper into him with every step.

A hump, a hill, some cover was what he needed now so he could take a shot at the pair behind him. Yes! He saw it 200 yards ahead. It was only a slight depression topped by a weathered upthrust of rock 20 feet in the air and 50 feet wide. Enough. He rode past it, angled to the side, and vanished behind it. He rode back to the base of the rocks, tied his horse to a sparse little shrub and pulled the Spencer out of the saddle boot.

Buckskin found an ideal spot for his sniping at the left side of the rocks. A niche in one of the base rocks could have been made by a rock fall thousands of years ago. It offered him a sighting slot and adequate protection. He hoped he could get in two quick killing shots and end this bounty hunter's game forever.

The pair riding behind him didn't seem to mind that he was out of sight. He had vanished a time or two before only to show up on the next rise. This time it would matter. He leveled in the Spencer carbine and wished he had that sharpshooter's Big Fifty to use. He could pick them off at three-quarters of a mile with a little luck.

Now he would have to wait until they were within a quarter of a mile. Five hundred yards at the most. He hoped the weapon had been properly sighted. He hadn't had a chance to sight it in to determine where the weapon fired. If it fired an inch high and left at 50 yards, that meant that at 500 yards the bullet would be ten-inches high and ten-inches to the left.

He had eight quick shots to make adjustments. At least he could kill the horses. The pair of hunters plodded along through the heat of the spring day. Even at 6,000 feet it would be blistering hot here in high summer.

Buckskin sat beside the rock resting his left arm. He checked the targets a time or two and now figured they were at 600 yards. He settled down behind the rock and aimed in on the pair. Elevation? He wasn't sure, there was no lift sight. Wind? Almost none. He leveled the weapon again and sighted at the smaller of the two men who he hoped was Warnick.

Three minutes later, he refined his sight, added a little elevation and fired. At once he worked the trigger guard whipping out the spent cartridge and plunging a fresh round into the chamber. The first round was low. He lifted his sights and fired again three seconds after the first shot.

Both riders had stopped and were starting to dismount. The round hit the larger man and he tumbled off his horse. By the time Buckskin levered in another round and sighted in, both men were out of sight. He fired at the closest horse and saw the round hit home and the animal go down, kicking and screaming.

Buckskin watched but saw no more movement. The second horse was down as well, but he wasn't sure how or why. He waited five minutes and when he saw no more movement, he went back to his mount and rode straight away from them behind the cover of the tall monolith. He was a mile farther on before he looked back. Both men came forward, riding one horse.

Buckskin couldn't believe it. One of them was wounded and they had one horse. He couldn't see any water for several miles. He would have to get to the Salt Wells River in the edge of the Aspen Mountains westward before there would be any water.

He figured about nine miles. The splash of green ahead could be a tributary to the Salt. He was going to find out. One way or another he needed to rid himself of Alonzo Warnick. All he had to do was figure out exactly how.

Thirteen

Buckskin slowly pulled away from the pair of riders behind him. The green swatch ahead was farther than he had guessed and when he at last got to it, the afternoon was almost over. The green was a small valley of pine trees watered by a tributary that probably flowed into the Salt Wells Creek that wandered north to Bitter Creek.

The railroad grade had followed Bitter Creek for 30 miles until it emptied into the Green River. He watered his horse well, then hid her in some brush and picked out his best point for attacking the riders coming in.

They would come, he was sure of that. Once a bounty hunter gets the taste of his first payday, it seems like easy pickings. This time it wasn't going to be half easy.

Buckskin found a sheltered place in the green

where he had a commanding view of a half mile stretch of the dry lands to the east. It was the track he had just rode on, and he expected that Warnick was still following him.

For a moment his conscience tried to whang at him, but Buckskin laughed out loud. That bastard Warnick would gut shoot him from ambush ten times out of ten if he had the chance. He came after him with four armed men in that hotel room.

Buckskin sat beside a foot thick pine tree and rested the barrel of his rifle over a small boulder. This time he would wait until they were within a hundred yards to make certain. After he dispatched both of the bounty hunters he could get a good night's sleep. The next morning he would follow the creek down to the tracks, turn east, and be back in Rocky Center before noon tomorrow.

He still had a kidnap victim to rescue.

The pair riding double on the horse came into his sight nearly a half mile away. As he watched, one of the men got off and walked ahead of the horse. The animal looked about used up. No way to treat a good horse, Buckskin thought, knowing he would gladly kill the animal if it would help him get Warnick. The two ideas did not seem to contradict one another.

He moved and his arm screamed at him with branding iron intensity pain. Buckskin moved the arm again to test it, trying to find out which motions caused the pain. He could turn his hand and lift his hand from the elbow with relatively little hurt. But when he lifted his elbow, the biceps bellowed in anger at him.

While there was still time, Buckskin stood and kicked the weeds and brush and rocks where he would be sitting. He didn't want to be surprised by a friendly rattlesnake at the wrong moment. Sure that the area was clear, he sat down and checked his victims.

They had stopped and evidently drank from a canteen, then looked at the landscape ahead. Again he wished for a Big Fifty that he could use to pick off both men before they knew they were shot. Now he had to wait.

As he watched them, the two men changed directions. One began an arc to the left, the other an arc to the right. They would stay out of range and still get to the cover of the woods. Then they would try to advance on him through the cover to a close confrontation.

Too damn smart. Although they were still out of effective range, Buckskin sighted in on the horse and fired. He wanted to let them know where he was. That would confirm their strategy. As soon as he fired, he pulled back into the cover and decided he would go north. The man with the horse was circling around that way and he probably was Warnick. If he could kill Warnick, the other man would drift away.

Buckskin hurried to his horse, mounted and rode cautiously, keeping out of sight in the timber but close enough to the edge so he could watch the progress of the bounty hunter. Twice the man stopped and checked the forested area ahead of him, then he came on forward.

When the hunter was 300 yards away,

Buckskin sighted in on him, then let the moment pass. He would come closer, why take a chance of missing him.

Buckskin moved north until he was near the point where the bounty man would enter the wooded area. His target was still 100 yards away and stopped for a moment checking the woods ahead.

This time Buckskin had sighted in on him with the barrel of the rifle over a tree limb. He was still mounted. Getting on and off was a struggle the way his arm hurt. Now he refined his sight and just before the man began to move, squeezed the trigger smoothly.

The Spencer barked and in a fraction of a second the bounty hunter took the round in his chest and jolted backward like he had been kicked by a wild mule.

Buckskin ducked and moved a dozen feet away from the pall of blue smoke where he had fired. When he looked back at the scene he saw the man sprawled where he had fallen. The horse had drifted off to the left, then moved forward, smelling the water, now free to move where she wanted to go.

Was it Warnick? He didn't know. He could ride out, check the man, catch the horse and ride on north. If the far man had kept his arc to the woods, he would be well out of rifle range.

Buckskin made the move. He rode out of the woods and galloped to the death scene. The man had fallen on his back and his hat dropped away. He was not Warnick.

"Damnit!" Buckskin blurted, then rode up to

the wandering horse, caught it easily and tugged on the reins until it followed. He rode back to the green protection and kept on his northerly route.

Warnick was on foot and over a half mile behind him. Before the cover ran out he should be able to gain a mile on the bounty hunter. He would decide what to do next. He could ride to the tracks and back to Rocky Center before dark. He figured he was no more than eight or nine miles from the town.

Yes, he would try it. If one horse gave out, he had the other. Before he left the stream to angle northeast, Buckskin made sure both he and the horses had a good filling drink of the cold water.

Then he turned and rode across a small ridge and down the other side. He could see the tracks in the distance from the top of the ridge. He was moving in the right direction.

Two hours later he turned in the found horse to the livery and went directly to the general store's back door. It was still open. He bought enough food to last him six days, a pot and pan for cooking, a plate and cup, eating utensils, matches, two blankets and a new six-inch sheath knife. When he checked his shirt he found blood oozing from his shoulder wound.

The doctor yelled at him for five minutes when he unwrapped the bandage. "No goddamn good sense, that's what you haven't got," the medic railed.

"Doc, better I bleed a little bit there than from three or four .45 slugs through my body. Now you just fix it up so I can get moving. Some folks hereabouts don't appreciate my being here too much."

The doctor nodded. "If it wasn't for gunshots I'd go out of business around here. At least you paid in cash. First cash I've seen in three days. How would you like to get paid in eggs, chickens and potatoes?"

"At least you have a good breakfast." Buckskin gave the doctor two dollars. The old medic looked at the money and gave back one of the paper dollars.

"I'm still overcharging you, but what the hell." He grinned. "Now get out of here and take care so that arm don't go busting loose again."

Buckskin waved with his right hand as he went outside and eased his way into the saddle. He had giving the dun gelding a good feeding of oats at the livery. He drank before they left and now was eager to get moving again.

The wounded shoulder had cost him a full day. He was that far behind the kidnappers. It was a long two hours ride to the old stage house at Black Buttes and he was sure he'd find it empty.

It would be well dark by then. He would stay there that night, or close by, and be ready to start tracking the three horses with the first light.

At least that was his plan as Buckskin rode along the right of way southwest toward the buttes.

Two hours later, when he could see the dim outline of the old stage station, he stopped and listened. For a moment he thought he heard the haunting wheeze of a harmonica. Then it was gone. He moved slowly toward the rock structure. There was no moonlight coming through a solid cover of clouds tonight.

Buckskin was within 50 yards of the structure when he heard the harmonica again, this time loud and clear, coming from the old stage station.

He got off his horse, tied it and pulled out his .45 Colt. Lee crept up cautiously toward the front door of the building. The harmonica came now and then, and he smelled smoke as the wind shifted and sent the scent toward him.

Almost at the same time he smelled something cooking, onions and something. Fried onions. Bacon and onions and fried potatoes. Someone inside was making a late supper. Could be a wandering cowboy. Could be an outlaw on the owlhoot trail. Could be the man behind the Big Fifty waiting for Buckskin to come back and start following the kidnappers.

After ten minutes of a cautious, patient approach, Buckskin eased up and looked through the lighted window. It was the same one that had four of the eight-inch panes broken out. Across the front room he saw the kitchen with a man there working over the stove.

On a table lay a six-gun and a rifle. But the long gun was covered by a jacket so Buckskin couldn't tell what make it was.

He stepped with infinite care and moved toward the front door. It had been left open and he edged inside. The sturdy floor did not squeak. In the faint light of a lamp in the big dining living room, he could see what he had spotted before, but not the kitchen.

Buckskin wanted to rush the kitchen door with his six gun ready, but that might be risky. He saw a plate, a cup of steaming coffee and a slab of bread on the long dining room table where hundreds of stage coach passengers had eaten in the glory years before the railroad went through.

Buckskin waited. It was more than five minutes later that the man came from the kitchen holding a hot skillet in one hand and scooped the contents onto his plate.

Buckskin cocked his .45 and the man froze.

"What'n hell?"

"Hold it just like that. Don't move an eyelash or you get hot lead for your supper."

Buckskin darted to the table, picked up the .45 and whipped the jacket off the long gun. A Big Fifty.

"We've met before," Buckskin said, "only you were on the other end of this Fifty. Put your hands on top of your head and lace your fingers, then lay down flat on your stomach on the floor."

"Rather not do that."

Buckskin shot a round an inch from the man's left boot. The lead tore into the wooden floor. Slowly the tall, lean stranger put down the hot fry pan on the table, backed away and knelt on the floor, then went flat out on his belly, face against the wood.

"Name?"

"Owen."

"Who you work for, the kidnap leader?"

"Poncho Saterlee. He's not a greaser."

"Where's he taking the newlyweds?"

"Don't know."

Buckskin shot him in the thigh. Owen screamed and sat up holding his bleeding leg.

"You shot me! You bastard, you shot me!"

"Sounds like what I said early this morning. Only your round was from that Big Fifty. Where's Poncho taking the kids?"

"Christ! East to the next old stage station."

"Mighty helpful of you. Why did you wait for me?"

"Figured you went into town to get patched up. When you didn't get back by dark, guessed you'd be along in the morning. Didn't know how bad I hit you. Damn clever, using that fire and the smoke to screen your move. Lucky I hit you."

"Not lucky enough."

"You ain't gonna shoot me down in cold blood?"

"Hell no, I'm mad already."

Owen tried to stop the flow of blood from the front of his thigh where the big .45 slug had taken out an inch wide chunk of flesh.

"You've got to stop the bleeding. Bandage up my leg."

"Yeah, I'll help you the same way you helped me."

Buckskin kept the Colt aimed at the marksman.

"Has Poncho sent a ransom note for the girl?"

"Yeah, $30,000."

"Where and when?"

"Don't know now. Was going to be at Bitter Creek flag stop. Now he'll change it."

"Why are you being so helpful?"

"Hell, I'm a hired gun. I work for the man who

pays the most. I don't get the ideas, got no loyalty. I'll side you against Poncho, if you'll pay me."

"Not a chance, Owen. I don't deal with sidewinders."

"My leg! Blood down all the way to my boot."

"Tough. I had blood dripping off my fingers."

Owen lifted his pants leg away from his boot top and Morgan tightened his grip on the Colt.

"Damn, but this is hurting. You gonna let me tie it up?"

Buckskin looked at the man, then away. He looked back at once and saw Owen's hand flash into the top of his boot and dart out with a derringer. He fired a shot before he had it well aimed. The first shot from the twin derringer missed Buckskin by six feet.

Buckskin shot his .45 Colt once. The round hit Owen in the chest and toppled him backwards from where he sat. The little hide-a-away pistol dropped from his fingers and his eyes glazed for a moment.

He lay on his back as Buckskin stood over him. His eyes cleared and he shook his head. "Damn, thought I could beat you."

"Poor bet drawing against a gun-in-hand."

"Yeah, I was dead soon as you got here anyway. Damn fool, I should have watched another day." He nodded at the table. "The Fifty. Beautiful weapon. Shoots a mite low and right at 100 yards. Never could site it in perfect. Half an inch low and quarter right at a hundred. Not much, but on long shots. . . ."

Owen shivered, then started to say something

else. His mouth came open and a torrent of blood spewed out, drenching his chest. His eyes glazed again, then stared unseeing at the beams of the ceiling ten feet above.

Buckskin Lee Morgan took a deep breath and let the hammer down on the fresh round. He had cocked the weapon automatically after the second booming shot in the small room.

Now he slid the weapon in his holster, grabbed the dead man by the shoulders and dragged him outside.

Buckskin slept that night 100 yards up the small creek from the old stage station. He didn't hear a thing all night.

Fourteen

The morning sun had burned the mists away and with them went the coolness of the 6500 foot altitude. The sun would be master of the planet today. Buckskin had used an old Indian trick and brought both horses along on his 20 mile ride from the first stage station to the one at La Clede. He had no idea what the name La Clede meant.

He rode his gelding hard for half a mile while trailing the horse Owen had in the back stables. Then he switched horses and rode the other horse hard for a half mile. In this fashion he covered the ground toward the next stage station quickly. He could follow the old stage road so the route was comparatively flat and easy riding.

After the second rotation of the horses he was sure that he was moving at least ten miles an hour. At that rate it would take him about two hours to cover the distance to the next stage station.

The stage road soon picked up Bitter Creek again and he followed it south almost to its origin. After an hour and a half, he began to watch for the station on the hills that were barren and dry once more. Only small shrubs and stunted brush grew on the hills now, giving them a dark color. It was some kind of sage and probably several kinds of chaparral. This whole area was more desert than high plateau, and nothing like the surrounding mountains with their lush growth and bountiful rainfall.

He spotted the stage station from more than a mile away and hunted for some sort of cover and concealment. The stage road was on the near side of the creek, so Buckskin took his mounts across the small stream and just past the struggling brush that grew there. It was the only concealment of any kind, so he had to use it. Otherwise he would have to wait until nightfall again.

Lee decided he would take a far different position at this station. First he would make sure the kidnappers and the honeymooners were still there. Then he would figure out some way to attack. He was through just waiting.

Cautiously he worked up the far side of the stream. He tied the second mount in some brush and kept going on the gelding. He had been riding generally south for the past eight miles, and now he could see that the creek was mostly dry to the south past the old station.

The concealing brush thinned dramatically and he knew it would not be enough to hide him.

This old stage station was not the same as the former. Logs and lumber had been hauled in, probably from the far edges of the Medicine Bow Mountains. It was a log cabin, built strong and large, being nearly 40 feet long and about that wide.

The roof seemed made from some kind of slate that had been dug out and would certainly turn away fire arrows thrown by the Indians. It was built more like a fort than a cabin. It showed only one window on the side he could see best, it was a three-by-five affair that had steel bars on the outside to prevent entry.

Now he could see smoke coming out of a chimney made of sturdy local rock and mortar. Someone was there. He could not see the stables which must be to the side. No one was showing outside and there were no other indications of humans except the fire.

Buckskin took nearly a half hour finding exactly the right spot for his vigil. He put the Big Fifty down and positioned two rocks to rest it on when he fired. He checked his supply of cartridges. He had found only 20 among the goods Owen left behind. It wasn't much of a bequest.

Down one side he could see what must be the front door. It faced north and he could barely make it out. Anyone coming or going from the place would be directly under his gun. He estimated the distance again and frowned. It was downright unfair. The Big Fifty was said to shoot accurately for more than a mile.

Here he was less than 200 yards from the front door of his target.

* * *

Inside the La Clede stage station of the old Ben Holiday Overland Stagecoach system, Poncho sat nursing a cup of coffee. He didn't like getting up this early in the morning. It was only a little after eight-thirty and already he had to make some decisions.

"How far are we from Bitter Creek, that little town?" he thundered.

"It's between here and the last place we was," Kelly rasped. "Nine miles at the most."

"Two hours on a good horse," Poncho said. "We get there today for the afternoon train eastbound and get the damn flag up so the big iron horse stops. Pretend you're a passenger, and then get the letter on board for Minderhausen. Only this time we make it better.

"Bring in that filly, Herta, or whatever her name is. Need to have a talk with her."

"Yeah, yeah. Where'n hell is Owen? He shoulda been here by now."

"Maybe the guy nailed him, who knows. That makes less people to split the money with. Bring in the girl."

Kelly scowled, then went to the room without a window and knocked, then unbarred it and opened the door.

"Herta, out here," he commanded.

"I'm coming, too," Joe said pushing along with Herta. "I'm not letting her out there without me along."

"Just the girl," Kelly snapped.

"Let them both come so the kid don't get in a snit," Poncho said.

The two young people came out slowly and stood in front of Poncho who sat at the long dining table with its practical built-on benches.

"Herta, there is pencil and paper. I want you to write a note to your father. Say anything you wish. What you need to do is convince your father it is really you writing the note, and that you are my prisoner."

"If it will help us get back home, I'll be glad to," Herta said.

"It should help," Poncho assured her.

Herta sat at the table and wrote two pages, telling her father that she loved him but that she had to run away and get married because she knew he would never understand. She said now all she wanted was to come home with her husband.

"Sign it," Poncho said when she had finished. She did. He put it in an envelope with another letter he had already prepared and sealed it.

On the outside he wrote Minderhausen's name and his address in Rawlins. Poncho handed the envelope to Kelly.

"Ride with this to Bitter Creek station and get the damned train stopped heading east. Be sure that it goes Railway Express and be sure that you pay the two dollar fee to have it hand delivered today. Do you have all of that? Repeat it back to me."

Kelly repeated it back, but forgot about the delivery today. Poncho slapped him on the side of the head. "Delivery today, dumbhead!"

"Yes, deliver it today," Kelly repeated. He looked at Poncho a minute, then headed for the back door. "Better get my horse saddled."

Five minutes later, Kelly cantered down the slight hill going with the current of Bitter Creek. He had a nine mile ride to the small village and he didn't want to be late.

In his hideout in the brush beside the creek, Buckskin Lee Morgan shook his head. He vaguely remembered hearing a horse riding by. He shook his head again. Had he passed out? His head felt light. He blinked until his eyes were clear and looked down the trail. Well down the old stage road he saw a man on a horse riding away.

"Damn, missed him!" Buckskin said. The sun had been too hot and when he checked his arm it was bleeding again. He still wasn't in the best of shape. He should be able to stay awake for a few hours even after losing some blood. He felt light headed and almost fainted when he stood up quickly to watch the rider. He leaned against a four-inch tree until his head cleared.

He recovered slowly. He hadn't lost that much blood. Or had he? He couldn't remember feeling this way for a long time. Buckskin drank water and chewed on some dried apricots he had brought from the store. He wouldn't pass out again, he would be sure of that. One man rode off to the west. Why? Communicate with Herta's father? A chance. The flag stop at Bitter Creek wasn't that far away.

So now might be his chance. Poncho would be alone in the log house with his two captives. If he would only come out the front door to check the weather, or get some firewood, Buckskin could nail his hide with Big Fifty. Back door. Firewood for the stove and the outhouse. Those would be the best reasons for the man to leave the log house.

Buckskin checked the angle of the creek. The side of the stage stop that faced the creek along the back had no windows. Even if the concealment of the brush wasn't as good, there would be no way for anyone to see him.

He worked up the creek another 200 yards until he could see the back door, the stable and the outhouse. Again he settled into a good concealed shooting position and looked at the back door. All he could do was wait. If nothing happened in three hours, he would move up and try to get inside.

If the rider was going to Bitter Creek, it would take him at least two hours each way. If the messenger waited for the train going east, he wouldn't be back until near dark.

Buckskin settled down to wait, but didn't get too comfortable. He was determined not to pass out again, and neither did he want to be lulled to sleep by the sound of honey bees buzzing around the splash of wild flowers near the bank.

Buckskin wondered what was going on inside the old stage station house.

Poncho stared at Herta. He grinned. "I've always liked pretty ladies with long blonde hair. You German?"

"Yes."

"You know you're my prisoner, I can do any damn thing I want to with you right now."

"Not and get your $30,000 for me."

"Oh, hell. You believe that? Your father is gonna hand over the money before he sees you, before you can tell him anything? Nah. I can mess with you any way I want to."

Poncho drew his six-gun. "You, Joey, get back in the room. Now. Move."

"No, not without Herta."

"You are no use at all to me, boy. I can shoot you down right here and not even blink an eye. You know that, don't you? You damn well better understand that."

"I know it."

"Then move. What good would you do Herta by getting yourself killed here and now?"

"No good."

"Then get in the room."

Herta nodded for him to go.

"Mr. Saterlee won't hurt me. He knows how valuable I am to him."

Joseph looked at her again. She smiled and nodded. Joey turned and walked into the room. Poncho used a rock and pounded the nails in on a two-by-four that acted as a bar across the door.

He went back to the table where Herta remained seated. Poncho stood behind her and smoothed down her long blonde hair.

"You know this makes you less than a man, Poncho. It proves that you can't get love without a gun. It makes you just another animal."

"I like being an animal, sometimes," Poncho said. His hand went down over her shoulder and inside her dress and cupped around one of her breasts.

"It makes you small and weak, and you are admitting that I am stronger than you are."

He spun her around, not moving his hand. "What the hell you mean?"

"You're so weak you have to force yourself on a woman. Can't you win a woman's love on your own? Are you so unmanly and crude that you can't be loved by anyone but a prostitute?"

"Hey, I almost got married once. She loved me. Two dozen times she spread her legs for me, and she liked it."

"Then how could putting your hands on me now be of any interest to you? Is rape better for you than the freely given true love of a good woman?"

"Hell, a woman is a woman, don't matter much to me."

He took his hand away from her breast and unbuttoned her blouse to her waist. She didn't stop him.

"Christ, nothing under that dress."

"You didn't give me time to clothe myself properly when you burst into our room."

"Yeah, I forgot."

He pushed the sides of the dress top back and stared at her young, pink-tipped breasts.

"Hey, good tits, really nice. I like good tits. Makes it all so much more interesting."

"You might call them breasts."

"Huh? Oh, yeah, breasts." He reached out for them.

"Don't . . . touch . . . me . . . again . . . or I'll find a way to kill you."

His hand stopped. He looked at her. "Damn, you're serious, ain't you?"

"Absolutely. Just because you're an outlaw and a kidnapper, is no sign that you really are a bad person. It would take a despicable man to force himself on me in this situation. You have been quite nice, actually."

"Yeah, I have, haven't I." He laughed. "But that's all over. I'm a tit lover, and I got to have them."

He caught her shoulders and stood her up, then bent to take one of her breasts into his mouth.

Her father had once instructed her how to hurt a man who tried to attack her. Now she remembered and she rammed her knee upward with all her might and hit him squarely between his legs, driving his scrotum upward, mashing one testicle between the hard bones of her knee and his pelvic bones.

Poncho screamed in terrible pain and let go of her, staggered to the side and fell on the bench. He pulled his knees up to his chest to lessen the pain.

Herta looked for his pistol but it still was in his holster under his body. There was a rifle somewhere but she couldn't find it. She rushed to the door where Joey was and tried to get the door open. The nails in the two-by-four held tightly. How did they get it off?

She gave up there and ran outside. Then she stopped. She couldn't saddle a horse. She had no idea where to run to if she did try to run away.

They were in the middle of a wilderness, a desert almost.

Slowly she turned around and went back inside the log house. She was just as trapped as she had been. By the time she got inside, Poncho sat on the bench and had his six-gun out.

"I think I'll kill you right now for what you did to me. Nobody ever did that before. Yes, no doubt about it, I'm going to shoot you five times and enjoy it."

He lifted the pistol and the pain at his crotch still stained his face, turning it into a painful, angry mask.

Fifteen

Poncho's .44 blasted a shot inside the dining room of the tightly closed log house that seemed like a massive explosion. The round dug a hole into the solid wooden floor next to Herta's right foot. She jumped back, her hands going over her ears to try to stop some of the sound pounding on her eardrums.

Joseph kicked on the door where he was shut in. His voice came through the heavy panel weakly. "Hey, what the hell is going on out there?"

Poncho ignored him. He pointed the weapon at Herta's half exposed chest. She had thought to button only two of the fasteners as she ran outside.

"Pretty tits, get your little round bottom over here or the next round goes into one of your legs.

How would you like to feel some real pain?"

She had moved her hands from her ears when she saw him start to talk. Herta shook her head and moved where he pointed.

His face still writhed in pain, his eyes were glassy and a tear slipped down his cheek. He wiped it away and groaned.

"Small cunt, you gonna pay for what you did. You gonna pay a lot. Right now, take off that dress! Pull it down, take it over your head, however you do it. I want you bare-assed in about ten seconds. Do it!" He roared the last two words at her and Herta's hands moved automatically.

She had tried her best to get away, she had hurt him. But it hadn't been enough. Now she unbuttoned the fasteners on her thin dress and lifted it off over her head. She had put it on hastily after she and Jopseh had made love back in the hotel and so she wore nothing else underneath.

Herta lifted her chin. She wasn't a quaking virgin any longer. She was a married lady. She had made love. Nothing he could do would be new or would hurt her.

"You never thought to ask if you could make love to me, did you, Poncho? No, you had to be the big tough man. Had to try to take what you wanted to make up for your coward's heart."

"Shut up! One more word and I slice off half your tit, you hear me, cunt?"

"Yes, I hear."

He moved and winced. Poncho sat up on the bench and it took all of his willpower and strength. He still ached. Her father told Herta a man hit hard enough in the testicles would not be interested in sex for at least two days. She hoped he was right.

"Come over here, woman!" Poncho growled.

She moved at once and stood directly in front of him. His face was only slightly above her waist.

"Bend down," he commanded.

She did and her large breasts swung out and down, hanging like two inverted peaks. Poncho's right hand came up and stroked her breasts. Then she understood. He was doing this to punish her, not for his own benefit. What would he do if she pretended to enjoy it?

"That . . . I hate to say it, but that does feel good. Makes me feel nice and good and all warm."

He took his hand away.

"Bitch, you coming in heat again?" He put his hand on the muff of honey blonde hair at her crotch. "Spread them, bitch in heat."

She did, without hesitation. His hand worked between her legs and up to the softly wet spot. He probed and then one finger plunged deeply upward inside her.

"Ooooooooooh! That's the place! That feels just wonderful, so sexy, like your big thing was up there. Do you suppose that you could. . . ."

He moved his hand at once and pushed her backwards.

"Get your ass out of here and put on your clothes. From now on, be quiet. Not a word. Nod that you understand me."

She nodded. Herta walked to where she had put her dress on the table, picked it up and turned her back as she dropped it down over her head and buttoned all of the fasteners up the front.

She watched him a moment and saw the pain on his face before he knew she saw him.

He grunted and pointed. "Over there by the wall. Sit down and be quiet. Go to sleep if you want to. You're no damn use to me for a while. Before this is through I'm gonna have more than a finger up your slot. You remember that."

Herta sat down and leaned against the wall. She let her legs drift apart so he could see between them. Poncho looked away quickly, knowing that he'd been caught. She snapped her knees together and let a small smile brighten her face.

She had taken him on at his own sexy game and beaten him each time. But what would happen now? What else could she do before Owen came back? She really didn't know. If she could get Joseph out he could do something. No, he would get himself killed.

That man the kidnappers were worried about, Buckskin, the one who found them first at the hotel. Where was he? Was he trying to find them? He must have been the one who shot the other two men who had been in the gang. Now there were just two of them left.

She heard Joseph pounding on the door, but there was nothing she could do to reassure him.

She simply had to wait.

Outside, Buckskin listened intently. He had seen Herta run through the back door, look around, and then before he could signal her she had gone back inside. After that he had heard what he was sure was a gunshot. But only one.

He wondered what was going on inside. This might be a good time to charge the place. Take on Poncho and get the kids out of there.

The back door had not proved productive. He checked the building again. No window looked out on his location. He left the Big Fifty in its firing position and checked the rounds in his six-gun. Just for luck, he thumbed a six round into the chamber and eased the weapon into his right hand. He walked silently toward the log structure. There was no need to run.

When he was 50 feet away he heard voices from inside. A man was yelling. Buckskin made it to the back of the log station and eased around the corner toward the back door. A small window looked out on the barren landscape. He lifted up without his hat and looked inside. It was the kitchen and no one was there. Through the only door, he could see a slice of what must be the main room for eating and getting warm after a long cold stage ride. He could see no one in his field of vision.

He ducked under the window and moved toward the back door. It had a screen door which now hung broken and unused at the side. There was a doorknob on the heavy back door which opened inward. A door was ten times easier to barricade if it opened inward. Also, it could be barred easier. Buckskin tested the knob, twisting it and pulling on the door.

Unlocked.

He eased the door inward an inch, then another inch. Buckskin squatted against the outside wall as he worked the door inward with only his arm in front of the door itself. When it was six inches open, a gunshot exploded inside and splinters flew from every edge of the heavy wooden door about three feet from the floor.

They barely missed him.

"You, at the door!" Poncho bellowed. "I know you're there. You get your ass out of there or Herta is one dead little girl. You hear me?"

Buckskin pushed the door open wide with his foot and peered through the opening six-inches from the threshold. He saw a man sitting on a long bench near a table. One of his hands held a six-gun hard against the blonde head of Herta. The other held her long hair in a tangled grip.

"Back off or she's dead and so is your fee, cowboy," Poncho said.

"I can put two rounds through your heart before you can pull the trigger," Buckskin snarled.

"Not so," Poncho said. "You try it and the girl's dead."

"So are you. I'll settle for that. I can find another job. Can you find another life?"

"I'll take the chance, cowboy, if you will. Blast

away."

Buckskin pulled back. His bluff hadn't worked. He ran for the barn. At least he could disable their horses.

A shot came from the door he had just left before he was within a dozen feet of the barn. He did a forward dive and came up behind an old stage coach with a broken axle. Another round whined away from the metal rim of the wheel.

"Keep running, cowboy," Poncho said.

Another 20 yards and he'd be out of range of the pistol, but not a rifle. They probably had one. He couldn't reach the barn. Lee took a shot at the door, thudded one round into the almost closed panel, and ran for the brush along the creek. He could still stop them from leaving with the Big Fifty.

He looked back once and saw the man pushing Herta ahead of him as they walked toward the barn. The kidnapper didn't look as if he was walking right, but Buckskin couldn't be sure. He grabbed the Big Fifty as soon as he got to his hiding spot. The pair was gone from the front of the small barn.

Buckskin worked his way along the creek until he could see the back side of the barn. No big door. He watched the front. Two minutes later a horse came out. The man was on front, and Herta was just behind him, her hands tied around the kidnapper's chest, Buckskin guessed.

A second horse followed on a lead line. Buckskin took careful aim and killed the second horse with a head shot. The horse slammed to the ground and rolled half over without making a sound. The animal was dead in seconds.

But he couldn't fire at the two riders on the other horse. The power of the Big Fifty would go right through the man and kill the girl as well. He'd have to wait.

"Don't shoot again, bastard!" Poncho called. "You do and you kill the golden goose here and you lose again. Back off."

For a moment, Buckskin frowned. There was nothing he could do now about keeping them there. It would be too chancy at this angle to hit the head of the horse they rode. He sighed and let them ride away slowly.

The man! Joey. Where was he?

Buckskin let the riders move to the east, get back on the old stage road and ride away at a slow canter.

Then he broke and ran for the cabin.

Joey had to be inside, but was he alive or dead? He stormed through the door, saw no one, then heard pounding on a door. Buckskin kicked the nailed two-by-fours off the door.

"Where is she?" Joey screamed as he ran out the door. He stopped and looked at Buckskin. "Oh, it's you. Where's Herta?"

"The kidnapper took her. They're both on one horse. I won't have much trouble catching up. You stay here so I'll know where you are."

"Absolutely not, I'm coming with you!" There was fire and fury and defiance in the smaller man's eyes.

"Look," Buckskin said, trying to be patient.

Then he exploded his right fist off the clerk's jaw and watched him slump to the floor unconscious.

This time it was Buckskin who ran. He rushed out the door back to where he left his horse. He didn't need two horses this time. He put the mount into motion, swept around the log stage station and on down the road east. The pair couldn't be far ahead.

He rode for fifteen minutes, then saw the double loaded horse. Herta was less than a quarter of a mile away with the kidnapper. He put on a spurt of speed and closed the gap to 100 yards, then worked into the thin sage and waist high growth off the stage road and pushed ahead faster. When he was parallel with the other riders, he brought up the Big Fifty and before the kidnapper even looked his way, sighted in and fired.

The horse went down, dying of a head shot.

Buckskin couldn't remember when he'd killed two horses in one day. Usually he went for the man. This time, the margin of error would be too costly.

Herta and the kidnapper spilled off the horse. The rope that had tied them together had somehow been severed and the man came up with his six-gun drawn and his eyes alert.

He saw nothing at first, then spotted Buckskin's horse. He began to crawl toward Herta.

"Hold it, I've got you in my sights," Buckskin bellowed. "One more move and you're a dead man."

Poncho held for a moment, then dove forward, grabbing Herta around the waist and twisting her in front of his body.

"Go ahead, cowboy. Go ahead and shoot. The odds are the same as they were before."

"You're right," Buckskin called. Then he fired. The round slammed into the kidnapper's right leg just below the knee where his leg was thrust out to maintain his control of the girl. He barked in pain and frustration, but didn't relax his grip on the girl.

He pulled his six gun and put it at Herta's head.

"Have it your way, cowboy. You want her dead, you got her dead. At least I'll have the fun of messing up your payday. So I might as well make sure and blow her head off right now. You hear me, cowboy?"

Almost ten miles away, Kelly put the letter in the hands of the Railway Expressman and gave him the two dollars for same day delivery.

"You sure you got it marked to be delivered today," Kelly asked.

"I do this all the time," the clerk said. "I know my job."

"All right, all right," Kelly said. "I just have to be sure that it gets delivered as soon as you get into Rawlins."

Kelly nodded and went back through the passenger cars to the conductor, paid for a ticket to Rawlins and settled in a seat. There was no chance that he was going to go back and find

Poncho.

Poncho had lied to him, had not even said he was sorry when two of the four of them were killed. Then today he had called him a dumbhead and hit him. Kelly knew that he should not even deliver the message. But he would do that much. Then he'd try to find a job in Rawlins or maybe even Cheyenne. Maybe he just wasn't cut out to be an outlaw.

The damn owlhoot trail wasn't nearly as interesting as he thought it would be. So far he hadn't made a penny by being an outlaw. Maybe it was time to stop and try something a little more honest and with less chance of getting himself shot and killed.

Kelly nodded then leaned back against the train seat. He'd have a small rest before they arrived in Rawlins. He still had almost five dollars. That would last him until he found a job.

Sixteen

The Special Delivery Express Mail envelope missed Hartley Minderhausen at the brewery and was taken by messenger to his home on the hill. It arrived just before supper and he glared at it a moment, then tore it open.

He read the first few lines and began to swear in German. Minderhausen dropped into an upholstered chair and continued to swear under his breath as he read the ransom note from the kidnappers.

"It's a kidnap demand, after all this time. He wants $30,000." Minderhausen shook his head as he stared up at Serilda.

"Pay him, do anything to get your daughter back," Serilda said. "Isn't Herta worth more to you than some money. When you look at it, what's $30,000 to you?"

"You're right, of course you're right. I just wonder how she is, if she's well, if they. . . ." He saw the other pieces of paper and eagerly grabbed them.

"It's from Herta!" He looked back at the letter and after reading the first two lines he bellowed in anger.

"She says she got married! That she ran off to get married! Why didn't I know anything about this?"

"She made me promise," Serilda said, cowering. She had a real fear of him now. "She said she would get me fired if I told you. What could I do?"

"My god! My own daughter!"

"Would you have let her go?" Serilda asked.

"Of course not! I'd have horsewhipped the upstart kid, whoever he was."

"That's why she didn't tell you. She said she tried to tell you more than once."

"My god, my god, my god! What this new world has done to my baby." He read the rest of the letter. "I have to go back to the office and get the money in cash ready to take on the morning train. I'm to go to Bitter Creek stop."

"Will it take you long to get the money? Should I hold supper?"

"Two hours, and I'll be back. Hold supper to then."

"You want your driver, Fritz?"

"Yes, call him. No, no, I'll drive the rig myself. Have him bring it around, the small rig."

Ten minutes later Serilda watched the one

horse rig swing down the drive and out into the street that led to Main.

When the rig was gone, she called softly. "Fritz, are you there?"

He came out of the living room.

"I hope you don't have it in your hand yet, a girl likes a few surprises."

Fritz was 18 but told everyone he was 21. He was tall, blond, German to the toenails and now he rubbed his crotch.

"Fritz, you know that drives me crazy. Where tonight?"

"It isn't dark enough for outside," Fritz said.

He had worked for Minderhausen for over a year and now was his only driver.

"How about on the kitchen floor, or the kitchen table," Fritz said.

Serilda had treated him like a servant until two weeks ago. Then she kissed him and put his hands on her breasts and invited him into her bedroom one afternoon.

Almost every day since then she had come to him. From what she said he had the idea she wanted to get pregnant, and didn't care by whom.

Now she rubbed the swelling behind his trousers as she led him into the kitchen. By the time they were there she had unbuttoned her dress and pulled it up to her waist. She flipped aside the chemise she wore and pulled his mouth down to her full breasts with their large pink nipples throbbing already in expectation and a surging hot blood supply.

"Chew me, sweetheart," she said. "Chew me half off but don't lose any in your pants the way you did last time. I want your very best seed. Do it now!"

She lay on the kitchen floor and pulled up her skirt. She had nothing under it and flashed her pink prize at him as he fumbled with his buttons. He tore the last one off, pulled down his pants and knelt between her legs, his thick short tool primed, hard and ready.

"Yes, now, Fritz!" she squealed and pulled him toward her.

He probed a moment, slipped by and she yelped when he dug into her brown anus an inch.

"That would be fun but not productive, darling," she said.

She pulled him up, nuzzled him into the right spot and surged upward against him until she felt his penis plunge into her.

"Yes, Fritz, yes. Your prick is so young and strong and potent. Not like some I've been using lately."

She caught his buttocks and slammed him all the way into her until their pelvic bones meshed and she moaned in the joy of being filled up.

"Go, Fritz. Do it now, hard and fast. Stick me hard, Fritz. I want all of you, right now."

He couldn't understand this woman. Either she just loved to be poked, or she had something else up her sleeve. She wouldn't pin a pregnancy on him. Hell, no! He could pick up and leave town within four hours of any warning. He would be far gone before he had to support some brat and this woman, even if she did have big tits and a pile driver for an ass end.

But then the stroking into her wetness got him started and her tightening and squeezing with her damn inside muscles set him on fire and long before he wanted to, Fritz shouted, growled and pumped harder and harder until he thought he would explode.

Then he did, and he let go with a wild scream that brought Serilda's eyes wide open and a surprised look on her face. He jolted the last of his fine German seed deep into her plowed field and when he was through, he fell on top of her.

She pushed at him. "I'm not moving for ten minutes, but I want you up and out of here. You must warn me if Minderhausen comes back. I need to stay this way. Now scat. Get out of here. Pull it back in your pants and button up and go watch for the old man. If he comes, you bust your gut in here and warn me."

She lay there, thinking how wonderful it was going to be. She wouldn't do a bit of work again for the rest of her life. She could marry anyone she wanted to. She could afford it.

Fritz looked down at her. "I don't understand you. You just like to get poked, is that it?"

"Yeah, Fritz, that's it, now get out of here and watch for the old man to come back. If he isn't back in half an hour, go back to your quarters. We don't want him to know about us, do we? He'd have you whipped and your prick cut off. Now git!"

She laughed at the expression on his face.

She calculated the time again. She had been in bed with old Minderhausen for almost three months now. Not every day, but enough so he wouldn't know the difference. If she didn't have any signs of being pregnant by the end of the week, she was going to tell him she was anyway.

She had sent the letter that morning so it would be out of town on the afternoon train. Her brother in Chicago could get there in two days. He would come at once, she was sure. With her brother here to help her, it would be simple. The whole thing had been easy.

She and her brother had traced Hartley Minderhausen from the days he had been in Chicago. From those dark days when her father had first suffered at Minderhausen's hands, and then sunk lower and lower and lower until one day he had taken a pistol and ended his life.

The brewery he had built was in a total collapse. Minderhausen's competing firm had cut all of their customers out from under them, lowered the price of beer and ruined him. Then Minderhausen offered to buy their father out at a ridiculously low price. Her father had finished it his way, and the family had lost every cent it had. There were still large debts against her father's name that she had vowed to pay off.

Now she would.

Serilda lay there half naked, exposed from her breasts down, luxuriating in the feeling of just being penetrated and bred. This might be the time when she really became pregnant. She shivered slightly at the thought, then lifted up. The fluids had been given enough time to fertilize her if they were going to. She pulled her clothing back in place and went to the small indoor bathroom and cleansed her body, then arranged her clothing and went back to the kitchen to check to see that the dinner was not overwarming.

The whole plan was simple. If she wasn't actually, she would pretend to be pregnant. She would tell Minderhausen with a great deal of put on fear and trepidation.

Her guess was that he would be delighted and would arrange to marry her at once as quietly as possible, probably in Cheyenne or Omaha.

Then she and her brother would decide what to do. At once, she would have some money at her command.

But they wanted it all, all the Minderhausen millions!

If he would not agree to marry her, she and her brother would assail him with threats. They would go to the police, claim that he had assaulted, raped and impregnated her against her will, kept her as a virtual prisoner in the house, used her for immoral purposes and refused to marry her when he got her pregnant.

They would bring criminal charges.

They would bring civil charges for support of her and his child.

It would work.

On the other hand, if Minderhausen cooperated, they wouldn't tell anyone how he had misled and criminally used her. They would quietly slip away if he gave them $500,000 . . . in cash.

Either way, they couldn't lose. Minderhausen was hog tied. All she had to do was keep a straight face.

She was quite sure that Minderhausen was so smitten with her that he would agree at once to a wedding to make his child legitimate.

She would be sure that the old fool had no idea at all that he might not be the father of the baby.

Then, after a couple of months when she didn't start to get large, she would have to go into phase two. She and her brother, Wilhelm, would work out the perfect murder, and the beloved Mr. Minderhausen would die quite suddenly of a terrible accident from which she would barely escape with her life.

She would inherit everything, of course, as his wife. The daughter might be a problem, but she could be dealt with. Especially now that she was married, as the note said.

Yes, it would work. She knew it would work. Even so, now she felt strangely unsatisfied, sexually wanting. She went to the living room and found Fritz reading a magazine and watching out the window for Minderhausen. It wasn't nearly dark yet.

She said hello and sat down beside him. Quickly she had the buttons on his trousers open and his erection came popping up through the opening.

"Need some more?" Fritz asked with a smirk.

She didn't answer him, she began stroking him with her hand.

"I want to see it squirt out," she said, smiling at him.

"I'll need some help," he said. He reached for her breasts and she let him fondle them, tweak them, pinch her nipples.

He growled and humped his hips, and she watched the bobbing, stroking purple head as she worked on him.

"Not yet," he said, reaching between her legs. She parted them and he probed and touched and at last pushed his finger deep upward inside of her.

"Chew on me," she said.

He looked at her in surprise. She hadn't put on any underpants yet. She spread her legs, pulled up her skirt and pressed his head downward toward her crotch.

"You want me to. . . ."

"Yes, now."

She went to her knees on the couch and pulled his face upward under her. As his mouth pressed against her she gasped, then grinned and felt his tongue probing into her, stroking at her clit.

She felt a gush of juices and he bleated, then licked her clean and probed again deeply.

Serilda felt the surge coming, the slamming, jolting climax. It hit her hard, making her tremble and then jolt back and forth. She held his face to her crotch as a series of spasms rattled through her once, twice, then three times.

Her juices gushed and she let go of him a little so he could breathe, then fell with him on the couch, his head still firmly against her nether lips, his tongue still working.

When the last trembling left her, she lifted him away from her and used her skirt so he could wipe off his face.

"Christ, what in hell was that?"

"You had your fun, it was my turn."

"Yeah, but my mouth . . . Christ, next time you suck me off, right? You take me in the mouth all the way. Christ, you must have climaxed ten or twelve times."

"At least," she said, "I don't have to wait a half hour between times like you men."

He looked out the window.

"The old man is coming."

She dropped her skirt. She'd have to quickly wash herself, then be sure his supper was still warm.

"Get yourself out of here," she ordered. "And remember, you tell anybody about you and me, and I'll have your cock cut in half. You understand?"

"Damn right!" Fritz said and rushed for his quarters over the stable.

Seventeen

For a moment, as Buckskin Lee Morgan watched the kidnapper put the gun to Herta's head, he thought the man might just be crazy enough to pull the trigger. Then after several seconds went by, he knew the man was thinking that he wasn't dead yet and that there still was some hope.

Buckskin still sat his horse. Now he rode slowly forward from where he had been with the Big Fifty Sharps at about 50 yards.

"Just ease up and we'll all live to see another payday," Buckskin said. "You aren't ready to die or you would have pulled the trigger by now. Why not just put the pop gun away. You know what this Big Fifty Owen used to own can do."

"You kill him, too."

"He pulled a derringer against a pointed six-gun. You wouldn't do anything that stupid, would you? What's your name?"

"They call him Poncho," Herta said. "Where's Joseph?"

"I left him at the stage station. He's fine. Let's talk about you, Poncho."

"What's to talk about?"

"You staying alive when this is all over."

"You've got the high hand—a horse, that Big Fifty, and no hole in your leg."

"You bleeding to death, Poncho?"

"Damn close."

"Let the girl go and tie up your leg. She'll sit there and wait. Then we decide what to do."

"Don't make sense," Poncho said. "Why don't you kill me the way you did my three men?"

"Two. Didn't even see the third one. They tried to kill me is why they're dead."

Herta looked at him, surprised. "You really killed two men?"

"It was either they kill me or I get them. Not a hard choice to make once it happens. This time it was them. That bother you, Herta?"

"Yes. It all seems so useless."

"Most criminals and their crimes are on the pathetic side. I know these four bank robbers I'll tell you about some time."

Buckskin rode closer until he was about 50 feet away, just out of accurate six-gun range.

"Poncho, from here I can blow that weapon right out of your hand before you can pull the trigger. Why don't you just put it down and let's work this out."

"You're talking like a lawman."

"Nope. Fact is, I've got a bounty hunter on my

trail right now. I lost him back in Rawlins, but I'll have to deal with him sooner or later."

"Bounty hunter? After you? Be damned! Who in hell did you kill?"

"It's all a big mistake. Christ, all this talk is making me nervous." Poncho moved the gun to Herta's neck.

"You put down the shooter and I'll take you back to Rawlins and turn you over to the sheriff for kidnapping."

"That sounds fair," Herta said. "It's certainly better than being killed."

Herta didn't look frightened at all. She was cool and calm and like she was at some woman's fancy meeting talking about sewing.

"If I'm convicted how long I have to serve?" Poncho asked. The gun was coming down a little now.

"If you get convicted, it could be two to five years. You didn't hurt her, rape her or anything. I'd say a jury would go easy on you."

Poncho lowered the gun and started to give it to Herta, then he tossed it on the dirt six feet away.

"Now you're making sense," Buckskin said and rode closer.

Herta hit him with her fist and jolted him to the side. Then she tore at him with her fingernails, slicing scratches down his face and neck. She screamed at him and hit and scratched him until Buckskin rode up and pulled her away.

"Christ, what a wildcat," Poncho said feeling his bleeding face. "Didn't figure she was that mad."

"Mad? After you kidnapped me and Joey and tied us up and ran us all over the country and then back there when you wanted to rape me, but couldn't, because I kicked you so hard in the crotch. You're right, I'm furious. If you'd given me that gun, I might just have shot you right in the crotch myself."

Buckskin pulled her away and sat her on a rock, then went back to look at Poncho's gunshot wound. That Big Fifty surely did make a hole. The slug hit the bone and probably cracked it. It took Buckskin a half hour to get Poncho's leg bandaged and splinted with a couple of sticks he cut from some of the low growing shrubs. Then he had to lift Poncho onto the horse.

"I'd rather walk," Herta snapped after Buckskin suggested that she could mount up behind the man. "I've ridden too close to him, too far."

It was almost an hour more before they walked back to the log stage station.

They saw smoke coming from the chimney and Buckskin fired a revolver shot to attract the attention of whoever was inside. Joey came out waving. He ran to Herta and kissed her, then hugged her and led her back inside.

All of the provisions Poncho's gang had brought were still there, and since it was an hour until dark, they decided to stay the night and leave in the morning.

Buckskin cooked supper for them, fried potatoes and onions, and cheese. They had bread from some nearly stale loaves, and ate from a small sack filled with dried peaches, apricots and prunes.

Buckskin nailed Poncho in the former jail of Herta and Joey, and the honeymoon couple took another smaller room that had a bolt on the inside of the door.

Buckskin bolted the main door and the back one, let the fire die down in the fireplace, and then eased his shoulder down on his blankets and tried to get some sleep.

Nearly 24 hours later, the four stepped off the east bound Union Pacific train at Rawlins, and Buckskin arranged for Joey to turn in Poncho Saterlee to the Carbon County Sheriff. Buckskin thought the less seen of him around town, the better.

The sheriff notified Hartley Minderhausen that his daughter had been found and the brewer stormed down to the sheriff's office to pick her up.

Buckskin watched the exchange as they came out on the sidewalk.

Minderhausen was still sputtering. "Damned foolish thing you did, daughter, running off like that."

"Papa, don't talk to me that way. I'm not a little girl anymore. I'm a married woman and I have responsibilities to my husband. We've talked it over and we're going to rent a small house over near his parents. We'll be able to get by on his salary from the store, so you see, you can't order me around any more."

"Never heard of such a thing. You'll stay at my

house. The two of you, of course. You can have the whole second floor and we'll hire a maid to take care of things."

"Mr. Minderhausen, I don't think you understand," Buckskin said. "Herta has become a woman, an adult. She's been kidnapped. She's been married. She put up a fine fight against the kidnappers, almost got away once but there was nowhere to go except the red desert. You've got to start thinking of her as an adult, as well as being your daughter."

"Ridiculous! Of course she'll stay with us at the big house."

"Papa. I'm married now. I want a house of my own, one Joey and I can afford. I don't care if it's just two rooms."

"I don't understand, you could have half of my mansion, and a rig and a driver, and. . . ."

"Papa, you really don't understand."

"I hear you went to Bitter Creek trying to find the kidnappers and that you had $30,000 with you," Buckskin said. "That would make a nice wedding gift for the bride and groom."

Minderhausen sputtered for a minute. Then he nodded. "Yes, yes, of course, done. Now, let's go home and talk about this."

"No, papa. First we're going to Joey's home and see his parents, then we'll all talk, and maybe celebrate. Oh, one more thing."

Herta became more serious and reached for Joey's hand. "We were married by the Community Church preacher in Rocky Center, but soon we'll go to Denver and be married in

Joey's church, a synagogue he calls it. I'll learn all about that."

Joey smiled. "That's right, Mr. Minderhausen. Mr. Morgan says there's a rabbi there who can marry us again. I just hope I can convince my parents that it will be all right."

"Convince them that it all right to marry my Herta? Who in his right mind could object to Herta?"

Joey smiled again. "Mr. Minderhausen, we're Jewish, and papa and mama take religion seriously."

"So do I," Minderhausen said. "I'm Lutheran, so what's the difference?"

Joey laughed softly. "Mr. Minderhausen, there's quite a difference, but nothing that Herta and I can't manage. Let's go meet my parents now. I don't think you know my parents, and I've waited so long for Herta to meet them. It's down this way."

"I'll call my carriage," Minderhausen said.

"No, Papa. Let's walk. I'm not going to have a carriage to take me places. Besides, I like to walk." She put one hand through her father's arm and the other through her husband's and looked at Buckskin.

"Thank you so much, Mr. Morgan, for all of your help. I'm sure father will be especially generous with you when he pays your fee tomorrow. Won't you, father?"

"Yes, yes, of course."

Buckskin grinned as the trio walked down the street. He put the newlyweds' bags in the

Minderhausen carriage and told the driver to follow them, then he headed for the widow's house. It had been a long time since he'd slept in a good soft bed. Then too, there was the widow Dutch Smith who might also be in the bed.

Dutch opened her back door when he knocked and looked at him.

"Who shot you?" she asked. Then she pulled him inside and kissed him.

"Some guy with a gun shot me. You got room for a boarder for a couple of days until I heal up?"

"Possible. Can you come up with rent money?"

"After tomorrow I can."

"You got a room and a bed and maybe some supper if you're lucky. Maud, look what the cat dragged in."

Maud ran in and gave him a big hug, then saw him wince and looked at his shoulder.

"Better let me check that out. Probably needs rebandaging. Who the hell shot you?"

Buckskin grinned and let Maud take over. It was good for a change not to have to worry about anyone or anything. He could just relax and lean back and rest up.

Maud looked at him again and shook her head. "No sense rebandaging that until you have a bath. Just get it all soaked. I'll put on some water to heat and you strip yourself naked." Maud grinned. "Not necessary in that order." She laughed and went out to the kitchen to build up the fire and put on the two buckets of water.

"Right now I wish we had one of them big mail order bath tubs," Dutch said. "The kind that's big enough for two people to get in."

"Woman, whatever are you talking about?"

Dutch laughed and poked him in his good arm. "Are you telling me you've never had a bath with a lady?"

"Lady, I'm not telling you anything I don't have to. Did Maud mention something about supper?"

"Not until after your bath."

"And you want to watch?"

"Watch, hell! I'm going to help. And I get to wash all the good parts."

She did.

Two hours later Buckskin luxuriated in the soft bed with real white sheets. He was in Dutch's bed. She sat down on the edge and bent over and kissed him. He reached down and caught one of her hanging breasts inside the loose dress and she murmured through the kiss. When it ended she nodded.

"Oh, glory! Sure you don't want to hang around my place here for ten or twenty years?"

"I'd be worn to a nub and so limp I couldn't even walk down the street."

"Not likely. You're good for six a night for a week without even taking a second breath. I've been in your bed before, remember?"

"You're a hard lady to forget, Dutch Smith."

"Good." She pulled back the sheet and slipped out of her dress and slid into bed beside him. "You won't mind sharing your sick bed then."

She was on his right side and Buckskin put his good right arm around her.

"Mind? I'd be mad as hell if you didn't try to seduce me at least once."

"Or twice, or four or five times. I'm ready. We're about to go on a new little banking project. Heading up to Medicine Bow in a couple of days. You're invited to come along if you want to. Going up by stage, a little wagon that's as rough as a just shelled corncob."

Buckskin laughed. "You do have a way with words, Dutch Smith. I might go along for the ride. I don't want to get in the habit of easy money."

He kissed her softly. "You still thinking about that gambling hall you want to open?"

"Thinking about it."

"Do it before you lose some of your partners. You're in a damn risky business. I've seen too many such partnerships suddenly dissolved by lead messengers."

"You say we're pushing the odds, running out of good luck? Hell, we all know that. Just that once you get started . . . Well, I'll think on it."

"Remember, you're thinking for all four of you, not just for yourself. Without you, the little game would be over for everyone. You have a responsibility, you know."

"I know, now shut up and kiss me and touch me all over, on every square inch of my body. I want your hands just all over me. I really like to be touched."

They touched, and touched again. It was well after midnight when Buckskin forgot and turned on his left shoulder and almost passed out.

"Enough," Dutch said. "My patient needs his bed rest."

At last they got to sleep.

Eighteen

Across the street from the Dutch Smith house, a man hunkered down beside a picket fence in the shade of a struggling tree next to the wall of an old warehouse and turned his attention to the white painted house across the street and down two lots. He had been watching that house every morning for the past six days.

Alonzo Warnick figured that Morgan would return to the house. He had been there more than once. He was not registered in the hotel or in any of the boarding houses. He would be back.

Warnick sipped on a mug of coffee he had brought from the cafe three blocks down. They were getting used to him drinking a cup there and then providing his own mug to be filled up to take out.

Warnick watched the front door and sighed.

Maybe this wasn't the best wanted poster man to try for. So far he had been nothing but trouble. Three of his hired hands had been shot dead, and he was lucky it hadn't been him. One more try. He'd invested too much time and money to simply walk away.

It would be ideal to nail him right here in town and drag his body down to the sheriff for verification. Then a telegram to Boise and his money would be coming back!

Someone came out the front door of the Smith house, but he relaxed. It was the shorter of the two women. Maud was her name. She was probably going to the market. One small downtown shop had produce and fresh fruits right off the train. Those two women seemed to have big appetites.

An hour later Maud came back and vanished inside the house. Most of the time drapes or blinds were down so he couldn't see much inside. He was a patient man. His watch here would pay off. He just had to be ready when it did.

Inside the house, Buckskin had the best breakfast he'd eaten in a week. He thanked Maud and she grinned.

"What the hell, got to cook for somebody. What I do best is cook. Course I used to be damn good in bed, but I ain't had much practice lately."

She went back into the kitchen and Buckskin sprawled on the couch for a minute, then checked the ticking windup clock on the dining room table. A quarter until nine. He should go collect his pay. He wondered how Herta had made out with Joey's parents. Herta would do fine, he wasn't worried about her.

He stood, checked out his fresh shirt and brown vest and clean pants. Should be good enough for a talk with his boss. He slid the Colt back into his holster after checking the rounds. His belt loops were full. Ready to go.

He found Dutch in her bedroom looking in the mirror.

"Hell, I don't seem to be getting any younger," she said when Buckskin came up behind her.

He put his arms around her and she moved them so one hand covered each breast.

"Yeah, you're an old broad by now. Bet you must be way over 19. Maybe pushing 20."

"You're nice. I don't care what all the other girls say, you're nice."

She stood, turned and kissed him gently. "Going somewhere?"

"Going to bring back some cash. Payday for the kidnapping. That's why I came to town. I was on my way back to my Spade Bit ranch up by Boise when I got the wire. This is just a stopping point on my way home."

"I'd like to have a home sometime."

"You will, that gambling hall. Place to make lots of money. I've seen a good gambling house take in $50,000 a week."

"That was in a big money town. Where, San Francisco?"

"Matter of fact, it was." He patted her round

little bottom covered by the print dress. "You hold the old body together now, I'll be back shortly."

Buckskin turned to the rear of the house and let himself silently out the back door that went through a small woodshed. He paused and checked up and down the alley. There was no one watching that he could see. Warnick might still be in town. He was a tenacious little bastard. So far it didn't look like he had hired anyone to watch the rear door.

Buckskin walked the long way out of the alley and then by Second Avenue to the Minderhausen Brewery. It was not on Main Street which pleased Buckskin. He wasn't sure why he was being so cautious, but that was how he had kept living so long.

At the brewery, he got right in to see Minderhausen. The man was smiling. Buckskin had never seen him smile before.

"Well, well, the man who brought back my little girl," he said, standing and holding out his hand. "I thank you. I also have a stack of cash for you, $5,000, as we agreed. Then Herta said she wanted to give you $2,000 for doing such a good job. I hope you won't carry all that cash on your person."

"I know how to take care of it, Mr. Minderhausen. You seem cheerful this morning."

"Why not. I have my daughter back. She's married to a good boy, and he's agreed to come into the firm and learn the business. It's what I've always wanted. Keep the business in the family. He's got a good business head, which is what is needed today.

"He can always hire good brewmasters to do the technical part of the job. But if nobody is at the business helm, even a good beer won't save a bad company. Now, what's next for you?"

"On my way west. See what I can find down the tracks."

"Thanks again for finding my daughter."

Buckskin went out a side door, found the general store and bought two pairs of town pants, a pair of jeans and two town shirts. He also bought a derringer. He'd thought for a long time that one might come in handy and so now he picked out a Remington two shot breech loading pistol.

It had a three-inch barrel in a .41 caliber and weighed only 12 ounces. The whole weapon was little more than four-and-a-half inches long and was easily concealed in one hand. It cost $9.40, but he figured it was well worth the price. He bought 50 rounds for it as well.

It fit neatly into a small shoulder holster he bought so the weapon went under his left arm. He put the device on under his vest to try it, then took it off. He would wear the holster only with a jacket.

Five minutes later he was back at the alley leading to the Smith house. He checked it out carefully before walking toward the residence. He didn't want any danger to come to the women simply because he was there.

Halfway down the same alley, Alonzo Warnick hid in a large packing cardboard box. He had cut out holes so he could see along most of the alley's length. About ten o'clock he decided he might be watching the wrong door.

The word around town was that the kidnapped daughter of the brewer had been found and returned unharmed. Warnick figured the man doing the finding had been Buckskin. Which meant he was back in town.

When Buckskin Lee Morgan came around the far end of the alley and stepped into the shadows to look it over thoroughly, Warnick knew he had him! The trouble was he couldn't get a shot at him from that distance.

When Morgan figured the alley was clear of watchers, he hurried down two houses and went into the back door of the second one from the far end without knocking.

He had him!

Warnick waited ten minutes after his target went into the house before he slid out of the box, stretched his cramped muscles and hurried down the alley the long way to Main and the saloons. He had to find a pair of helpers, or at least one.

Warnick drank and watched and asked questions and watched again. Finally he found the man he wanted. He wore his gun low and had a two week stubble and needed somebody to buy him a drink.

Warnick set him up twice, then motioned him into the alley. The negotiations took about two minues. The man could shoot, didn't mind working for hire, and jumped at the dollar a day pay. Warnick gave him 20¢ so he wouldn't be falling down drunk and told him they started work at midnight.

Warnick had learned one thing in his recent bounty hunting work. That was to hire a man to do the dangerous work, then move in behind him and mop up what was left.

It was supposed to work that way. He still didn't see how Morgan had slipped out of that hotel room with four of them trying to kill him.

This time he'd be certain. If the two women got in the way, they would be dealt with. He'd never shot a woman before, but there had to be a first time.

They would watch the lights and see where the bedrooms were. Then they would both go in the back door which he was sure would be unlocked. Nobody locked their doors in Rawlins. When they found the right bedroom they would put a slug through Morgan's heart, push aside the woman he was sleeping with, and drag his body down to the sheriff's office.

Neat, clean and quick. That was the way Warnick liked it. If they had to kill one of the women, it would be an accident. He couldn't be responsible for accidents.

Warnick grinned. He had done a good day's work already. He would pick up his gunhand—his name was Vince—at the Crooked Elbow Saloon at midnight.

Warnick went to the hotel where he had been staying and ordered a full steak dinner for his noon meal. He could afford to eat well now. The Wanted poster said $2,000 for the hide of Buckskin Lee Morgan. Yeah. This time tomorrow, he'd be in the money!

In the small white house two doors in from the cross street, Buckskin listened to the plans of the four women. Pris and Navaro had come for the meeting. Pris was as cold and standoffish as ever. She wouldn't even look at Buckskin, which was fine with him.

Dutch had got things moving quickly. "Then we agree, one more run, one more bank, and we'll each have enough money for a long, long time. We close up our little shop after that. Agreed?"

Maud nodded. "Damn right, I'm getting tired of this."

Navaro looked up. Dutch had talked with her before, using what little Spanish she had until Navaro understood. She watched Dutch and said, "*Si.*"

Pris looked at Navaro with anger. "Why don't she learn English, for shit's sakes. Yeah, fine. Last job. Then I move on."

Dutch picked it up. "We'll take the stage to Jeffrey City. Not a big bank, but no guards, and just two people work inside. We'll do our usual closing up technique right at three. This one even pulls down a shade at closing time."

"We get horses again?" Pris asked.

"Yes, we'll have them if we need them. We'll take our dresses with us, and if we have time, we'll change clothes in the back room where nobody can see us, and slip out the back bank door in our dresses.

"We wander down the alley, throw our men's

clothes in a burn barrel and walk to the hotel one at a time. Should work. If there's any shooting and anyone gets wind of us, then we'll have to use the horses and make a run for it. Jeffrey City is only 65 miles or so if we have to ride for it."

"That's a long ride," Buckskin said.

"I doubt if we'll have to make the ride. We'll be careful, professional and neat," Dutch said.

The other two women left shortly. Dutch, Maud and Buckskin sipped at a late night cup of coffee.

"Does Navaro understand about the last job?" Buckskin asked.

"Yes. She's going to take her money and go to Mexico. With that much money she can live like a queen down there. Buy a husband if she wants one."

"You still thinking about the gambling operation?" Buck asked.

"You bet!" Maud said quickly. "I sure as hell don't want to rob banks for the rest of my life. It could be a short life."

"Sure you want to risk it again? The four of you could ride out of here well fixed without the final fling."

Dutch shook her head. "Not a chance. Part of it is the fun of the deception, then walking around right in their faces while we wait for a stage. Probably only one a day. I forgot to ask."

Maud looked at the clock. "Morning comes early. We got to catch that eight-thirty stage."

"Yes, Mother," Dutch said.

Maud took a swing at her and missed.

Twenty minutes later, Buckskin and Dutch lay in the soft bed in each other's arms.

"Not even once tonight, just some kissing," Dutch said sternly. "We have to save our strength for tomorrow. The stage office said it will take us 12 hours to get up there."

"We stay in the hotel and hit the bank the next day, right?" Buckskin asked.

"Yes, then we catch the morning stage out the next day."

"Sounds reasonable. Now you move over there and don't touch me and just maybe I can get to sleep."

"After we get back we'll make up for lost time," Dutch said. "Then we'll figure out where to go to get our saloon and gambling emporium going."

"Denver might be good," Buckskin said. "San Francisco would be better. We'll talk about it."

He got up and went from the bedroom to the kitchen and on to the woodshed attached to the back where the rear door was. In front of the door he stood up a dozen empty gallon cans. There was no lock on the door, but if anyone tried to come inside they would make one hell of a racket. He threw the bolt on the front door and went back to bed. He slept at once.

Just after one A.M. Buckskin came upright in bed. The cans in the woodshed had tumbled. Someone was coming in the house, maybe Warnick.

He grabbed his six gun and motioned for Dutch to get against the wall. Heavy footsteps pounded through the one story house. Buckskin raised his six-gun and cocked the trigger aiming it at the bedroom door.

Nineteen

Alonzo Warnick was the first one into the back door of the small one floor white house about one A.M. that night. He heard the first can fall over and knew he had been outguessed. He charged in, rushing to the kitchen, then through to the bedroom on the right where he figured Buckskin must be. He kicked in the door and fired twice at the shadow of a bed, then saw the flash of a gun to his left and tried to swing his arm around that way, but his right arm didn't work anymore. He was shot!

Furiously, he spun and charged back toward the kitchen. He tipped over a chair, heard the person slam into it and by then he was out the door and racing down the alley. Behind him someone fired three times, then the footrace began.

Warnick felt something dripping off his fingers. Before he looked he knew it was blood. Damnit, what had gone wrong this time?

He sensed that the man behind him was gaining. He cut through a yard to the street, ran down aways, then cut back to the same alley and rushed on. He was looking for a horse, any horse. There had to be one here somewhere. How much farther could he run?

Warnick knew he was running slower. His right arm hung limply at his side, no help in running. His left pumped hard. He turned back toward Main Street. There would be a horse or two next to a saloon. Somebody always got drunk and forgot where he left his mount.

Behind him he heard the man puffing. He was getting tired, too. Was he losing too much blood? Warnick didn't know. If he passed out, then he'd be dead, because he knew this time Morgan would stomp him to death.

He went past the first blush of light from a house and he saw the man behind him, running slower now. Warnick was gaining on him, getting away! It surged his efforts and he ran around the next corner and spotted two horses at the Gunpoint Saloon. He rushed up to one, put his left foot in the stirrup and swung up on the mount, then reached down with his left hand and undid the one wrap of the reins around the hitching rail. He kicked the horse in the flanks and it jolted down the street away from Morgan.

Buckskin Lee Morgan puffed around the last corner on Main Street and stared down the block. He wore only a pair of pants he had jerked on when he got up buck naked from the bed and before Warnick stormed into the room. He was barefoot, bare chested and about ready to fall over. Warnick was getting away. The damn Big Fifty gunshot in his arm had taken more out of his hide than he realized. Now he could only stand there and watch as the man grabbed a horse, lifted into the saddle and galloped down the street. The man's right arm still hung useless at his side.

Buckskin walked slowly back to Dutch Smith's house. He was exhausted. For a moment he wasn't sure he could get there. Now that would be stupid, to pass out in the middle of the street and have some cowboy find him early in the morning. He gritted his teeth, balled his fists and marched back up the alley to the door.

Dutch Smith stood in the backyard wearing a robe, a six-gun in one hand and a shotgun cradled in the other arm.

"Missed him?" Dutch asked.

"He got away. Had to be that skunk Warnick, the bounty hunter."

"One of them didn't get away. Come take a look."

Maud sat in the living room rocking slowly in the chair. A lamp glowed brightly against the pulled drapes. Six feet from the front door lay a body.

"Dead?" Buckskin asked.

Dutch nodded and pointed at Maud who still held her six-gun. She looked straight ahead.

Morgan rolled the body over. A black smudge showed just over his right eye and a big bloody splash stained the back of his head.

"There were two of them," Buckskin said. He caught the dead man by the armpits and dragged him to the front steps. There he got under him enough and heaved him on his shoulders.

Buckskin wasn't sure how far he could carry the man, but every block would help. He got him over two blocks before Buckskin's left knee buckled and they both fell in the dirt. Morgan pushed away from the corpse, dusted off his pants and hurried back to the small white house.

At the steps he saw Dutch washing the blood away. By morning it would be clean and pure. He helped her work on the floor in the living room, and the wall where the blood had splattered. Not much could be done about the wall. At last they hung a picture over the spot even though it was low.

When they were done, they went in and sat beside Maud.

"Hell, don't baby me. I'm all right. Just the first man I ever killed and it don't feel too damn good." She shrugged. "First thing I heard was some clatter out in the woodshed. I got up thinking that damn tom cat from down the street was prowling again and I'd fire a shot over his head to scare the gizzard out of the varmint.

"Before I got out of my bedroom door somebody pushed the door open and next thing I knew he fired three shots into my bed, then he turned and ran for the front door. I ran behind him and yelled. He looked back just as I shot."

Maud stood and went to the kitchen. She wrung out a cloth with cold water, washed her face and put it over her forehead. Cooled the cloth and did the same thing again.

"Lucky shot, I'd say. I was so damn mad I'd have shot even if he didn't turn around. He tried to *kill me.*"

"So he got what he deserved," Buckskin said. "I carried him over two blocks. Won't be anything to connect him with you come morning."

Maud looked up. "The other one. I heard somebody else shoot. He get away?"

"I'm afraid so. I had him dead, and only hit him in the arm. He might not use it much anymore. He had to be Warnick, the bounty hunter who's been trying to kill me."

Buckskin slammed his flat palm against the wall. "Damnit! I didn't want either of you to be in danger because of me. This is the last night I spend here. From now on I'm gone, or in a hotel, or out along the river somewhere. No more will I put you ladies in danger."

"If this is your last night here, I have a favor to ask," Maud said. She looked at Dutch. "Smith, it all right with you? Just want to borrow him for a while. Hell, I'm probably a virgin again, been so damn long."

Dutch nodded and turned and walked back to her room. Maud caught Buckskin's hand, blew out the lamp in the living room and led him into her room.

"Oh," she said in the darkness. "I mean, I didn't even ask you, Morgan. You want to ram an old shitter like me? I'll understand if you don't want to."

Buckskin laughed softly. "You want a light on

or you remember about the plumbing?"

"Hell, I remember, but I'd like a light. Been so long since I seen a stiff cock I forget what one looks like." She found a match, scratched it and lit a lamp beside the bed.

Maud stood there and looked at him. She wore a white nightgown that hid her chunky figure. She reached up and ran her hands over Buckskin's bare shoulders, down his arms and across his chest with its black hair.

"Christ, but I'm liking this. I always did like bedding a good man. I mean, *I loved having sex*. Lots of women don't. Their bad luck. Then suddenly, I'm a widow. What they say about widows was true of me. I wanted a man damn bad. But in most small towns, there ain't no way to get laid without half the town knowing about it the next morning."

She sat on the edge of the bed and Buckskin sat beside her.

"Maud, I'm sorry I let that bastard break in here and shoot at you."

"I'm not. Now I get your ass in my bed." She grinned. "I told you I like it. In your weakened condition you should be good for three or four, at least."

She knelt in front of him and unbuckled his belt, then opened his fly. "You mind me taking the lead, undressing you?"

He shook his head. She pulled down his pants and when she saw his limp penis she grinned. "Damn worm. I can help him." She bent and kissed the base of his tool, then whipped off her nightgown. She was chunky, but fronted with large breasts that had big brown areolas and thumb sized nipples.

She stood and pushed a breast at his mouth and he sucked it in.

"Yeah, yeah! Been too damn long since somebody chewed on my titties. Damn good!" She pushed her hands down to his crotch and laughed. "Hey, that worm we had down here done got himself some prick of a back bone."

She lifted his legs on the bed, and he edged over laying on his back. She went on hands and knees over him letting her breasts hang down toward his mouth. They were the biggest breasts he had ever seen. He chewed on the nipples until she squealed in delight.

She moved lower, lifted his erection and positioned it, then slowly lowered herself down on him as he lanced upward into her throbbing vagina.

"Oh, lord, Oh, lord, oh lord, but that is fine. I like to get it rammed up my pussy. Yes! Don't worry, I'll do all the hard work. Glory, but I ain't had a good poking in two years. You know how long that is? You probably get pussy every couple of days. How'd you like to go for two years without some snatch, not even jacking off? Hell, you'd go crazy with wet dreams every night. I know about you men."

Then she began to puff and pant and she began rocking forward as she worked up and down his pole. She rode him like a stallion, pumping and puffing and squirming around and around.

"Oh, hell, I forgot," she said and laughed. Then she began to squeeze him with her internal muscles on every stroke and within a half dozen plunges Buckskin climaxed with eight hard upward thrusts.

She grinned. "Yeah, it always works. I'd make one hell of a whore, you know that? If the men weren't so damn ugly, so mean and so shitty smelly, I'd enjoy the work."

She lifted off him and lay beside him on the bed.

"Didn't you make it?" he asked.

"Oh, shit, I never climax. Never can. Last time I did I was 13 and my uncle had my panties down around my ankles and his hand inside his own pants and he diddled me with his finger. I climaxed that time, lordy it was good. Just then my old paw came into the outhouse and surprised us both and he damn near killed his wife's brother. Uncle Ned never come around the place again, and I got my bottom paddled.

"Since then I ain't never cum in my life. Oh, don't think you can do it. My sweet, loving husband tried everything we ever heard about. One night we tried thirty times and I just never come off.

"Don't worry about it. I enjoy the contact, the pumping, feeling your big whanger sliding up my chute. I get lots of jollies without having to climax. Might even be more fun my way."

"Maud, you over killing your first man?"

"Hell, no. Won't never get over it. But, hell, I can live with it. Like not cuming, I guess. It's just part of me now. I won't worry about it again, and I'll know how it feels. I just might be a little more cautious how I shoot at the next man I have to.

"Like in a couple of days when we rustle that bank. Sure, I'll know how powerful that six-gun is now. I'll realize it a little more. But this is the last time. I might never pick up a gun again. Who knows? I really love the idea of opening a gambling hall."

She looked at him. "How long you need to get hard again?"

Buckskin laughed. "See what you can do."

She padded into the kitchen and brought back a small wash pan and a pair of cloths and a towel. She washed him off, dried his genitals, then nestled at his crotch with her head.

"Remember, I got three holes where your big cock here can fit. Before this night is over, you're going to be in all of them. Hell, I'm not worried about you keeping up your strength. You can sleep all the way on the stage ride tomorrow.

"Course if we five are the only ones on the stage, I might do you once on the ride. I've never been pumped on a stagecoach before, have you?"

Buckskin said he hadn't and laced his fingers behind his head as she began working on him down below. It didn't take long for her mouth to bring him to full excitement.

A little later she lifted up and looked at him. "Since I'm down here already, no sense in moving. You better turn over on your hands and knees, though. Most men can't climax very well on their backs. Bet you never knew that. True." She slid under him and then began to work on his erection pumping back and forth with her mouth.

An hour later, Buckskin eased down on the

pillows beside Maud and shook his head.

"You're as hot to go as when we started. You've convinced me, you really do like sex, any hole, any position. You've got to promise me one thing. After we get you two established in your gambling hall, that you'll get yourself married. You're too much woman to go to waste this way."

She lifted up and kissed him. "Glory be, marvelous young man. That's the nicest thing anybody's said to me in years. Are you available?"

"Afraid not. I'm just not in the marriage market."

"Oh, shit." She laughed. "You about done for the night?"

"I think so."

"You don't have to leave, you can stay here. Been a long time since I slept all night with a man."

"It's almost four A.M."

"So I let you off easy. Now go to sleep."

He did, but only after he assured himself that Alonzo Warnick would not be back tonight. By tomorrow it would be too late for him to find Morgan.

Twenty

Buckskin was up and dressed, took a small carpetbag with two changes of clothes and headed for the North Wyoming Stage Lines just at daylight. He wanted to be away from the Smith house.

He made it with no contact from any hostiles. He had a good breakfast at a cafe on Main, then sat inside at the stage station to wait for the rig to come.

One by one the women came in and bought a ticket to Jeffrey City. He pretended he didn't even know they were there. Each wore a nice dress and a hat. Each had a carpetbag and they waited primly. Buckskin still had trouble believing that these four women could be bank robbers.

That was part of the beauty of their method.

Nobody would suspect four women in town, even if they were strangers. Women just didn't go around robbing banks. Everyone knew that.

Buckskin asked the station agent why they used the old celerity wagons on this run.

"Don't rightly know, young feller. Probably because the owner could buy them cheap when so many stage lines went out of business cause of the train. Best reason I know. We don't get a lot of business up that way. Why you going to Jeffrey City? Ain't much of a town."

"Looking up a relative."

"That so? I used to live up there. Maybe I know him."

"Agnew, Charles Agnew."

The agent shut his eyes and thought a moment. "Nope, he must be new. I don't know no Agnew."

The stage was on time since it began in Rawlins. Besides the five of them there was one other man. He looked at the ladies, tipped his hat and promptly went to sleep in one corner of the bouncing little wagonlike coach.

The celerity coach was really only a wagon. They had been used in the high mountains for particularly difficult terrain that required a light rig and a lot of clearance. They looked like a light farm wagon with five wooden uprights on each side that held up a light roof. Curtains were provided along the sides to keep out the wind and rain. Benches on each end and two in the center provided the seating accommodations.

It was going to be a long, rough ride.

The first 15 miles up the stage road northwest seemed the hardest, Buckskin hoped. He'd had

Maud rebandage his left arm before he left the house that morning, but each jolt of the unsprung rig sent needles of pain into him. He gave a sign of relief when they pulled into the stage stop after almost three hours.

The driver yelled at the wranglers who had a new team of four horses ready to hitch up. He stepped to the side and looked in.

"Won't be here long enough for you to step down for more than a minute. There's a convenience out back if'n anyone has a call of nature. Don't take long. I got me a schedule to keep."

Buckskin wished desperately for a cold beer or a hot cup of coffee, but the relay station was little more than a barn and corral for the horses and a lean to for the two wranglers. He had no idea where they cooked.

They made a food stop a little after two that afternoon. The stage station was not nearly as good as those Buckskin had seen on the old Overland Stage route. This one was only a rough cabin made of rock and mortar with a pole roof.

The meal was some kind of stew, but it had lots of vegetables in it and some meat which could have been venison or beef, Buckskin wasn't sure. Coffee and bread and butter finished the meal. It was 50¢, take it or leave it. They all ate and had seconds on coffee.

A half hour stop and they were moving again. Dutch lifted her brows at Buckskin. He sat on the far back of the rig facing forward and Dutch sat on the front seat. For some reason, the back of the rig was the bumpiest.

It was nearly eight that evening when they rolled into Jeffrey City and eased cramped muscles to get out of the rig. The hotel was just across the street.

"Ladies, are you going to the hotel?" Buckskin asked as they stood in front of their bags. "If so I'll be glad to help carry your luggage."

He toted three and his own, Pris held on to her own small bag with a look that said "touch it and I'll kill you." At the hotel he let the women register first, then took the one room that was left. The man who had started with them had gotten off some place enroute. Evidently there was a ranch back off the track somewhere.

Dutch's room was 22 on the second floor. He was assigned room 24. Upstairs he waited a few moments, locked his own door, then went to 22 and knocked softly. The door opened at once.

Inside Dutch kissed him fervently.

"I nearly attacked you twice on the trip up here." She leaned back so she could see him clearly. "And thanks for what you did for Maud last night. She's going to talk about you for years, I know she will. That was most gallant of you."

"Hell no, not gallant at all. I enjoyed myself. You should see what she can do with her....."

Dutch put her fingers over his lips. "That part I don't need to know about."

They dropped on the bed and one of the boards fell out. They giggled.

He kissed her and pulled her on top of him. "It's not too late, you know. You can call the robbery off."

"I wouldn't mind, but the others would be

disappointed. Pris would throw a fit and probably shoot all of us just for practice."

"That girl is crazy, you know that."

"Yes, but a good shot. She saved our skins once."

"I'm glad of that."

"Are we going to waste the whole evening?"

"We could get some dessert in the dining room downstairs."

"It probably wouldn't be much better than that soup we had at the stage stop. No. Let's stay here."

"Would you take a look at my arm. Does the bandage need redoing?"

She checked it. "It doesn't show any bleeding."

"Good, we'll leave it alone."

"I want to get out of these clothes," Dutch said.

"Good, I'll watch."

She took off her traveling clothes as if he wasn't there.

"How was it being married?"

She looked down at him as she combed her hair. "It was good. I was protected. I felt safe, secure. I was loved. I was happy. Any time I wanted to make love, I could. Any time he wanted to make love, we did. It was . . . perfect."

"I never tried that kind of a commitment. Maybe someday."

She sat on the edge of the bed wearing a thin cotton nightgown.

"Are you going to sit there all night or are you going to undress and come to bed?"

"I'm not sleepy yet."

"Good, neither am I."

* * *

The next morning they had breakfast at separate tables. Maud and Dutch had breakfast together, then did some shopping.

They had decided to get the horses the way they usually did: they asked the hotel clerk to rent the horses and saddles for them so they could do some riding and bring them around to the back of the hotel.

The room clerks thought little of it as long as they got a good tip. This time they did.

After the noon dinner they all met in Dutch's room.

Buckskin wanted to make one last try to talk them out of the shot at the bank, but Dutch had warned him not to. They were this far along on it, and raring to go like race horses. There was not a chance they could be stopped now.

They made last minute plans. Buckskin wouldn't help them this time. He would be sitting across the street in one of the chairs leaned up against the general store.

"Remember, we work it as usual. No changing clothes inside the bank. That wouldn't work here. I was in the bank this morning to change a twenty dollar bill. There's an old warehouse about two blocks down from the bank that is not being used.

"Buckskin will take one of our carpetbags down there and drop it off. Inside will be all of our dresses, so be sure to get to me what you want to wear back here later on and I'll pack it. That's our only change. If we have to ride, the way we are, Buck will catch up with us in a few hours."

Dutch looked around at the other three women. "Any questions? Any problems? Let's be damn sure we don't fire a shot unless we have to. If we don't use our guns, we don't have to ride astride some damn horse for sixty-five miles."

They slipped out one by one and came back with the dresses they would change to in the warehouse.

An hour later, Buckskin hid the carpetbag with the dresses behind a board at the big warehouse. There was nobody in it or around it. He walked in one door and out another and went back to Main Street by a different route.

At 2:45 P.M. he sat in a chair across the street from the bank. It was a long ten minutes. Then at 2:58 the women began to wander into the bank one by one. They all wore men's clothes, and hats pulled low with smudges of dirt on their faces.

They were the last ones inside the bank. He wished he were inside.

Promptly at three o'clock, Dutch locked the front door and pulled down the shade. The clerk had just come around the counter to do the job when Dutch pulled up her bandanna and pushed her six-gun in his face.

"Stick up!" Maud bellowed in her baritone voice. One little old woman at the teller's cage fainted. The manager ran to get his pistol from the drawer but Pris slammed her weapon down across his head knocking him senseless.

"Clean it out!" Maud rasped.

They worked quickly, cleanly. Dutch pushed the teller down on the floor and tied his hands and feet, then put a gag in his mouth. She tied the unconscious woman the same way, then helped them push the bills and gold coins in the convenient bank bags of stiff canvas.

It took them three minutes to loot the bank, clean out the vault and walk to the back door. They checked outside and saw the horses where they had left them just across the alley and down two doors.

They pulled down their kerchief masks and walked to the horses, stepped into saddles and rode away, two in each direction out of the alley and headed for the old building.

As soon as Buckskin saw the shade go down, he walked toward the warehouse. He walked quickly and was almost there when he saw two men ride toward him. Then he grinned. Dutch and Maud. They went past him without a glance and on to the warehouse. They rode behind it, and he lost sight of them.

By the time Buckskin got to the warehouse he heard the women in the far end of it. They chattered quietly. Pants and shirts flew and dresses dropped in place.

Dutch stuffed the men's clothing in the carpetbag and left to get her horse. She led the animal out the far door and walked as she took the horse back to where they had picked them up behind the hotel.

Buckskin hurried and caught up with Dutch, took the reins of the horse and the carpetbag. It was much too heavy to have only clothes in it.

"Careful, you're also carrying all the bank booty," Dutch said.

"Any trouble?"

"Not a bit. Just one customer who fainted and two men. They won't know what hit them."

They tied the horse at the rail in back of the hotel and went inside. Dutch led the way and Buckskin came a minute behind her.

She waited for him on the second floor. "It was so easy that I was bored. That was no fun at all. It's getting to be like work. I'm glad we're done. All we have to do is have the clerk return the horses and give him a dollar tip and we're free and clear."

"The men's clothes," Buckskin reminded her.

"I'll dump them in an alley somewhere tonight."

"I'm in the mood to go shopping," Dutch said. "I bet there's not a single women's dress shop in town."

"This isn't exactly Omaha."

"Then let's go to Omaha on the train and go shopping."

"I think you should. But I've got to go the other way."

The other three gathered in Dutch's room one by one. They took out the bank bags and began counting. They had a little over two thousand dollars.

"Five hundred each ain't bad," Dutch said. "Everyone going back to Rawlins, I'd guess. The stage leaves here at eight-thirty tomorrow morning. The agent promised me it would be a Concord stage, so it should be easier riding."

One by one the women drifted out of the room when no one else was in the hall.

"Now let's go shopping," Dutch said. They went shopping and she found a dress she liked in the general store. It cost almost four dollars, but she said it was for her anniversary. The woman in the store understood the extravagance.

Twenty-One

Buckskin and Dutch came out of the general store and started walking slowly down the block. Dutch wore a tight fitting calico print that covered her from neck to wrist and swept the uneven boardwalk in front of the stores. Buckskin thought that she was as pretty as a newborn fawn trying her legs for the first time.

Each store owner built his own boardwalk out to the street. Sometimes there was a step up or down betwee stores when owners decided that they wanted the walk at a different height than their neighbors.

They were across from the bank when somebody stared in the partly shuttered front door.

"People in there are tied up!" the man yelled. "The bank's been robbed!"

A dozen people gathered quickly. A deputy sheriff ran up and looked in the door. He kicked it hard and the lock inside gave way. He hurried in and a moment later he was outside telling somebody to run and get the sheriff.

The bank had been robbed!

All around them people were staring at the bank and making comments. Dutch looked at Buckskin and shook her head.

"Can you imagine that? Goodness sakes. In this modern, enlightened age you'd think people would be more respectful of authority."

Buckskin nodded solemnly but came within an inch of bursting out in laughter. She took his arm and they walked back toward the hotel as the sheriff ran up with three deputies and went in the bank.

Shortly after, the woman customer Dutch had tied up came out shrilling in anger. She talked to anyone who would listen.

"There were six of them, all over six feet tall. Mean and nasty. One of them hit me three times and made lewd suggestions. He made us lay on the floor. They tortured the bank clerk until he opened the vault. They weren't local men for sure, because I saw them all before they pulled up their masks. Mean and ugly as sin they was, probably some bank robbery gang from Missouri. They got a lot of them down there."

Buckskin grinned. "That lady said the robbers were big and mean and ugly. I guess I'll have to go along with that."

Dutch punched him in the ribs. "Tonight I'll show you just how mean I can be," she said, but she was enjoying this part more than the robbery itself.

The five of them caught the stage the next morning and were back in Rawlins a little before seven that evening. Buckskin slipped in the back door of Dutch's house and packed his carpetbag, gave both Maud and Dutch a kiss and hurried out into the night.

He took a room at the hotel under the name Jason Pollack. He made sure the room was on the second floor where he pushed the dresser in front of the window and put a stiff backed chair under the door handle. He slept well. The next day he would decide just what was next on his travel plans.

Just down the hall, Serilda met with her brother from Chicago. Karl Schwartz was short and fat with reddish cheeks, blond hair and beady eyes that shaded from brown to almost black when he was angry.

"We'll get this pig and make him pay," Karl spouted. "At last he will pay for killing papa. I took what you wrote out and had it copied twice. Now all you have to do is sign your statement of charges against Minderhausen and we have our ammunition."

"It's just as I wrote it, Karl?" Serilda asked.

"Almost. Even better in spots, especially how we described his taking of your virginity. Don't worry, it will stand up in court. He'll wish he had never heard of the brewery business before we're through with him."

"Karl, I know you read for the law some, but are you sure we're doing this right?"

"Absolutely. We have signed, sworn statements that he seduced you, that he kept you in sexual bondage here for almost six months, that he raped you, and now that he's the father of your unborn child. The threat of the publicity alone will be enough to make the old brewmaster crumble. Mark my words, Serilda."

She signed the papes and Karl folded them and put them in a leather case.

"These statements are our back up case if he does not agree to marry you. Oh, I quite agree that marriage is by far the best plan. That way we can have all of his estate, every blessed dollar he ever earned!"

"It would be the slower way Karl, and remember, he's only 52. He could live 30 years yet."

"Could, but not with our plans. A widow is a much nicer term than a wife. I guarantee that if you do marry the old bastard, he won't live more than two or three weeks before the two of you have a tragic accident. You'll come out of it scratched and bruised but fit. Poor Minderhausen won't be so lucky. Then we have it all!"

"What about the daughter, Herta?" Serilda asked.

"Under modern jurisprudence, a minor daughter, even married, would not be in line to inherit anything. If he writes a will, we'll contest it sharply in court and win easily."

"I guess that covers it all," Serilda said. "We

must never be seen together. That could spoil it all. I'll talk to Hartley tonight and tell him my great news. Tomorrow I'll tell you his reaction. Now I have to go, I've been away far too long visiting my sick friend as it is. The driver will cover up for me. He's in my debt."

She touched her brother on the shoulder, then saw there was no one in the hall and slipped out. She went down the steps and out the side door. The carriage waited there and five minutes later she was back in the big house on the highest point in the low lying town.

Minderhausen was reading a German language newspaper when she came into his study. He put the paper aside.

"Serilda, you are the one great joy in my life. Did I tell you that? You make my days worth living."

She came and sat on his knee and stroked his cheek and bent and kissed it.

"My darling, that makes what I have to tell you all the sweeter. Today . . . today, I found out for sure." Her eyes glowed as she pushed near him and stared in his face. "Today I know that I am pregnant with your son!"

For a moment she misjudged his reaction. His face reddened and his eyes shut and then he leaped up shouting and yelling and running around the room. At last he came back and grabbed her face with both hands and kissed her lips so softly she hardly felt it. It was the sexiest kiss she had ever known.

His hands held her face tenderly, his dark eyes stared into hers.

"Those are the most beautiful words that I have ever heard! You make me so happy, so exceedingly, so wondrously happy! I don't know the right words in English. I'm overwhelmed. I am so thankful, so pleased."

Then his brow creased. "Oh, *mine got*!" He clasped his hands behind his back and paced the room. "*Mine got*! What can we do? What will people think?" He turned to her, his face solemn. "How much are you pregnant, how many months?"

"Oh, just one month, but I'm sure. I'm sure."

"Then we be married tomorrow. I arrange with the judge to have the date on the papers set back three months, and we will be married tomorrow. All quiet and just the two of us, but nice. And I get the big ring for you tomorrow, and best dress in town for you to wear with the judge. So happy! We will be so much happy!"

He caught her and they danced around the den, then out into the hall to the great living room. Minderhausen danced a good solid German waltz without music and his face glowed.

"How can I be such a happy man! Everything good is happening to me. My Herta is safe and married. Her husband is working with me now and someday will take over the business. Then we will travel to Germany, to Rome, to Paris, to all of the great cities of the world. Just you and me, and my new son!"

That night he touched her and fondled her and asked her if it still would be all right. She smiled and said it would be fine for three or four months yet, so they made love, and for a moment she was caught up in the drama of it all and she believed, too, that she was pregnant with his son.

Morning brought a flurry of activity. They scoured the dress stores but found nothing suitable. At last she wore her best dress, a light pink with ruffles and bows, and he put on his best black suit and they went to the courthouse where the county judge married them.

The judge himself had back dated the marriage license and everything was legal and proper. They went home at once and consummated the marriage in the big master bedroom where he never before had allowed her to come. Now that she was his wife he insisted that she move in with all of her clothes and goods.

"If you want to sleep in your other bed sometimes, that is entirely fine. When you are more pregnant this may be your wish."

She lay there watching him. He wasn't that old. Maybe it would be nice to be married to him for a long time, and have all the money she wanted. She was sure that he would buy her anything her heart desired.

As if anticipating her thoughts, he took her to the best jewelry store in town that same afternoon and bought her a wedding ring set with six diamonds, and a large solitaire diamond ring for her short engagement.

When she admired pearl and jade earrings, he bought them without even asking the price. They were almost $50! When she left the jewelry store with Minderhausen, Serilda was wavering in her plans for becoming quickly rich.

Later that afternoon, Minderhausen went to the

brewery to take care of business. He had hired a cook and housecleaner and the Irish woman would be there the next day. That evening they would eat out. She was not going to have to do a bit of work around the house.

Serilda left the house and walked to the hotel where she went up the back steps and knocked on her brother's door.

When he saw the rings, he tried to take them off.

"I could cash them in and play at the gaming tables for a week, even if I lost, with what I could sell those for," he said.

"No, these are symbols of my marriage. They can't be sold, not while I'm married."

Her brother drank from a bottle of beer he had brought in. "Heard about the good news, Mrs. Minderhausen. The old boy sure didn't waste any time. How soon do you want the accident to happen?"

"Karl, I've been thinking about that. Maybe that's not such a good idea. We can get plenty of money this way. I'm sure he'll give me money each month for spending. We can do quite nicely."

"Goddamnit, no! We worked up this little plan to get even with old Minderhausen once and for all. He killed your daddy, how can you forget that! The man has to be punished, and the best way to punish him is to kill the bastard!"

"Karl, you're half drunk. We better talk about this when you have a clear head."

"Clear as I'm gonna be for weeks. I'm gonna start playing poker tonight and I play best when

I'm relaxed with a few dozen bottles of beer. Don't fret. I'll take care of everything. You just be a good little wife to the old bastard. The accident will come as a surprise to you, too. Then you can't give it away."

"Karl, we're going to talk about this again. I think it's a much better plan to wait at least a year before the accident. People in this town will talk. The sheriff might even get involved. We have to be careful."

"Baby sister, you did your part with your cunt and your big tits. Now it's my turn to do my job and kill the old bastard so it looks like an accident. You just go on home and play the proper wife and keep your knees apart so he'll be zonked out half the time. That will keep him in line when you tell him you'd like a little cash to spend downtown. A hundred a week should be about right.

"Now get the hell out of here, I got to do some planning and figure out just how to make it look so good, nobody in his right mind would even speculate that the death of beer magnate Minderhausen was anything but a tragic accident."

Serilda started to argue with him again, but it was too late. He was too drunk to be rational. She wold have to do it later. She was more convinced than ever that a slow approach to getting his money would be best.

What if it did take a year? That way it would be certain and completely safe. She shivered. She had no intentions of spending even one day in custody of the law, and certainly not 20 years in a woman's prison for murder.

* * *

Mrs. Herta Minderhausen Radowitz stood at the hotel window and looked down on the street. She had just spent ten dollars bribing a worried and frightened hotel clerk to remember if Buckskin Lee Morgan was registered at the hotel.

"If I tell you and he finds out, he'll whip me good, break my legs probably, if he don't kill me," the clerk had whined.

She assured him that she was a special case and she would caution Mr. Morgan against any violence on the clerk's person.

Reluctantly, the clerk gave Herta the room number and she wasted no time in presenting herself to a surprised Lee Morgan.

"Mr. Morgan, you can be a most difficult man. I have thanked you in good measure for rescuing Joseph and me from the clutches of Poncho. I have made a simple request for your further services and you turn me down."

"Ma'am, I've been on my way to Idaho for two months now. I have to get back there and take care of my ranch, the Spade Bit. I raise horses there, and I need to attend to it now and again."

"I understand that, but this is as important! Much more important than your rescuing me. I've known this woman for four months, she is not what she seems. Now, this morning, I hear that Judge Barnes has married my father and Serilda. I don't even know her last name.

"I was certain that for the past three months while she was our cook and housekeeper, that she was something more than that to my father. I'm sure now that he had been sleeping with her all that time. She is an opportunist. She is a healthy young girl who has grabbed the affection of a man almost too old to be her father. She is after only one thing from him—his money.

"All I want you to do is make some inquiries in Chicago by wire, and find out what you can about her."

"If this is true it will come out quickly, don't you think, Mrs. Radowitz? Then he can divorce her quietly and it will be over."

"A divorce takes two years in Wyoming. A lot can happen in two years. I've heard of such cases, where younger women have been known to deal harshly with a rich husband. So harshly that their very lives were in danger."

Buckskin looked up quickly. "You have some evidence that the woman might kill your father?"

Herta looked out the window again. She had seen them in the jewelry store that morning and knew it was the beginning.

"Mr. Morgan, I lived in the same house as that woman. I confessed my love for Joseph to her and saw her reaction. I saw how she treated my father, and what she said about him when he wasn't there to hear. She called him an old man, said he was fat and old and really ugly. She was angry with him, and I couldn't figure out why.

"Yes, Mr. Morgan. I think my father's life is in serious danger right now, and for as long as he's married to Serilda."

"His will. Will he change it to favor her?"

"I assume he had left everything to me, but under Wyoming law, now that he's married, that wouldn't be possible. The widow must receive three-quarters of all goods, as I recall. I'll check it for you with a lawyer friend of Joseph's."

Buckskin sighed.

"Mr. Morgan. I'll put you on a retainer of $50 a day while you investigate, and a payment of $1,000 if you do find that there is a danger to my father from Serilda and prove it to my satisfaction." She held out her hand. "Do we have an agreement of employment, Mr. Morgan?"

Buckskin took her hand wondering how long this was going to take.

"We have an agreement, Mrs. Radowitz."

Twenty-Two

That same afternoon, Buckskin went to the court house and checked the application file for marriage licenses. He found the entry and saw it had been dated three months ago, but in the register is was entered after three licenses issued this day. Someone had adjusted the date. The name was more important to him: Serilda Miller. A good German name. Nothing wrong with that.

He wandered back to the hotel, keeping a sharp eye out for a man with a bandaged right arm. He didn't see Mr. Warnick. At the hotel, Buckskin waited until the room clerk wasn't busy, then he came up to him with his Colt against his chest so the clerk could see it.

"You owe me, dead man," Buckskin said in an even, flat undertaker's tone.

The clerk's eyes went wide. "I didn't think it

would hurt. She's a nice lady, and wouldn't harm you."

"You still owe me. You know Serilda Miller, the former housekeeper and now wife of Mr. Minderhausen?"

"Seen her around."

"She ever use the hotel, for an hour or two say, or come to see people?"

"Not much. Did see her last night. She asked me what room a Karl Schwartz was in. Said he was her brother."

"Interesting. What room is he in?"

"Twenty-Two."

"Thanks. Did you tell me this?"

"Not me, Mr. Morgan."

"Have you seen me here or around town last couple of days?"

"No sir, not me!"

"Have you ever heard my name before?"

"What name? No, sir."

Buckskin eased away from him and slid the six-gun back in leather.

"Nice not talking to you," he said and grinned as he walked away.

He made it to the railroad station quickly working up his ten word message as he went. The telegraph operator took the message and held out his hand for the six dollars.

The telegram went to an old friend who ran a detective agency in Chicago and knew the town from the glitter to the whorehouses. He asked for back ground on Karl Schwartz and sister Serilda Miller. He was to telegraph anything suddenly important, and send the rest to him by Railway

Express, care of the station master.

It would take two days to get his response. He decided to try for a look at Mr. Schwartz and see what he was up to.

Buckskin got to the lobby just as someone brushed past him on his way out. The clerk looked up and motioned him over.

"That man in the black suit and fancy vest was your Mr. Schwartz," the clerk said.

Buckskin nodded and hurried after him, then followed him into the Smoking Gun Saloon and Gambling Palace. He bought chips and settled into a poker game with a house dealer. Buckskin bought ten dollars worth of chips and waited until there was finally an empty chair at the same table where Schwartz played.

Three hands into the game, Buckskin knew Schwartz was cheating. He was palming cards and holding them back. When it was his turn to bet next, Schwartz eased up the ante. Buckskin folded and saw Schwartz turn over four kings. He'd waited until he drew one or two and used his sleeve cards.

Schwartz played smart, cheating only to win big pot hands, and folding and cursing his luck on the small pots.

Buckskin bowed out of the game, and hurried back to the hotel. A skeleton key opened room 22 and he searched the place quickly but thoroughly. Only an extremely sharp eye would know the room had been checked over.

He found the papers of testimony about rape and sexual slavery of the girl Serilda by Minderhausen. Why such papers if he married her? Perhaps that's why he married her. Buckskin couldn't take the papers, but when he looked farther, he found some earlier drafts of the same statements. He took the most damaging with Serilda's signature on the bottom. He found a stack of newspaper clippings in an envelope and briefed through them.

All were about a big contest between two breweries in Chicago, and how one won, the other lost. He took two of the most detailed clippings and put everything back as it was and slipped out of the room. He went down the far steps from the second floor as he saw Schwartz coming up the front steps.

Back in his room in the same hotel, in room 29, Buckskin read through the clippings. Two familiar names came at him. One Hartley J. Minderhausen's brewery had been in a death struggle with another brewery, Schwartz Old Lager, and the death knell had been struck. Schwartz filed for bankruptcy two days before the date on the clipping. And that morning Wilhelm Schwartz blew his head off with a shotgun.

It was just a little after suppertime when Buckskin found the house where Herta lived with Joseph. He knocked and she came to the door wiping her hands on an apron.

"I'm learning to cook," she said. "I've never done any cooking before. Joseph is helping me learn and his mother is so nice."

He showed her the clippings and the signed paper. She looked up in wonder.

"You say this Mr. Schwartz is Serilda's

brother? Then her real last name must be Schwartz as well. It was their *father* who killed himself in Chicago. I don't understand."

"The only thing I can figure is that after Chicago, Minderhausen moved west and Serilda came to find him. She and her brother could have planned this whole thing. After they found your father, her job was to worm her way into his fancy, and into his bedroom. Then if he wouldn't marry her, they would use the sworn statements to blackmail him and threaten to expose him and subject him to criminal prosecution for rape and sexual slavery. That would just about ruin his business."

"Revenge," Herta said softly. "The brother and sister are looking for revenge because my father was a better businessman. Father didn't kill their father. He just beat him in business."

"By now it's so emotional, the facts are probably not of much importance to either one of them."

"My father always wanted a son. I was trying to figure out why he would suddenly marry a girl so young. Then I wondered if she told him she was pregnant . . . that she would bear him a son . . . Father would be moved by that. Of course, Serilda couldn't know if she would have a son or not if she were really pregnant. But she could swear she was pregnant and be faking it."

"For a while."

"They don't need much time if they want to kill my father so they will inherit his fortune."

"You have to tell all of this to your father."

"No, I couldn't. He would laugh at me."

"Even when you show him the clippings, and the fact that Karl Schwartz is here and claims to be Serilda's brother?"

"As you say, this is a highly emotional situation for my father. The facts won't mean much to my father either if he thinks he can sire a son to take over his business."

"Then I'll talk to your father, today. Something like this can move extremely fast once the players are all in place, such as they are now."

Minderhausen had left his office. Buckskin walked up to the house on the rise and rang the front bell. An Irish housekeeper answered the door.

"Mr. and Mrs. Minderhausen are having supper right now and can't be disturbed. Could I give them a message?"

"He seems to be right behind you," Buckskin said.

The woman turned and he stepped past her and walked down the hall toward what he figured was the formal dining room.

"See here, laddie, you can't go storming in there," the servant woman said impotently.

He opened the double doors and looked at the twelve-foot long formal dining table. Two places were set but no food had been served. Minderhausen and a woman fancifully dressed stood near the table.

"See here—" Minderhausen said.

"I need to see you, Mr. Minderhausen. Right

now would be a good time in your den or library."

"Morgan, what is this? I thought we finished our business."

"We did finish *that* business. This is another matter of extreme importance. Would you mind leading the way?"

The brewer scowled, shrugged and walked toward the door. Serilda began to follow him but he shook his head. "You don't need to be bothered with this. I'll take care of it."

In the den he closed the door and turned.

"Mr. Minderhausen, if I were a betting man, I'd give ten-to-one odds that your life is in danger."

His head snapped up, his eyes stared hard at Buckskin. "Who put you up to this?"

"No one. I understand you spent some time in Chicago."

"Yes, five years."

"And that you had a successful brewery there. Why did you leave?"

"Too much competition. I couldn't brew the beer I wanted to at a fair price."

"I understand you also eliminated some of the competition, a man by the name of Wilhelm Schultz."

"How do you know that?"

"Public record, it was in all the newspapers."

"Yes. I beat him in business, I didn't kill him."

"His son and daughter think so."

"And who might they be?"

"His son's name is Karl Schwartz. He's now staying at the hotel. I'm positive he's seeking revenge for his father's death."

"I'll have a talk with him about it tomorrow."

"This man is not in a mood for talking. He won't listen to a logical argument. He wants blood. Your blood. It's my suggestion that you hire some bodyguards for the next few weeks. That you never go anywhere alone, and that you pay special attention to visitors in your office."

"Preposterous. You have no proof."

Buckskin showed him the newspaper clippings. "I stole these from Schwartz's room less than two hours ago. The man is wound up tight as a Comanche in a ghost dance. He's playing poker to whet his nerves, I'd say. He's a dangerous man."

"I've done nothing wrong, why should I protect myself?"

"To stay alive. Oh, one more caution, no one but you and I must know about this. No one else must be told, not your people at the office, not your secretary, not your housekeeper, not your wife."

"Not even. . . . Yes, I see what you mean."

"By being with her and near her, you could be putting her in danger as well."

Buckskin had decided not to tell the man his own wife probably was in on the conspiracy. The shock might be too much for his heart and Serilda would have what she wanted.

Minderhausen paced to the far window and back, toyed with things on his desk, and at last looked up. "Yes, there were some threats at the time, but the children were young then. That's part of the reason I left the Chicago area. All right. I suppose it's possible that I do need some protection. Are you asking for the job? If so, you're hired, at whatever fee you say."

"No, I'm not asking. I'm due to leave in the morning. I've been here too long now. You can find three or four good gun hands around town. Keep one with you at work, keep another one at your house during the night, and a third to be on hand when you go outside of your office. That should discourage Schwartz."

"And if that doesn't help?"

"Then go to your judge friend and get a restraining order keeping Schwartz at least 20 miles from your residence and your place of business."

"Goddamn!"

"I agree entirely. But the situation must be dealt with."

"How did this get started? You didn't dig all of this up on your own."

"Herta has been concerned about this. Perhaps she saw Schwartz and it brought back memories of Chicago, I don't know."

"Herta. Yes, she would know about something like ths. How can a man be so blessed." He threw up his hands. "All right. We'll go downtown tonight and hire the three men you suggest. What should I pay them?"

"Enough so no one else can outbid you for their loyalty. I'd say ten dollars a day."

"A day?"

"That figure impressed you, it should win their total loyalty."

An hour later they had hired the three men. All moved to the stable house. Two would patrol the grounds at night. The cook would feed them when they were there.

Buckskin watched Serilda closely when Minderhausen explained to her why he was hiring some guards.

"Them brewers in Denver been saying they planned on ruining me. Quickest way is to shoot me full of lead. Figured a little protection wouldn't hurt a thing. Other men have bodyguards, why can't I?"

"You can, darling," Serilda said. "Yes, you should. I approve. You do know that you haven't had your supper yet. Cook is keeping it warm for us. Are you ready now to eat, it's almost eight-thirty?"

Buckskin Lee Morgan walked into the darkness, then stopped and looked back at the mansion. He figured she would be leaving in about three hours. He found a patch of grass near a board fence and settled down for a long wait. He'd bet his left handed monkey wrench that pretty little Serilda would be making a midnight visit to her brother at the hotel.

He waited.

An hour later he checked the Big Dipper in its nightly circle around the North Star. The two pointer stars on the outside of the dipper cup were aimed up at the star from an eight o'clock position. Midnight. He hadn't missed her. He had almost dozed off once, but the ground was too hard to let him go to sleep.

He'd give it another hour, then lose his bet with himself.

Half an hour later he heard a screen door

squeak and soon a slight figure worked along the house, then down to the street and began walking determinedly downtown.

Buckskin gave her a half block lead, then moved along after her. The figure in a long raincoat moved directly toward the hotel. He closed the gap when she went in the back door. He ran to it and saw her climbing the steps.

On the second floor he saw her knock gently on room 22, then she used a key and let herself inside.

Buckskin grinned as he went into his own room and wedged the chair top under the door. Serilda had taken the bait just as he figured she would. The next move was up to her and her brother, the revenge siblings.

Twenty-Three

The next morning, Serilda spent most of the time searching through her husband's study. She hunted the will as her brother had told her to. They could do nothing before that point was determined. She figured there would be a copy of the will in the wall safe, but she didn't know the combination.

Each place she searched she left exactly as it had been. It was almost noon when she spotted the folder with the will in it. She didn't understand the legal terms but one line stood out for her.

"I hereby bequeath all my worldly goods to my daughter, Herta Louise Minderhausen, having no other living children and no spouse."

She put it back carefully and tried to decide

how to bring up the subject with her new husband. She thought she had a method.

That noon when Minderhausen came for dinner with his wife, she kissed him affectionately, then frowned.

"A man came to the door this morning saying that he was an itinerant lawyer helping people to write their wills. I told him that was foolish, I'm young, I don't need a will, but he insisted and got his foot in the door. At last I jumped up and squashed his foot. He left then. I've never heard of anything so silly in all my life. I'm a married woman, that's my life and my protection. I don't need a will."

Her husband paused with his soup spoon half to his mouth. "That's quite true, my love, you don't need a will, but I definitely must make a change in mine. Now you will become my major heir, until we have our child, of course. Then if he's a son as you promised. . . ." he smiled. "But that change we can make later. Yes, I'll have my lawyer come by today and make some changes."

Later in the light meal he told her about Joseph, Herta's husband.

"I think he's going to do exceptionally well. He has a fine grasp of business, and is excellent at figures. I'm going to start him on the receiving dock and he'll work two weeks at every job in the plant. At the end of a year he'll have been in 26 different positions and ready to step into a management role. I am just as pleased with him as can be."

"We should have Herta and Joseph over for

supper one of these evenings. I've yet to meet the young man."

"We will, we will."

Minderhausen called for his bodyguard and they went out to the rig and rolled down the hill. Serilda wasn't comfortable yet having that man with a gun prowling around the grounds, but she would have used him if a salesman actually had come to the door that morning.

She would go shopping that afternoon and tell Karl about the development. Within a day or two the will should be settled and they could move forward with their plans. She had changed her mind again. They would gain little by waiting a year. If her husband were to die, she agreed that it should be within two weeks. Karl would make all of the arrangements. Not even the bodyguards would prevent him from getting the old man, Karl had assured her.

Buckskin had reported to Herta his talk with her father and assured her that he had picked out some good guards for him. Now it would be up to Schwartz to make the next move.

"What do you think he'll try?" Herta asked.

"I'm not sure. He might just give up and walk away. He might hire six men and come at your father with guns blazing. Which reminds me of one more small task."

He left Herta's house and went to the three main saloons in town that had the most clients. He invested five dollars with each of the head bartenders with a small suggestion.

"Just keep your eyes and ears open. If a guy called Schwartz is around hiring any guns, or anyone else is looking for some gun hands, you let me know damn fast."

None of the aprons asked him why he wanted to know. They knew a good deal when they heard it. For a quarter they could get somebody to run a message any time of the day. Buckskin had a beer at the last place and tried to decide when to leave Wyoming. He should have been in Boise two weeks ago.

He felt some responsibility to Herta and her father. Another three or four days. He was sure something would happen by then, if it was going to happen at all.

He got some paper from the barkeep and wrote a message, then found a kid on the street and told him to run it down to the white house with the picket fence, number 12. The kid looked wide-eyed at the quarter and took off on a run.

Twenty minutes later Dutch knocked on his hotel door and scurried inside as she heard someone coming up the steps.

"Hi cowboy, got your lariat ready?" Dutch asked.

"I've been missing you, long and tall. When do you head out for Denver?"

"Be a week or so, maybe more. I made the mistake of buying that little house. Now we have to sell it."

"Dig up the money from your backyard before you sell."

"Money isn't in the backyard."

"Oh, I'll stop digging then."

She sat down on the bed, opening the buttons that fastened the print dress up to her throat. "You going to talk all day, or can you figure out what the two of us all naked might do that would be more interesting?"

"Figured it out already. You settle on Denver for your gambling house?"

"Just about. You coming along?"

"Might. Might also have some cash to invest. I picked up $7,000 by honest labor."

"You get paid that much?"

"Minderhausens don't come along very often."

"Figured maybe you had fiddlefooted away from this town by now."

"Not without a goodbye."

Dutch kept on unbuttoning the fasteners at her chest. "Can you be any help to a girl taking off her clothes?"

"Fair to middling help. That works both ways, though."

Buckskin pushed his favorite chair back under the door knob and then stepped to the bed where he did a quick disrobing of one rangy lady with long brown hair and soft brown eyes. He kissed her bare breasts and pushed her down on the bed and she made soft little noises in her throat.

"Now, right now, cowboy. Let's get to the good part."

They knew each other by now, what each liked and wanted and they satisfied each other for as long as Buckskin could hold out. Then they both climaxed gloriously and collapsed on the bed.

After a regenerating time, Dutch pushed up and watched him where he lay beside her.

"Pris lit out for Salt Lake and points west. She's riding. Said she likes it better than going by train. She can afford the train. She's probably going to lose her money along the way. I couldn't talk her into doing anything else.

"Navaro has decided to go to Denver with us and throw her money into the business. So right now I'm trying to figure out how to move about $48,000 to Denver."

"Hire a good gunman to go with you."

"I tried, but he keeps yapping about Boise."

"Nothing is chiseled in stone about Boise."

"Damn good," she said. "Hey, I'll even offer you my body daily if you'll come along."

"Sell the damn house fast, and it's a deal."

They negotiated other aspects of the move to Denver through the afternoon.

It was almost five that afternoon when there was one sharp knock on the door and a white envelope slid underneath. Buckskin pounced on it and read the message inside. It was from the Rawlins Saloon.

"A lowlife I know is asking about gunhands. Says he needs three. Didn't say what the pay is. He's in a poker game. Should stay around a while." It was signed Al.

Buckskin pulled his pants on and his boots, then his shirt, and looked down at the still naked Dutch.

"Stay put, I got a man to find. Could be important. Just be damn sure you don't put on any clothes while I'm gone."

She threw a shoe at him as he hurried out the door.

The Rawlins Saloon was the worst of the three big ones in town. It had a beer bar, a dozen tables for free lance poker playing, a monte table and twelve girls upstairs. They did most of the whoring business in town.

Buckskin bought a beer and looked at Al. He slid over to Buckskin and muttered. "Brown hat, first table. Goes by name of Arizone."

Buckskin watched him until he went through the back door toward the outhouse. Lee waited for him to come out. He looked up at the larger man with caution.

"Hear you're looking for gunhands," Buckskin said.

"So?"

"I fit the bill."

"Maybe."

"Hear you're working for a guy named Karl Schwartz."

"What is this? How'd you know that?"

"This is an invitation to stay alive." Buckskin drew his Colt so fast the other man frowned.

"What the hell?"

"How many men he want?"

"Four, including me."

"When are you working?"

"Tomorrow afternoon."

"Where?"

"Out along the river."

"The river's six miles from here."

"That's the one, the North Platte."

Buckskin motioned the man to move down the alley where they could stand in an indentation between two buildings.

"What's the job?"

"He didn't say. He's paying good, so I didn't ask."

"How much is he paying?"

"Three dollars a day and twenty dollar bonus if we get the job done."

"He mention any names?"

"Nope. Just some older guy going out with his new bride on a picnic."

Buckskin let the hammer down on his Colt and holstered it.

"What the hell?"

"Yeah, about right. Tomorrow, Schwartz is going to have you kill a man. He wants him dead. I want him alive. This is what you're going to do, and you're going to make it look good. You bring it off and each of you gets an extra $100. Is that clear? You keep him alive and make Schwartz think he's dead and you each make $100 extra, besides what Schwartz pays you."

"Hey, great! I can get those guys to do anything for another hundred."

"Will Schwartz be riding with you?"

"Said he would. We go out early, hide in the brush, then they come for the picnic and we hit them. Said he wants us to beat up the old man, then we drown him."

"I'll be trailing the buggy or carriage by a half mile, just out of sight. You convince the old man he's getting killed, but don't even break a bone. Fake the whole thing. You understand good?"

"Yeah, yeah, sure."

"What's your name?"

"Arizone."

"Ever been there?"

"Time or two."

"You bust up the old man, or accidentally kill him, and I'm coming after your ass, Arizone. No place in this country will be safe enough for you. Your butt is going to be shot so full of holes, it'll sink in a sand pile. You understand me, Arizone?"

"Yes, sir. Should I know your name?"

"No, you shouldn't. Make sure your men understand the double cross on Schwartz, then make it look good. I'll be there shortly after you ride away, leaving the old man in the water and supposedly dead."

"Yeah, and then somebody's supposed to come along and discover the tragedy and bring the girl back to town and notify the sheriff."

"What time you leave tomorrow?"

"Just before daylight."

"Don't be late."

Buckskin watched the man walk back into the saloon. He took the alley exit and walked to his hotel. The more he thought it through, the more certain he was that it would work. If the four hired hands couldn't do the job of protecting Minderhausen, Buckskin knew that he'd level in a few rounds with the Big Fifty and then ride in and take charge.

There were a lot of things that could go wrong. But if it all went right, by tomorrow night he'd have Schwartz in jail on an attempted murder charge, and loyal wife Serilda sitting in another cell right beside him with the same felony charges against her. It couldn't happen to two more deserving young people.

Twenty-Four

"I know it's Sunday," Hartley Minderhausen said. "That's why I'm not down at the office."

"This is the day you promised me we could go on a picnic over by the river," Serilda said. "Cook has fixed us a wonderful picnic basket, and I'm going to drive one of the smaller rigs, and there'll be just the two of us talking about our new son."

"We can talk right here."

Serilda opened her dress top and let one big breast swing out of the fabric. She walked toward him.

"Hartley, look up here. There'll be just the two of us and we can take off all our clothes and play in the water and roll around nude in the grass and then you can make love to me. We'll be like Adam and Eve."

She walked up and eased her breast against his

cheek. He turned and nibbled on the pulsating nipple.

"Damn, woman. You have the best arguments I've ever seen. Yes, yes, we'll go. Let me get into some country clothes and my boots. Don't want to kick up any snakes out there."

An hour later, Buckskin watched the young woman driving the buggy as they moved out the river road. He had been up since five-thirty watching the road. Just before light he had seen five horsemen ride in the same direction. That meant brother Karl was with them. He hoped the gunsharps could play the part the way they were supposed to. By now they should be safely hidden away in their ambush well up the road at a spot they had selected in advance.

Serilda and her brother deserved whatever punishment they got out of this. He mounted his rented horse and rode slowly up the road so he could keep the rig in sight about a half mile ahead. The Big Fifty buffalo Sharps rode in the boot and he had a dozen rounds. That should be more than enough if anything went wrong.

The buggy ahead moved out a little faster and Buckskin lost it for a moment. Then he trotted his mount and soon had the vehicle in sight.

He rode for almost an hour, went past a small community off to the left on a stream and near the tracks. Then they came to the North Platte River and the buggy moved downstream a quarter-of-a-mile and stopped.

Buckskin had turned into the woods along the river and worked through them staying out of sight as he moved up on the victims. He kept a sharp lookout and figured that the ambushers would be on the far side, downstream from Minderhausen. If they weren't, he would be able to spot them coming up silently. He had tied his horse just inside the cover and now worked up like he was a Comanche.

At a hundred yards he saw them through the cottonwoods. They had spread a blanket and were eating. Serilda kept looking around as if expecting something. Buckskin stared across from them in thicker brush and trees but couldn't see any movement.

The guard! Where was the guard who was supposed to be with Minderhausen wherever he went? Buckskin snorted. Serilda must have talked him out of bringing the guard. Figured.

Buckskin worked closer. He was within thirty yards of them now behind a two-foot-thick cottonwood and could hear them talking. He couldn't make out the words.

Now Buckskin could see movement across the way. The five men were moving up on the target. It would be simple to use the Big Fifty and blow them out off the woods. But that wouldn't prove them out of the woods. But that wouldn't prove the act.

A booming pistol shot shattered the woodsy silence and the five men rushed out of the woods almost on top of the Minderhausens.

Buckskin could hear every word now.

"What the hell? Who are you?" Minderhausen brayed.

"You don't remember me, Minderhausen. I was a little kid of fifteen. That's when you ruined my father and kept pushing and pushing until you killed him."

"Karl Schwartz. I knew you were in town. I didn't think you would be this stupid."

"I'd love to shoot you down right now, but we have to do this neatly," Karl said. "An accident."

"It'll never work, nobody will believe it."

"Sure they will, your wife will be your survivor and an excellent witness."

Minderhausen turned to Serilda. "He's lying, isn't he, Serilda? Tell me this maniac is lying."

She turned away, stood and went to stand beside her brother.

"It took me half the night but then I remembered Wilhelm Schwartz's daughter's name, and I didn't want to. I told myself it just wasn't true. Serilda, did the two of you plan this whole thing? You came here hunting me, got a job with me and now you are going to do this?"

"Yes, Minderhausen. You killed my father."

He sagged, then quicker than they expeccted, he pulled a derringer from his inside pocket and shot once at Karl, but missed.

"I've got another round," Minderhausen said. "Don't lift that six-gun or I'll kill you."

Karl laughed. "At 20 feet you couldn't hit the river." He snapped up the revolver and fired. The round hit Minderhausen in the right arm and the hideout spun away.

"I still have five shots, Minderhausen, don't move. We'll tear the bullet wound so it looks like an injury. Now, move down toward the river. We've got a good place where you tried to ford and didn't quite make it."

Buckskin watched all of them walk toward the river and slightly downstream. He followed feeling helpless. If the four goons got over-enthusiastic in their work, they just might kill Minderhausen. Before that happened, he'd step in.

At the bank near a ford, Schwartz nodded. "You men know what to do. Arizone, it's your responsibility. Pound him around and use a limb and tear open that gunshot wound. Then drown the bastard. I'll bring down the rig and we'll all tip it over."

Schwartz stared at Minderhausen.

"Now you know how my father felt just before he died. He wanted to die, you don't. So you'll have to sweat a little more. Too bad you left your gunslinger home today. I was looking forward to shooting it out with him."

Schwartz walked up to Minderhausen and spit in his face, then slapped him hard on both cheeks. When the older man lifted his hands, Schwartz showed off his boxing skill by peppering Minderhausen's face four times with stiff blows, then crashed a right fist into his jaw and knocked him down.

"Bastard! You killed my father!" Schwartz kicked Minderhausen in the stomach, then turned and marched away to drive the rig and one horse down to the river.

The North Platte was narrow and almost looked like a river here. It spread out a half-inch thick in spots, but here it was banked properly and more than ten-feet deep at the center. A gentle current moved down the channel.

Two of the men picked up Minderhausen and dragged him down to the river. He fought them at first, then Arizone talked quickly with him. They hit him a few times but not hard, and he splashed water and they kept pretending to batter him until the buggy drove down by the water.

Then one of the men gave a mighty tug at Minderhausen's head and he floated away in the current, face down. Slowly the body turned over so they could see his face and his staring eyes. He turned again face down as the current carried him downstream.

Schwartz ran down to the water's edge where the four men stood waist deep in water.

"Bastard really put up a fight for an old man," Arizone said.

"He's dead already?" Schwartz asked.

"That's what you wanted. We don't mess around and make a quick job last a long time. Charlie there broke the bastard's neck. I'd forgot how a neck snaps when it breaks. Just like at a hanging."

Schwartz watched the body floating downstream. He took out his six-gun and sighted in and fired but the body was well out off range. It rolled again in the current and for a moment he saw the hated face, then he grinned.

"Yes, good work. The bonus is yours. Now, help me turn over this buggy in the water. Lead the horse in to its belly. Then we'll turn over the rig.

It took them ten minutes to coax the horse into the water, then another five to tip over the light buggy. It splashed at last, half in and half out of the water. The horse stamped in the water and moved over a few feet but remained standing in the traces.

Serilda sat on the bank on some grass crying.

Schwartz dropped down beside her. "Hey, what's the matter? We did it. You're the widow Minderhausen, owner of all his lands and goods and businesses."

"Sure, I know. But he was good to me. He really was. He loved me. And he wasn't all that old. I sure took good care of his needs."

"Yeah, but now his money is going to take care of both of us. Fact is, I know the brewing business. With his operation I can take it over and really make us some money."

She stopped crying. "I guess."

"No, no, you keep on crying. It'll look good for the widow. Next we got to get you dirtied up. Go jump in the river and get soaking wet. Remember, you got pitched out of the rig into the river but your husband was hit by the buggy and floated downstream. You don't know what happened to him."

She sat down in the water and he splashed water over her and soaked her hair. Then before she could protest, he took a stick and scratched her forehead and both arms until blood came.

"Easy!" she screeched.

"Now, drag yourself out of the water and up to the grass. Make lots of marks where you crawl so anybody can see."

Arizone came up. "Mr. Schwartz, I been watching like you told me. There's a buggy coming down the road. You want me to call to him that I saw a rig tip over down here?"

"Yes, yes. Good timing. Run out there. You don't know the folks. You was fishing upstream. We'll all be gone but Serilda here."

Schwartz and the other three houligans faded into the brush downstream. Arizone went running toward the River Road. Buckskin shook his head. Schwartz had it down to a science. It looked like he murdered men for a living. Buckskin's only worry was that the four men had been too rough with Minderhausen.

When the brewer rolled over in the current, Buckskin figured he was getting a big breath of air. The man must be a good swimmer to fake his drowning so well.

Two or three minutes later Arizone came back leading the light buggy. It held a single man driver. He rushed up to Serilda who lay apparently unconscious on the bank. He patted her cheeks trying to bring her back to consciousness. He put his ear on her chest and looked up nodding.

"She's breathing and has a good heart beat. Help me get her into my carriage and I'll take her to the doctor in Rawlins. Was there anybody else in the rig?"

Arizone shook his head. "Don't rightly know. I was fishing upstream and saw the rig trying to ford. Just didn't make it. Didn't see nobody else but could 'a been."

"You stay here and search. I'll drive this lady into town and send the sheriff back out."

Arizone nodded and stood there shaking his head. "Don't know why the fools tried to ford with the water this high."

The man stepped into his rig. "I'll send the sheriff right back. You look for somebody else, or a body downstream." Then he cracked the lines on the black's back and the buggy jolted away toward the road.

When the rig was out of sight, Schwartz and the other three men came out of the brush. Schwartz took out his wallet and passed around the cash.

"Twenty for the bonus, and five dollars for each man. Arizone, you get an extra twenty for recruiting these fine lads. The three of you I want out of town for at least a month before the sun sets. Don't want no loose ends. Arizone, you'll have to hang around here and talk to the sheriff when he comes. Look bad if you vanished.

"That's what I'm going to do, vanish back to town and get in a whale of a good poker game. Nice doing business with you. Arizone, I'm going to be around town. I might be able to use you on my payroll. I'll look you up in a week or two and make some arrangements. At a good salary, I'll add. I can always use a man who's good with a gun and can keep his mouth quiet."

Schwartz turned and walked to where he had hidden his horse, mounted and rode leisurely toward the River road and the way back to Rawlins.

When he was sure that Schwartz had gone, Buckskin ran from the woods, signalled to

Arizone and he and his three men hurried into the woods and brush downstream.

"First we find Minderhausen," Buckskin said. "I hope he's not hurt too badly."

"We already found him, sir," Arizone said. "He's about a quarter-of-a-mile downstream. He's drying out in the sun. Right down this way."

Hartley Minderhausen sat on the bank in the sunshine. He had stripped off his pants and shirt and had them drying on the brush in the sun. He sat letting the sun's rays warm him. He looked up when the men walked to him.

At once he stood in his underwear and held out his hand to Buckskin. "I understand I'd be dead if it wasn't for you. I'm angry with you, though. Why didn't you tell me yesterday that Serilda was one of the Schwartz family?"

"I wasn't sure you would believe me and it might spoil the whole scheme. Then too, I was afraid the shock of such a fact might be too much for you. I could see how much you loved the woman."

"Yes, I love too easily. She had me fooled completely and I enjoyed it at the time."

"There isn't a man alive, Mr. Minderhausen, who would not have been fooled by that sexy bundle of woman. Me especially. And I know I would enjoy it."

"I was up half the night worrying about it. Finally decided she must be the Serilda I'd heard about in Chicago. Not exactly a common name. That's why I took my derringer, for all the good it did me."

Arizone had been tending to his shot arm. The bullet went in but didn't come out. He bandaged it to stop the bleeding.

"Mr. Minderhausen, we'll get you to the doctor just as soon as we figure out a few things," Buckskin said. "Do you want to be alive or dead for a few hours?"

The German's eyes twinkled. "I see, let them think I'm dead and see what they do. Yes, might be interesting. But my people at the office and plant. . . ."

"By tomorrow morning you'll be back at work," Buckskin said. "We can meet the sheriff and show him exactly what happened. Arizone here, I'm sure, will testify how he was hired by Schwartz to murder you, and how Serilda went along with the plan making her an accessory. No charges could be filed against Arizone or the other three men."

Arizone looked up. "Sure, I'll testify. Didn't like that slimy Schwartz guy from the first time I saw him. Be glad to put him behind bars."

"About your marriage, I'm sure your judge friend can get it annulled on the grounds that she married you under false pretenses with plans to murder you."

"I can't do that, she carries my child."

"Mr. Minderhausen, I'm not overly familiar with these things, but Herta said she figured that was why you married Serilda. Herta guessed that Serilda told you she was pregnant. Herta said there is a very good chance that Serilda isn't pregnant at all. You could have the union annulled now and if she is pregnant, decide what to do about it later on."

"Yes, yes, good planning. I just hope that my clothes are dry by the time the sheriff gets here. Hate to talk to the sheriff in my underwear."

They were dry.

Twenty-Five

The wait for the sheriff was a little over two hours, which meant he had left immediately after he heard the news from Serilda.

The men stood in a group as the sheriff and one of his deputies rode up on horses that had not been pushed hard. They swung down and looked at the buggy and the horse still standing in the water.

"Could of taken the horse out of there," the sheriff growled at them.

"We wanted you to see the rig just as it was," Buckskin said.

The sheriff glared at him.

"Which one of you found the rig?"

"I did," Arizone said. "My name is Arizone Cawley. I flagged down the driver on the road and brought him in here and he looked at the woman and we loaded her in his rig. Was she injured bad? We couldn't tell."

"Cut up some but in good shape. Leastwise, she isn't dead. You find the body yet?"

The six men looked at each other. At last the older man stepped forward and held out his hand.

"Sheriff, I'm the dead man, Hartley Minderhausen. As you can see I'm not really dead."

"Your wife said you were. Said she saw you get hit by the buggy and sink and then float downstream dead as a rat."

"That's what she wanted to think," Minderhuasen said softly.

"What the hell is going on here?" the sheriff demanded.

"Sheriff, we've got a story to tell you about revenge and plans for murder and sexual entrapment and at last a bold move to murder Mr. Minderhausen so his brand new wife and her brother from Chicago could take over his business, all of his property and his fortune."

The sheriff frowned. "Better be a damn good story. I left church service to rush out here and hunt for a body."

"You found it, Sheriff," Buckskin said. "It's just more alive than the killers wanted it to be."

Buckskin told the story, shortening it for the lawman who looked glum at the start but got interested as it moved along and then a little irate.

"Goddamn, the murdering bastards!"

"I'd say you have a good case against the two of

them. Conspiracy to commit murder. Hiring another to do murder. Attempted murder, assault with a deadly weapon, aggravated assault from the wound." The sheriff was smiling now. "And this man, Arizone, you say you'll testify that Karl Schwartz hired you to help him kill Mr. Minderhausen?"

"Yes, sir, but we decided just to pretend to kill him."

"Something has been left out here. You, storyteller, what was your name again?"

"Buck, Buck Smith." He told the sheriff about finding out about the plot, and how Herta Minderhausen Radowitz had hired him to investigate, and that he hired the four men not to kill Minderhausen.

When they were done the sheriff turned to Mr. Minderhausen.

"Sir, what do you want to do?"

"Bring all the charges against both of them that you can in his name and her maiden name. I'll be getting an annulment of my marriage tomorrow morning. Prosecute them with all deliberate speed, sheriff. I hope you can arrest them today."

Arizone and his three men righted the buggy and led the horse out of the water. They dried it off and found it functional, so Minderhausen drove it back to town, but let the sheriff go first to call at his home and arrest Serilda. He would do the paper work later.

Buckskin held back and when the others were gone, paid the four men their $110 each. They grinned.

"Damn, that's half a year's pay as a cowhand," Arizone said. "Maybe I should take up this detective work full time."

"Now and then somebody takes a shot at you," Buckskin said.

Back at the hotel, Buckskin sent a note to Dutch. She came after doing some window shopping and having a cup of coffee in the dining room, trying to see if anyone followed her. She saw no one.

She slipped into Buckskin's room.

"The bitch! It's all over town what she and her brother did. Both of them are in jail. How could she do that? Sleep with him and trap him into marriage and then try to kill him?"

"I guess some women are like that," Buckskin said. "I call them Black Widows."

"Good name for them." She stopped being mad and looked at him. "Christ, you're as pretty as ever. Did I tell you that I really like you? I want to keep you around to tickle my fancy and anything else you can reach. Am I being too bold? Hell, I rob banks for a living, I have to be bold. You want my body?"

Lee grinned and pulled her down on the bed. He kissed her and rolled her over and laid on top of her. "That's the worst example of a hooker I've ever seen."

"Hooker? What's that."

"A chippie, a fancy lady, a whore. During the war, General Hooker wanted to keep his officers in line, so he hired a dozen women to move from camp to camp with the troops. As I remember, they serviced only the officers for a price. They got to be called Hooker's women, and eventually, just hookers. I figured the word is in the language now and will be around for a long time."

"You telling me I couldn't sell my ass if I wanted to?"

"Oh, yes, you could sell it, you'd just fall in love with every man who screwed you and keep running off with them and getting fired and never making dollar one."

"Good, I quit being a hooker. Now, about serious. I sold the house. Got the money, almost $800. I signed the papers yesterday. So when do we go to Denver?"

Buckskin kissed her and tried to think fast. He had't really thought about going to Denver. Not seriously. Damn!

She broke off the kiss and put her hand down to his crotch.

"That kiss was delicious, Buckskin Lee Morgan. But it doesn't answer me. You aren't trying to toy with my affections, are you? Just stringing me along so you can have my body and then walk away and let me lay there alone and crying."

"Hell, Dutch, I'd never do that. Got me two more little projects here. Probably have to testify at the trial. If it don't happen soon I'll leave my testimony in a sworn deposition with the district attorney."

"Yeah, that's a day at the most," Dutch said, rubbing at his crotch and producing a swelling. "What's the other one?"

"The guy who shot up your house, Alonzo Warnick, the bounty hunter."

"Right, he has to be dealt with. I don't want him chasing us all the way to Denver. So what do we do?"

"First we get your hand off my crotch if you want a serious statement out of me."

"Sorry, I kind of like your friend down there."

"Good. Now about Warnick. I'm tired of him surprising me. This time I'm going to be ready for him. Been thinking on it. I want to be the one to pick the time and the place, then I should be able to convince him that he shouldn't hunt me any more."

"How'll you do that?"

"Convince him one way or the other."

"I could put on my bank robbing clothes and go out and have a shootout with him."

"No, you'd probably whip him, then I'd be overshadowed and my fragile male ego couldn't stand that."

"What the hell did you just say?"

He grinned and kissed her. "Don't have a shootout with him. I don't like tall girls with big breasts who have holes drilled through their bodies."

"That I understand." She laughed and rubbed at his crotch again. "How about right now?"

"In the afternoon?" He tried to look shocked, then laughed as she rolled on top of him and tried to smother his face with her breastworks.

"Just so you leave me enough energy to go see Herta and Papa Minderhausen."

"I'll let you save just about that much."

She pulled off his clothes and then slowly stripped out of her own as he watched.

"I like to see that old worm of yours get interested and then hard as a poker and start throbbing and jumping around."

"Damn strange, woman. I like that to happen, too."

She lay on top of him, both her hands around his stiff rod.

"Something different this time. Something strange and wild and . . . and . . . weird."

"I could bring in a nice big male dog."

She hit him. "You know what I mean, the two of us, but something wild."

"Like you standing on your head?"

"Can't be done."

"Let's try!"

"Yeah, but you have to hold me up."

"Let's start with you standing up and bending down and touching the floor."

She did. "Wow! I feel so . . . so exposed."

"It sure is, smiling at me and wet and ready." He slid into her and got everything loosened up.

"Now lift up one leg and put it on my shoulder."

She tried, she couldn't. It just wouldn't go that far. He held her leg at his waist.

"Lift up the other leg and lock them behind my back," he said. "Stand on your hands."

She tried it. "Damn, I made it!" she squealed upside down.

The pressure on him was so intense that it nearly broke him in half. He tried to stroke but there was no chance. She squeezed him and he lunged a little. They broke apart, laughing so hard they fell on the bed.

"Now that was different," she said. "My climax was so different, gentle yet powerful. I—I couldn't say a word for a couple of minutes."

He kissed her and held up his hands. "I've got to go see Herta and tell her what really happened. Her father is probably still at the sheriff's office."

"I'll stay right here and we'll have supper sent up from the dining room. They do that here if you pay extra and I'm buying supper, just . . . for fun."

"Done," he said. He waved and went out the door after checking the hallway.

Buckskin walked the back streets to Herta's new little house. She was there reading three cookbooks spread out over the table. Herta smiled and let him in.

"Now I want to hear what really happened out there. I've heard six different versions and I only talked to three people."

Buckskin just started when someone knocked on the door. Herta let in her father, gave him a big hug and a kiss on the cheek.

"I'm getting popular," she said. "Two visitors the same day." Her smile was full and honest. Herta blinked back a tear. "I'm so glad you're all right, Papa. I don't know what I would have done. . . ."

Hartley J. Minderhausen hugged his daughter again. "I'm the one who owes the thanks. If you hadn't talked to Mr. Morgan here, I'd still be floating down that river. I never expected young Schwartz to be quite so bloodthirsty."

He went into the living room and they all sat down.

Herta sat close to her father. "Papa, I'm so sorry about Serilda."

"Yes, no bigger fool than an old fool. She had me totally convinced. Fine little actress, that one. You never were convinced about her, thank goodness."

Minderhausen looked at Buckskin. "I didn't mean to interrupt your report to Herta. But I guess I can fill her in on most everything. Herta, I'm getting an annulment tomorrow. Percy said there would be no problem, since she married me with ulterior purposes and promptly proved it."

"Well, I better be going," Buckskin said.

Minderhausen held up his hand. "First we have some business. I'm writing you a draft good at the local bank for $10,000 in partial payment for saving my stupid neck. You can call on the bank at any time with a draft by mail or in person and tap your account there. An account book and some blank checks will be ready for you tomorrow by noon."

"That's an overpayment by far, Mr. Minderhausen."

"Are you telling me that my life isn't worth $10,000 to me? Anyway, I bought the bank two years ago. Not many people know about it, but it's got lots of cash reserves. The draft is good."

"Oh, no sir I didn't mean to suggest. . . ."

Herta giggled.

Her father looked at her and smiled. He

glanced back at Morgan. "I understand that you raise blooded horses out west somewhere."

"Yes, sir. Idaho. Best stock I can find."

"Good. I'd like to make an investment in your ranch. I'll give you a draft tomorrow for $50,000. You put it in your bank in Boise and it should clear and be paid in two or three weeks. That money should buy me a 20% ownership in your ranch, fair enough?"

"More than fair. I'm not used to having any spare cash around."

"Get used to it. You deserve it."

Buckskin stood and shook Minderhausen's hand.

Herta jumped up and hugged him and kissed his cheek. She put her arm through his and walked with him to the door.

"I can't tell you how much I appreciate what you did. I'm too young to be an orphan, and I would have been if you hadn't started checking on Serilda."

"We were lucky, Herta. I'd suggest that you ask your father to keep his bodyguards around for a while. No sense in taking any chances."

"Yes, I understand. Will you be staying for the trial?"

"I doubt it. I have to go to Denver, and then get back to the Spade Bit in Boise."

This time she shook his hand. "Thanks again, Mr. Morgan. And good luck with your ranch."

He went out the door and looked around. He saw no one lurking in the shadows or ready to challenge him. Maybe he had a chance yet to be the one to surprise Alonzo Warnick. He was going to do everything he could to make it happen.

Twenty-Six

Buckskin Lee Morgan walked back to the hotel without attracting any attention by using the back street route. He rode the roan he had rented that morning to the livery and told them he wanted the same animal the next morning about eight.

He whistled softly as he worked his way to the back door of the hotel. Buckskin was doing his best not to be spotted by Warnick, at least not until he wanted to be.

Dutch looked up and lifted her six-gun when he stepped into the room.

"Gotcha," she said and blew imaginary smoke from the muzzle of her gun.

"I'm easy. We need to talk."

She had dressed and now watched him closely.

"You dead set on Denver and a gambling palace?"

"Yes," she said.

"The other gambler hall owners won't be happy about having more competition."

"That's why I want you to front the place for me. Nobody is going to get rough if they know they'll have to deal with Buckskin Lee Morgan."

"And I can move around, stop back and make a show, and move on again. Sounds fair. You and Maud will run the place?"

"Maud worked in a gambling operation in Texas. She was manager for a while. She knows how to get us set up and where to get equipment. We'll start small and grow and build."

"Might work. I just came into another $10,000. I can invest $15,000 now."

"Easy come. . . ."

". . . seldom missed."

He picked up her hat and reticule. "Your hat and purse, young lady. Time for you to be walked home."

"But you don't want to be seen with me."

"True, I've got my reputation to think of."

She swung the reticule at him, missing by an inch.

"You're right, I better stay here. Tomorrow I'll be calling at your place about eight-thirty A.M. on a horse. I'll be packed for the trail and ready to move. I figure Alonzo Warnick will be either watching your place or having somebody watch it looking for me. He'll get the word fast that I'm riding out packed for the trail and he'll be there quick.

"Only by then I'll be moving out of town without a lot of hurry. Idea is I want the man to follow me. I'll get him in the outback without any supplies and not much of an arsenal and I'll pick the time and place for the showdown."

"He could bring three or four men with him."

"True, he's tried that before. He'll have some sneaky idea, but I'll have to beat him at it."

Her face twisted into a frown. She put her arms around him and held him close.

"We could just forget about him and slip out of town one at a time for Denver. He'd never find you."

"He might. I'm tired of his tracking me. This is the time for our settling it."

"Buckskin, you goose, I don't want to lose you in some man-to-man battle to see who is the best."

"Won't be that. Not a chance. He doesn't believe in fair play, so that makes it downright easy for me to play his kind of game." He watched her.

"I better go before it gets dark," Dutch said. "You promise me you won't get yourself killed, and I'll write a note to your teacher letting you go."

She kissed him and went to the door.

"Damnit, Lee, don't get killed."

She closed the door softly.

Buckskin went down to the room clerk, the same one he had paid before, and gave him a five dollar bill.

"Have the dining room bring me up a steak

dinner, a big one, with everything, and two bottles of cold beer. Keep the change. You still don't know who I am and that I'm not staying here, right?"

"Yes sir, that's right. Medium rare on the steak?"

"Medium rare."

The steak was a pound slab of beef, done exactly right at medium rare and the whole dinner was worth waiting for. After he finished eating, he put the dishes outside the door. Then he jammed a chair under the door handle and pushed the dresser in front of the window. Too many times he'd had a man or a bomb swung into his room through a closed window. Not tonight.

Nothing bothered him that night.

Morning brought a big breakfast, a stop at the livery for his horse and another stop at the back door of the general store. He bought a blanket, a small sack of food and a fry pan, kettle and tin plate, a cup, knife, fork and spoon. The food was all tinned and dried, plus a fresh loaf of bread and a half pound of bacon, thick sliced. The store man neatly wrapped it all in an old flour sack and Buckskin tied it on behind his saddle.

He spent almost seven dollars for food and gear. He got a 25 count box of shells for the Big Fifty and stowed them in his saddlebag.

Then he rode slowly down Main and turned toward Dutch Smith's house. He hitched the mount to the gate and walked up to the front door and knocked.

Maud almost jerked him inside.

"Dumb, shit dumb! You trying to get yourself

killed? I seen two different guys watching the house last few days. Somebody always there and he was today. Just took off like a castrated bull yearling out of a chute right after you hitched your horse out there. I'd say you got about five minutes to live or to ride."

"And a good morning to you too, Maud." He lifted her and kissed her lips and put her down.

She snorted, grinned, then hugged him and led him into the kitchen where Dutch sat working on coffee.

"Maud says we made contact. I better be moving on."

Dutch came up and kissed him, then put his hand on her breast and kissed him again.

"Gonna miss you, cowboy, if you don't ride back."

"Oh, I'll be back. He unbuttoned his shirt and untied a cloth money belt from his chest and dropped the cash on the table. "Should be $5,000 there in greenbacks for the new business." He took a draft from his pocket that had been pushed under his door inside an envelope sometime last night. It was made out to him and good for $50,000.

"Keep them for me. Little insurance so I'll be damn sure to get back."

"$50,000?"

"Minderhausen said his life was worth more than the $50 a day I was getting paid. He bought in for 20% of my horse ranch up in Boise. Course, it don't cost him nothing if I don't live to cash in on that paper."

He kissed Dutch seriously, then pecked Maud

on the cheek and walked out the front door. He waved once, then rode away slowly back through the middle of town and due south toward the Medicine Bow Mountains, toward a far off green tinge that he could barely make out through the early morning haze.

Buckskin was a half mile south of town when he saw someone following. He pulled up and watched closely. Three men on horseback came toward him. They didn't seem in any rush to catch up with him.

He patted the Big Fifty in the boot and grinned. All he had to do was figure out which one was Warnick, then he would cut down the odds to one-on-one.

That was when the real game of deadly hide and seek would start. There would be only one winner.

The loser died.

They rode for two hours at almost the same distance apart. The land kept rising. Buckskin remembered that the Continental Divide was nearby, on the ridge to the right, he thought. The hills were still mostly barren, with small shrubs and some sage growing. No timber, no real concealment. No streams.

He made his first move a half hour later. A sharp water course cut down from the ridge and gouged out a six foot deep ravine. Buckskin dropped into it and went out of sight of the other three. At once he kicked off his mount and drew out the Big Fifty.

Now the game would get more interesting. He crawled back up to the lip of the gully and looked over. The three horsemen had put their mounts into a trot forward. They were a half mile behind him and slightly downhill.

He settled the Big Fifty on the edge of the ravine and found a comfortable shooting position, then pushed a round into the chamber and eased down to sight in on the trio below. He wanted a man, not a horse.

He figured the boss, Warnick, would be in the middle. The one on Buckskin's right seemed the larger of the two. He shifted his sight to the man who seemed to be constantly in motion. They wouldn't be stopping. He'd have to chance it.

The riders came almost directly toward him. Not much adjustment there. There was almost no wind yet this morning. Unusual. He looked away, then sighted in again, zeroed in on the man's chest and slowly squeezed the trigger.

The Big Fifty sounded like a cannon going off in the clear, thin air at more than 7,000 feet. Below and almost a half mile away, the larger man jolted backwards out of the saddle with a bullet through his heart. He sprawled in sudden death on the rocky ground. His horse shied away to the left and galloped 50 yards away.

Buckskin lifted his head and watched the other two men. Both rode rapidly away at a right angle to their previus route of travel. There was no place to hide. Ahead another 100 yards, Buckskin saw the start of another ravine. He had reloaded as soon as he shot, pushing another round into the chamber.

Now he lifted the big gun and sighted in and fired. Quickly he pumped another round into the breach loader and this time sighted in better and squeezed the trigger.

Downhill! His round hit the horse and the animal went down and screamed in the morning so loudly Buckskin heard it. Before he could sight in for another shot, the last rider was over the lip of the ravine and out of sight. The horseless bounty hunter ran for the gully in a zigzag manner and spilled down the slope and was hidden from Buckskin before he could get off an aimed shot.

"Better odds already," Buckskin muttered. He didn't want to kill Warnick long range. Buckskin wanted to see the man close up. Wanted him to know he had played a dangerous game and lost. He would find a way.

The terrain wasn't going to favor him. He figured he might be ten miles yet from the first creek that ran into the North Platte. Ten miles to any kind of timber cover. He had to do it here, out in the open, in the high desert.

Buckskin mounted up, made sure his rifle was loaded again, and then rode downhill and to the left so he could see into the ravine where the two men hid.

They might have ridden down the gully. Possible. Would Warnick share his horse? Maybe the on-foot man would try to get the other horse the first man rode.

Buckskin rode for five minutes and could see the gully plainly. There was no one in it. The dead horse lay to the right of it. A pair of carrion eaters circled high above. The water course extended down some ways and bent in half a dozen twists and turns.

He could ride well below where they should be and wait for them. He could follow the ditch down and find them. No. They would hear him coming and lay a trap for him. It wasn't supposed to work out that way.

What other choices?

None. He rode well away from the side of the gully hoping they wouldn't hear his mount. He trotted for a ways down the slope, walked his roan a ways, then trotted another half mile. When he figured he was well below the pair, he pulled over by the edge of the ravine and looked down. Here it was still only 20 feet deep, with numerous crumbling sides and little tributaries of sandy ditches that led down to the main dry watercourse.

Winter rains must cause gushers down here with no growth to soak it up or hold the moisture. The winter snow pack would give the ground a warm coat in the winter, but the spring runoff again would turn this ditch into a river.

He checked the sandy bottom of the gully. There were no horseshoe prints. He moved upstream slowly looking for a good defensive position. He found it 100 yards ahead. The gully made a sharp turn around a house sized boulder. He put his horse behind the boulder and found a place where he could see up the gully without being seen.

Now it was a matter of waiting.

It was nearly an hour later before he heard them talking as they came down the gorge. He couldn't make out the words. When he saw them about 75 yards up the ditch, they both rode on the horse.

Buckskin tried but could not get a clean shot at the man riding behind Warnick. It was the bounty hunter, all right. The bastard was talking like he was still king of the hill.

Buckskin let them come forward. A new plan formed in his mind. Yes, it would work. He let them come until the horse and its two riders were only 30 yards away. Then he stood up in plain sight of the pair and leveled the Big Fifty at them.

"Hold it, Warnick! This is the end of the line for you."

Twenty-Seven

"How the hell you get down here?" Warnick screeched at Buckskin in surprise and frustration.

His rifle held on them. "Wasn't hard. For a bounty hunter you're plain asshole dumb. Why you suppose I led you out here? For a picnic? Who's your friend?"

"Hired hand."

"Hired hand, you want to wind up the way your other friend did?"

"No, sir!" a voice said from the man still hidden by Warnick.

"Both of you lift out six-guns and drop them in the dirt, damn careful, or you'll be eating a fifty-ninety slug."

"Damn, a buffalo gun?" Warnick asked.

"Yes, a Big Fifty. Now drop the iron."

They both let revolvers fall into the sand. They didn't discharge.

"Now, both of you, get off that nag. Down to the ground. Do it."

They slid off on the same side.

"Hired Hand, climb up the side of the gully and start running for home. I want to see how far you can run before I nail you with a hot lead slug. You might get lucky."

The man looked at Buckskin. He was maybe 24 or 25, wore old pants and suspenders outside a plaid shirt. A dirt brown hat sat on his head.

"He said you was Wanted, Mister, and he said the three of us would bring you back alive. You musta had doings with Mr. Warnick before. I don't want no part of that. I don't want to die neither."

"Get running. Next time get some references before you go out on a man hunt."

The man scrambled up the side of the gully and lit out running north toward Rawlins.

Buckskin looked at Warnick. "Face down, little bastard. Lay down on your face and stretch hands and feet as far as you can."

"What . . . what you gonna do?"

"You'll find out."

When Warnick was face down in the sand, Buckskin gathered up the two revolvers and pushed them in his belt, then climbed up the side of the ravine. Hired Hand was 200 yards away. He looked back and saw the gun and ran faster. Buckskin put a shot past the man close enough so he could hear it, then let him go. He'd probably run all the way to Rawlins without stopping.

Warnick hadn't moved a muscle.

Back in the gully, Buckskin got his horse and mounted up, then rode almost on top of Warnick.

"On your feet, big bounty hunter, we're taking a walk upstream."

"What . . . what you gonna do to me?"

"Ain't rightly figured it out yet. Been thinking that just shooting you would be too fast. Right well like to roast you head down over a slow burning fire, Cheyenne style. That way you'd last for two, maybe three hours, before your brains boiled and blood poured out of your ears and nose just before your skull exploded. Makes a damn strange sound when a skull explodes that way. Cheyenne have it down to a science. Trouble is, we're ten miles from a good sized tree and don't look like you can make it that far."

"That really doesn't appeal. . . ."

"Shut up! I don't care if you like it or not, bastard! You shot up a house of some friends of mine. Damn near scared a nice lady half out of her underwear. She was the one who killed your man that night, not me. Then you came at me with four men in the hotel. You're a real bastard, Warnick. Think you'll ever change?"

Warnick looked at him from where he lay.

"Get up and start walking north. And let's move right along, I don't want to waste the whole day just killing you."

"My horse. . . ."

"Should do fine right there. Probably will get hungry in a few hours and start back to the livery stable."

"How far. . . ." He looked at Buckskin and stopped.

"I'll probably have to settle for an ant hill. You seen these Wyoming giant red ants? Damn near half-an-inch long and got the sharpest little beaks I ever been chewed by. Had a bet with an Indian how long it would take a hill of them to kill a man. Never did get to find out. He wanted me to be tied down and I wanted him on the hill."

"You wouldn't do that. I'm a white man!"

"Not that I can tell. You act like a damn savage."

They walked for almost an hour and came to the end of the gully and near the top of a low ridge. There was another ridge behind it and between a small dry canyon a quarter-of-a-mile across. Two stunted cottonwoods grew near a flat place where a watercourse leveled and in the rainy season and runoff probably formed a small lake. It was all dry now.

"Over the top and down to those two poor excuses for trees. I might just as well hang you and get it over with. Course won't be enough drop to break your neck, but in two or three minutes you'll strangle to death just fine. Whatever works, I always say."

Warnick watched him, then looked away. His face was drawn now, showing the strain.

"Why don't you just go ahead and kill me?" Warnick asked as they walked down the slope.

"Is that what you did? Caught a Wanted man, shot him dead, and took his body to the closest sheriff for verification?"

"Couple of times."

"Then you've got the same treatment coming, don't you?"

At the pair of trees, Buckskin got off his horse and tied her to a branch of the straggly cottonwood. Warnick had dropped down in a small patch of shade the undersized tree made.

It was time.

Buckskin wanted to gut shoot the smaller man and watch him die in agony. But he couldn't do it. Warnick was a bastard who had shot down unarmed men and earned a living doing it. No more.

Buckskin stared at Warnick.

"Stand up, bounty hunter. It's time."

Warnick came to his feet, his eyes looking around for a way out. There was nothing to help him, no one.

"Catch," Buckskin said, tossing one of the six guns from his belt at the man. The bounty hunter grabbed it while it was in the air.

"Holster it, or you're dead before you can lift it."

Warnick looked at Buckskin's .45 leveled in on his chest. He pushed the weapon into his own leather. Slowly Buckskin holstered his own.

"Anytime you feel lucky, bad man," Buckskin said. They stood ten feet apart at a can't miss range.

Warnick's face worked, his eyes widened, the color drained from his cheeks, his mouth opened slightly and his chin quivered. His right hand hovered over the weapon. Suddenly he jolted backwards and ran to the right, then the left, in a quick series of zig zags. A wild scream of terror ripped from his mouth.

Buckskin drew and shot him twice. The first slug took him high in the side under his arm and daggered downward past his heart through his left lung.

The second round ripped through the back of his neck, tearing lose a section of his spinal cord and killing him instantly.

It was over.

He turned, slid the Colt back to leather and walked to his horse. Buckskin Lee Morgan stopped and looked back at the figure doubled up in the sand and rocks.

Somewhere a mother would wonder what happened to him. Buckskin shrugged. She bought that worry when she raised him to walk all over other people. It was partly that mother's fault. Now she would reap the agony.

Three hours later he rode up to the livery and turned in the two horses. Told them he found the spare one wandering to the north of town.

At the general store he gave them back the goods he had just purchased and told them to give them to the first needy family he found.

It was just before three o'clock when he opened the rear door of the white house with the white pickets in front.

A shotgun poked out the kitchen door.

"Move a step and you're buzzard bait!" a woman's voice barked at him.

"Easy, Maud. Easy with the scattergun."

The door came open and Maud grinned. "Ain't taking no damn chances this close to us all being out of here."

"Good idea."

Dutch ran past Maud and grabbed him, hugging him until he yelped. Then she kissed him properly.

"Glad to have you back, cowboy."

"Good to be here. When do we go to Denver?"

"Day after tomorrow. We transfer at Cheyenne."

Dutch brought Buckskin a bottle of Minderhausen beer that had been cooling in a bucket of water overnight. He flipped the cap and tasted it.

"Good idea, thanks for the beer. Now. What kind of gambling house we going to run in Denver?"

Maud moved up with a sketch she had done in pencil.

"We'll have faro tables, craps and a roulette wheel. Them's the fastest action games, and the suckers eat them up. Course we'll have monte, Boston, seven-up and black jack as well as poker tables. Poker is too slow for this type of gambler. But we'll offer high stakes tables with the house taking ten percent of every pot with the deal rotating."

"How do we get started?" Dutch asked.

"We rent a building and get our equipment in, and tables and chairs, then hang out a big sign and hire a six man band to play in front of the place and offer free one dollar chips to the first 50 players every day. We'll be mobbed."

In the short silence that followed, Buckskin suddenly looked up sharply.

"I heard shots," he said. "A lot of them. I'm going to go see what happened."

"Me too," Dutch said grabbing her hat and reticule. They went out the front door and saw someone running toward Main. They hurried that way.

The Rawlins Home Bank sat on the corner of Main and First, a block and a half from Dutch's house. They walked quietly down First and soon saw a group of people around the bank.

"Be damned," Dutch said. "A real bank robbery."

It was. The sheriff was there trying to keep the people back.

"Back off!" he bellowed. "We got a shot up man here and the doctor is trying to get through. Give him room."

"How many of them, Sheriff?" someone shouted.

The sheriff pushed back his gray hat and shook his head. "That's the curious part. Near as we can tell, just the one. He came in just at closing, locked the front door and pulled a gun. But the manager was in the vault and came out with his own pistol and began shooting.

"Hit the guy once and he turned and bolted out the front door. Old Charley kept on shooting and hit the varmint at least twice more. Think he's stone dead, but Doc will tell us.

"Nothing missing from the bank, folks. Your money is safe and sound. Now you better just move on home. We can take care of this. Don't make it no worse than it already is."

Half the crowd split up and left. Buckskin and

Dutch moved forward to see the robber. He lay on the boardwalk on his side, with one leg dangling into the street. Blood pooled under the body.

The medical man hurried up and eased the body over. He touched the man's throat and shook his head. Then he took the man's hat off which had slipped down over his face.

When the face came into view, Dutch gasped. Buckskin turned to look at it and saw the silent, still frowning face of Pris, the crazy wildcat who had been in Dutch's bank robbing gang.

"Oh, Lord!" Dutch whispered and sagged toward Buckskin.

He held her tightly.

"She didn't go to Salt Lake."

"Looks familiar," somebody in the crowd said.

"Just a kid, don't even shave yet."

The doctor opened the shirt to look at a chest wound. He saw the woman's breasts and quickly covered the chest and looked up.

"This one never would have shaved. This is a woman dressed up like a man. Ain't no man at all."

The crowd chattered in response. Somebody pushed up closer.

"Yeah! Yeah, I remember her. Used to eat at the cafe all the time. Unfriendly type. Seems to me people called her Pris. Never did know her last name."

Sheriff snorted. "Damn foolish thing to try. Hell, women can't rob banks. She should have known better." He sighed. "Well, two of you carry her down to the undertaker. See if anybody claims the body."

Buckskin supported Dutch as they turned and walked home. Dutch hadn't said a word after she recognized Pris. Tears came slowly, then in a flood. She was sobbing by the time they got in the back door of the white house.

Maud looked up, curious, then alarmed. "What the hell?"

"It was Pris. She tried to rob the bank all alone. She's dead."

"Oh, Christ! That poor child. She told me once she had been run out of two towns already. Her family wasn't much, I guess. Pa got shot dead when she was six. Mother ran off with another man and she and her brother made it on their own since she was eight and he was ten."

"Why did she think she could do it alone?" Dutch asked. "She always said we should hit the local bank, but we talked her out of it. They knew about the closing up robbery gang. I heard that the owner had special protection, and that every person who worked there had a revolver at hand at all times. The manager had a sawed off shotgun, too. Maybe I didn't tell Pris."

"You told her, three times I can remember," Maud said.

Buckskin headed for the door. Both women looked up.

"Figure we need to give her a proper burial. I'm least known in town. I'll do it anonymously. Headstone and all. She have a last name?"

"Barker, she told me once," Maud said.

Buckskin nodded and hurried out the door.

He left $20 with the undertaker for the burial and a proper marble headstone with her name and age, 19, and her death date.

Back at the house it was quiet. The women were packing. They would leave the furniture in the house for the new owner who had paid an extra $30 for the lot.

"What about Navaro?" Buckskin asked.

"She left yesterday. She wants to go down to Texas for a month or so, then will join us in Denver. We have her investment, and she understands it's a gamble, but wants to go along with it.

Buckskin nodded. "She has a better chance than Pris had. Damn, but that makes me angry. She could have been set for life."

Dutch put her arms around Buckskin and set her head against his shoulder. "At least three of us got out of it. We'll have to be thankful for that."

Twenty-Eight

Buckskin paid one more visit to Herta Minderhausen Radowitz and found her reading cookbooks again.

She hugged him and stepped back. "I still can't thank you enough for all of your help. Serilda and Karl are in jail. They have enough money to hire a lawyer but not to post any kind of bail, so I'm sure they'll be there until the trial.

"Oh, the sheriff asked me to tell you he wanted to see you so you could make a deposition, just in case you left town."

"I'll see him today. I am leaving tomorrow and I wanted to say goodbye and wish you all the best."

"Things are just fine, right now. Joseph is learning the brewery business, and doing extremely well. There was no challenge for him at the store. Now he can really develop. Father is happy with his work and the way he's digging into the business."

"Good. Say goodbye to your father for me."

He left and went to the sheriff's office where he was sworn by the judge and then gave testimony that was written down by a court secretary. He covered everything except the break in at the room. He described the whole story of hiring the already hired men, and redirecting them, and watching the supposed killing directed by Karl Schwartz.

When he finished he went to the general store and found a good gun case he could use to carry his Big Fifty to Denver. Never know when he might need it later.

The afternoon train out of Rawlins was right on time and left them at the depot in Cheyenne 148 miles later at just after nine in the evening. They took hotel rooms and found out the Denver spur line railroad passenger train left at eight the next morning.

Morgan took a room as well and when the ladies were settled in he slipped into Dutch's room and found her waiting.

"Cowboy, I'm a long way from home and I need some tender loving care. Can you help me?"

"Let's start with some supper downstairs before the dining room closes. Yell at Maud, I'm buying."

The train left the next morning at eight o'clock and they were on board. It was a 100 mile ride to Denver through some spectacular mountains.

They arrived a little after two that afternoon and Buckskin took them to a good hotel that wasn't overpriced.

They toured the gambling halls which were located on Sixth Avenue and Broadway. Maud was not impressed.

"Bunch of pikers," Maud said. They don't have free snacks for the players. Don't have any entertainment at all, not even a piano player. Place looks like a barn. We're going to have some class."

She made some inquiries and before dark had found the best place to buy gambling equipment.

Buckskin and Dutch went to the Rocky Mountain Bank where he already had a small account. He told a clerk he needed to see the bank manager and they were ushered into an office that was neatly decorated but conservative.

"I'd like to make a deposit to my account," Buckskin said.

The manager was slender, rail-like, with a pinched face and wary eyes.

"I believe the teller can help you, sir."

"No, I'm afraid he can't. I'll need more guarantee than that. I'd like to deposit this draft to my current account." He handed the paper to the manager who looked at it, and then looked again.

"Oh, my. Yes. I understand. We'll have to hold the account for three or four days to be sure we collect on this draft."

"You mean you question Mr. Minderhausen? He owns the bank in Rawlins."

"Of course, we know Mr. Minderhausen, but it's bank policy to be sure we collect. We could make, say $400 available to you at once."

"Fine. Then we also wish to open another account."

He loosened two buttons on his shirt and took out two money belts. Dutch removed a large package from her reticule and they laid the three items on the man's desk.

"I believe you'll find $63,000 there in cash. We want to open up the account in the name of Smith-Lowden Enterprises. We'll be setting up a business here in town, but we're not free to tell you just what it is yet."

The manager's eyes popped when he saw the cash.

"Mr. Morgan, I'll bring in a teller to verify your count on this cash, and open the account at once. You'll want checks printed I would expect. We can take care of that in two days and I'll have a stack of checks for you to use at once as well. Just write your name and your address on them."

"We don't have an address yet," Dutch said. "I'll be signing the checks. Do you need a sample of my signature to verify it?"

Two days later they were settled into a former general store that had gone out of business. It was half a block from Sixth Avenue on Broadway and had a great number of people walking by.

Maud had taken charge of the operation with a vengeance. She barked orders at carpenters and other workmen setting up the three faro tables, the two roulette wheels and three craps tables.

"We'll have high stakes poker games at the back with curtains so the rabble won't know what's going on," Maud said.

She had the gambling equipment paid for and set up in a day. Next she worked with a sign painter to get the name of the place just right.

"It's the El Dorado Casino," Maud said. "Been thinking up the name for weeks. El Dorado, the place of abundant wealth, and goods and opportunity. Great name. Now, excuse me, I've got to talk to the liquor distributor. We'll serve nothing but Minderhausen beer of course, by bottle or on tap. The whiskey is trickier. I've got a gentleman to talk to up front."

Two more days and the El Dorado Casino was nearly ready to open. Maud had hired only experienced dealers and table men. She had chips stamped with the El Dorado logo in denominations of one, five, ten and one hundred dollars, and stood there while the presses did the job and collected every misprint and destroyed it.

Maud hired an armed guard to haul the printed chips back to the casino with her. Each bit of cardboard was worth its face value and they were treated the same as cash. They were counted, double checked and stacked away in packages of various dollar amounts in the large safe Maud had installed.

A standup bar at the side of the long room was staffed by three women bartenders, and three more young, attractive girls served as waitresses to bring drinks to anyone who ordered them.

Denver's mayor, Ronald Hardesty, would be

there at noon the next day to open the doors and roll the dice for the first time. Customers would get the snacks of cheese and fruit and small cakes they would get ready in the morning for the noon crush.

"I've passed out over a thousand leaflets announcing our grand opening and pushed the idea about a free one dollar chip for the first 50 customers through the door," Maud said.

"The whole operation seems in fine form," Buckskin said. "No problems of any sort so far."

"You were wrong about the trouble we could expect," Dutch said. She had discarded her more mannish attire for frilly dresses and some with a flair for the more stylish.

"Yes, Dutch, I was wrong. Things look great. Are we going to have the grand opening party tonight? Tomorrow night we'll be working."

"True, we'll talk about it."

Instead of a party they closed up the El Dorado and went to dinner, then back to the hotel to bed. They would have a hard day tomorrow, Maud reminded them.

Buckskin thought he heard something about midnight, but when he sat up it had quieted. He was up first the next morning and hurried to the El Dorado Casino three blocks over from the hotel to make sure the painters were finished.

When he rounded the corner half a block from the Casino he stopped, stunned. The whole front of the casino was black and burned. Some smoke still drifted up from the burned structure. Denver firemen were putting out the last of the hot spots when he ran up to them.

Half ruined!

He stood in the doorway. The sign had been burned to a cinder. The front doors burned away. The entire front half of the wooden structure was singed and burned and sooty smoke had clouded the whole building inside.

Half ruined, a dream shattered.

He found the head fireman who said a witness said someone had thrown buckets filled with flaming liquid through the front windows about midnight.

The fire station with the latest in pumpers was just two blocks away, or the whole building would have been a loss.

"Too bad, I was planning on being here today for the grand opening. Now it looks like it will take a while to get it back in shape."

Buckskin hired three men as guards to prevent anyone from entering the building, then checked it more thoroughly. The actual damage looked a lot greater than it was. Repainting, a few new tables and chairs, a new wooden facade up the front and a new sign.

The damage to the roof was not serious. The firemen had done an excellent job. Quickly he estimated the cost. Another two thousand dollars would do it, and the work would delay the opening no more than a week.

He heard a scream at the entrance and ran back to find Dutch there bellowing in fury at a policeman.

"I own this firetrap," Dutch screamed at the officer. "Now stand aside and let me see how much money I've lost!"

She came inside and saw Buckskin and ran toward him.

"We're ruined, we're wiped out!" she brayed.

He caught her and hugged her and kissed her cheek. "Easy, pretty lady. Easy. It isn't all that bad. We won't open this noon, but I'd say no more than $2,000 will put us in good shape. In the meantime, I'm going to find out who set us on fire and return the favor. If they think they can scare us out, they're crazy. Where's Maud? We've got a hard day's work to do."

Maud came a half hour later, stepped through the rubble of the entrance and looked around. She came up to Buckskin and shrugged. "They caught us. You said they might. My bid is $1,500 to put us back better than we were."

"I'll take your bid. I'd figured $2,000. Any of the basic gambling equipment need replacing? That's your specialty. Dutch, you get those same carpenters we used before and start them working on the front of the building and the first 15 feet. We need it framed in by tomorrow night and ready for the painters two days later."

He looked around. "I hired three guards for now. We'll have a guard on inside and outside from now on. There won't be any repeats of last night's easy pickings. Right now I have to go call on a few old friends in the gaming business."

There were four major gambling casinos in Denver that year. Buckskin knew the men who ran two of them, had met the third, but the fourth was a newcomer. Some said he came from San Francisco.

Buckskin thought about the two men he knew

best. No, they would not resort to firebombing a competitor. They both would fight hard to attract business, but they would not try to burn out a new casino.

That left Lefty Naidier, the man he knew least of the three, but had met when he came through Denver a year ago. He looked like a French prince and talked like one. Buckskin decided he was not the one either.

That left the Lucky Lady Gambling Hall. It was new since he had been through. He found it quickly and walked past. There was no activity there yet. It would open at ten o'clock, the usual starting up time for the gamblers in Denver. That wasn't for a half hour yet, but surely the management was there.

He tried the main door. Locked. He rattled it seriously and a moment later a guard opened it a crack.

"We ain't ready for business yet."

"I'm not gambling, I want to see the owner," Buckskin said and rammed the door inward. The guard, caught by surprise, bounced backwards. The guard's hand grabbed for a revolver at his waist, but Buckskin's drawn .45 probed at his ribs and his hand stilled.

"I asked you nicely to see the owner. If you want me to become insistent that's the next step before I get rough. Where is the man who runs this garbage dump?"

"That would be me, sir. I own this gaming establishment. If you wish to speak to the owner, please come this way and I'll accommodate you."

Buckskin turned and saw a nattily dressed

man in his thirties watching him. He was in formal attire, complete with ruffled shirt and tails, and carried a black walking stick with a gold head on it. He was not over five feet tall, clean shaven with a mass of red hair that looked as if it had been waved and set and varnished in place.

The small man leaned on the golden head of the walking stick as he stared at Buckskin. "And who sir, may I have the honor of addressing?"

"Look, you stupid little shithead. Last night you hired two drifters to burn down the El Dorado Casino. It halfway worked. I believe in an eye-for-an-eye, you bastard. Tonight your nice little place here is going to burn to the ground. Just thought I'd let you know. If you want to be rough, I can be twice as rough. You have a name?"

"I can assure you that I had nothing. . . ."

"Shithead! I asked if you had a name?"

Buckskin hadn't put away his six-gun when the small man first spoke to him. When he turned he still had it in his hand and now it came up trained on the small man's chest.

"Yes, yes of course. I'm J. Arthur Ihander. I own the Lucky Lady. I did not hire anyone last night to burn down your casino."

"Tough shit for you, Sylvester. If you don't tell me by midnight who did burn up my casino, your place is nothing but ashes in the morning. You doubt it, just ask around town. Buckskin Lee Morgan is the name and you'll find out I do exactly as I promise."

He spun, fired one shot and blasted a whiskey

bottle off the bar spraying the back mirror with splashes of whiskey and shards of glass.

Buckskin holstered the revolver and walked out the door without a backward glance.

Twenty-Nine

Just down the street, the Bonanza Gambling Hall had opened for business. A hawker out in front announced the fun had begun for the day and urged people to come inside.

Buckskin walked through the doors and past the tables that were beginning to have customers, and on to the stairs that climbed one wall to a small balcony where the big spenders would risk the ranch or deed to their home on the turn of a card.

A well dressed, sturdy man lounged near a door without any name on it.

"Is Mr. Herkimer in? I'm an old friend," Buckskin said.

"Mr. Herkimer has lots of old friends."

"Buckskin is the name."

The man looked up sharply. "Yes sir, Mr. Buckskin. Right this way. He said you might be calling."

They went through the door, down a short hall and to another door that opened into a fancy office.

"Mr. Buckskin is here," the bodyguard said and retreated out the door.

The man behind the desk looked up, a grin spread across his face and he came around the mahogany slab and shook Buckskin's hand. He was solidly built and as tall as Buckskin, about 60, silver hair neatly trimmed and with a white, neat moustache. Blue eyes sparkled and he seemed pleased to see his visitor.

"Damn, it's been more than a year. Hear you're backing the new gaming hall. Congratulations. Sorry about the little misunderstanding with the fire. You know I don't play that way."

"Any idea who might?"

"Got a couple."

"I have just one. I don't think Lefty would stoop that low. But this J. Arthur Ihander seems about the right breed of gutter rat to do it."

"Met him once. I tend to agree with you."

"Smokey Altman still in town?"

"Yes, but he's reformed. Deals for me now. Doubt if he's back in his old trade."

"Mind if I talk to him?"

Buckskin watched his friend who didn't hesitate at all.

"I'll have him come right up." He pulled a small rope twice and spoke into a speaking tube. Then listened.

"He's on his way. How long before you can

open?"

"A week. I'm taking $20,000 out of somebody's hide for the cost and the lost profits."

"Don't blame you. How's the ranch in Idaho?"

"I'm not sure. I've been gone too damn long this time. Might not even be mine anymore for all I know."

The guard brought in Smokey who stood with his green visor in his hands turning it slowly. He glanced at Buckskin, nodded and watched his boss.

"Smokey, talk to Buckskin. He's a friend. Tell him whatever he wants to know."

"Yes sir, Mr. Herkimer."

"Good to see you again, Smokey. You been working your old trade recently?"

"Like last night? No sir. Quit cold. Almost landed in jail for good. Mr. Herkimer give me a job and got me out of the lockup."

"And if Mr. Herkimer told you to burn down something, you'd do it?"

"Oh, damn right. I say that 'cause I know Mr. Herkimer's a fine gentleman and never would tell me to do that."

"Did you torch the El Dorado Casino last night?"

"No sir." He said it without a trace of hesitation.

"Do you know who did?"

Smokey paused, rubbed his forehead. "No sir. Don't reckon, Mr. Buckskin. See, it didn't burn down. Now, to do it right, you start at both ends and you have somebody get tangled up with a wagon just when the fire team is coming out.

Insurance, you know? An extra ten minutes at the start of a good fire makes it almost impossible to put out."

"Then you think some amateur set the fire?"

"Heard it was two buckets of burning coal oil thrown through the front window. Not a professional way to start a real fire."

Buckskin slapped Smokey on the back and thanked him. Herkimer nodded at him and he grinned and walked out the door.

"Looking more and more like Ihander." Buckskin reached across the big desk and took Herkimer's hand.

"Thanks. I'll be around a while. Got to get the ladies off to a good start."

Herkimer frowned. "Two women running it, I hear, with you as a partner. Are these ladies tough enough to stand the gambling trade?"

"Tough?" Buckskin laughed. "Don't tell anyone, but the first time I met Dutch Smith and Maud, they and two other women were dressed as men, had just robbed a bank, and were in a shootout with a scroungy deputy. Yeah, Roger, these ladies are tough enough."

Herkimer looked at Buckskin, not knowing whether to believe him or not. At last he lifted his brows. "I think I should believe you. I won't mention a word."

"Thanks. Now I'm off to see Eldridge."

Buckskin had a good talk with Charles Eldridge, another friend who now ran the Western Casino, the last of the big four casinos in town. Charles had been walking the floor watching his dealers and floor men but mostly talking with the customers when he saw Buckskin come into the casino.

His handshake was firm. "Lee, sorry about last night. You know I didn't have a hand in it."

"Wanted to tell you I figured that way. You hear anything this morning, any rumors?"

"Not a word. Which usually means it's somebody close to the trade."

"You heard about any hired men who specialize in setting fires for profit?"

"Not since Smokey quit. We've got a police chief who really comes down on fire starters."

"He hasn't called on us yet this morning."

"He will."

"What do you know about a little slime ball named Ihander?"

"Too much. Waltzed into town with a big bundle of cash and bought away my best dealers and board men about a year ago. Even hired away my general manager. He runs a good casino. But he hasn't made any friends in the trade."

"Where's he from?"

"San Francisco. Heard something about how he was run out of town by the other operators, but don't know for sure."

"Thanks, Charles. Always good to know what kind of stripes the polecat is wearing when you're hunting him."

They stood. "Buckskin, one caution. Things aren't quite so open as they were here in Denver on your last visit. We got a new mayor and a new bunch of city fathers and a police chief who thinks he's god himself. Be careful."

"Careful is my middle name. Thanks again."

Back at the El Dorado Casino, the burned facade on the building had been ripped off and hauled away and new lumber was going up. Structurally the building was sound. Inside, a dozen women were washing down the soot and smoke residue and getting the walls and ceiling ready for repainting.

The dealers and table men had been sent home to change clothes and came back to clean up chores. The three bartenders were washing glasses, washing off whiskey bottles, and polishing up the twenty foot mirror behind the bar.

Maud walked around with a four-foot long stick directing the operation. There was no doubt who the ram rod of the outfit was.

Maud saw Buckskin come in and marched over to him. "Moving along. Four more days. Got us something different working for tomorrow noon. Heard there's a foot racer in town. Been a hoot since I've had a foot race. This guy will challenge any of the local talent to a race. We pick the fastest one and he races against our champion. I found him this morning and he agreed to run. He places his own bets as usual, we place ours."

"How can we make any money that way?"

"Gets us some publicity. Hold the race in front of the casino here for 100 yards. And we bet all we can on our man. He's a college boy, a sprinter from Harvard, where he won lots of medals. I'd figure he can't lose. Had 500 handbills printed to scatter over town this afternoon. Race at high noon tomorrow."

She moved off grinning.

Maud was going to do just fine, if he could get the bastards who fire bombed them last night. It still figured to be the Lucky Lady owner, J. Arthur Ihander. If it was Ihander, he'd defend his casino. The best way to stop it getting burned down was to stop the man who threatened him . . . Buckskin.

Ihander himself wouldn't do the dirty work, he'd hire someone. Still, it would give Buckskin a good tip off that Ihander had dropped the buckets of fire.

All of this meant Buckskin had to make himself available to be shot at. He walked the streets again, found a place where he could buy coal oil and four one gallon glass jugs. He'd get them at two different places later. Then all he needed were some wicks and a couple of matches. He had even figured out how he would get the fire bombs inside the casino after it closed. But that would wait until he was sure.

He wandered past the gambling strip, went down side streets, and without being obvious checked to see if anyone was following him. Nobody was.

Maybe he'd jumped to the wrong conclusion about Ihander. No, it had to be him. He was the only one who fit the mold.

It might happen when he stopped thinking it would. He would pretend to give up and give that a try. Buckskin walked down the street to a small cafe and went inside. He sat against the far wall facing the door and ordered a cup of coffee and a cinnamon roll.

Only a few seconds after his coffee came a man slipped in the door with a neckerchief over his face waving a pistol. He spun around looking at the tables and when he looked toward Buckskin his revolver came down to aim.

Buckskin shot him from under the small table, the round hip-aimed and slammed through the right handed gunman's right arm spinning his weapon away. He jolted backwards into the wall and slumped there keening in pain.

Buckskin was beside him within seconds, his gun holstered and his hands around the man's throat.

"Who paid you to shoot me?" Buck demanded.

"Don't know what you mean," the man croaked.

"Tell him it didn't work, and this is one more I owe him."

Morgan stood quickly, picked up the gunman's revolver and pushed it inside his shirt, dropped a dime on the table for the coffee and roll and left quickly, not wanting to explain anything to the tough Denver police.

Outside, Buckskin walked rapidly down the street and away from the cafe. There would be only one. He felt easier now that it had happened. He bought the gallon jugs and took them to the El Dorado and put them in a corner. An hour later he bought the five gallon can of kerosene at a hardware store and stashed it next to the glass jugs. He was ready, except for some cloth to use as wicks.

Maud caught him. "Did you like the first sign? We can change it if you want to?"

"It was fine, Maud. Have the man paint one again just like it. You still planning that foot race? I've seen lots of them. Almost every small town has a champion foot racer. First time I ever tried to make any money off one."

"The secret is to have the ringer, a real champion from the whole east coast. Then it's hard to lose. Course you can just do it once in a town. You can't let the champion become too well known. Never any newspaper stories." Maud grinned and went back to the sign painter.

Buckskin looked around. Already the acrid smell of smoke and soot and charcoal was being replaced by that of paint and soap and wood polish.

Maud was putting Humpty-Dumpty back together again faster than he thought possible.

Thirty

Dutch grinned that night when she rolled over on top of him in their hotel room bed.

"Hell yes, I can do a little job like that. I can find that spot easy. It's an old run down house standing alone on the end of the block and nobody lives there. I set the fire promptly at three A.M. and then walk away."

"Right, and I take care of the rest."

"You sure it was this Ihander who set our place on fire?"

"As sure as I need to be. He didn't deny it. A man tried to gun me down in that little cafe. The two fit together like the broken halves of a dinner plate."

"Once more," Dutch said. "We've got plenty of time before we go up to that vacant house. It's a mile from here, right. And that will put the fire wagon a long way from the Lucky Lady when it just happens to start burning."

"Yeah." Buckskin rolled her over and nibbled at her breasts. She lifted her legs over his back and then put them all the way on his shoulders.

"Do me this way. You never have."

He was ready. Buckskin plunged into her in one deft stroke and Dutch moaned with a whole delicious group of sensations. It was a strange angle and set her on fire at once. The increased friction fired Buckskin's desire as well and in moments they both were panting and rutting and grinding and climaxing in a fury.

"Oh, god! Best ever!" Dutch crooned.

Buckskin could only pant and grunt and drive harder and harder until he vaporized himself in his last thrust and knew he would never live again in this world or any other.

Then they both floated back to earth and to the hotel and into each other's arms as they recovered slowly.

Promptly at two-thirty A.M., Dutch and one of the guards from the casino walked away from the hotel. She carried a paper sack shielding a gallon can of kerosene.

They walked to the right street and Dutch looked across the way and saw the abandoned house. Yes. Perfect. Nothing else around it to catch fire. She told the guard to walk back a block and wait for her. She hurried across the street, faded into the back of the building and opened the can of fluid letting it soak into the dry wood of the floor and back wall. Then Dutch lit three matches and started the fire. When she was sure it would keep burning, she slipped out of the old house, walked around the block and met the guard.

"Now we can go back to the hotel," she said.

Buckskin had made his preparations. He had emptied the kerosene into the four jugs, stoppered them with easy burning newspaper plugs, and carried them to the top of the brick building next to the Lucky Lady Casino. It had closed down and he had spotted only one guard near the front of the building. He usually left shortly after three A.M.

The brick building on one side of the casino would not burn and the Lucky Lady sat on the end of the block, so it could not set the whole block on fire. He had got to the roof of the brick building by a steel ladder up the back, and now waited patiently for the fire wagon men to be alerted.

He heard the first noises about three-fifteen, and soon the big horses were hitched and the heavy fire wagon tanker rolled out of the station a block over, its hand cranked fire bell clanging as it raced away up the street.

Buckskin grinned and lighted the first newspaper wick that had a cloth core to keep it burning. He let it flame up well and then tossed it the three-feet into the skylight that opened directly onto the casino floor below. All was dark. The first crash of glass was followed by a second and then a third as the three gallons of kerosene fell to the floor below and the burning paper and cloth quickly set the fluid on fire and the flames begn to lick at the front and the back of the building.

Buckskin took the last jug of fluid, lit the wick and tossed it at the outside of the roof, next to the three-foot high beam, and watched the tarred paper begin to burn. He could see light and flames through the broken skylight now.

He slipped down the steel ladder at the back of the brick building and walked the long way around the block and back to his hotel.

Dutch came into the room shortly after he did and they both stood at the dark window and looked toward the Lucky Lady which was hidden a block over behind a large stone building.

It was ten minutes later before they could see a glow in the sky and then shrill voices shouting, "Fire!" Right then the fire wagon and the firemen were a mile away putting out a pesky fire in an abandoned house.

"Done," Buckskin said. "We have six extra night guards around the El Dorado tonight. All should be well in the morning."

The next morning they heard about the fire at the Lucky Lady before they had breakfast at the hotel. They walked within half a block of the place and looked. It had burned to the ground. There was nothing left but a few charcoal black timbers and a large safe that now lay tipped on its side.

"What a shame," Dutch said as they moved away from the ruins toward their own casino. All was well as they checked with the guards. Someone had run toward the place about five that morning, but they drew their revolvers and the man turned and fled with his two gallon can.

Inside, the reconstruction work continued. It was almost done. If all went right they would open the next noon. When Maud came in, she was grinning about the Lucky Lady's bad luck.

"Couldn't have happened to a nicer lady," Maud said. She laughed and went to check with the people who would furnish the snack food for the bar.

By ten that morning a crowd began to gather outside. Dutch and Maud went out with pads of paper, set up a table and began accepting bets against Henry, their favorite racer. The betters bet even money that Henry would lose to their local champion.

Maud and Dutch put down the better's name and how much he wagered, then took the bet in cash. Private bets were being made all over the street. It seemed like half of Denver had crowded into the block to see the challenge race.

By noon the street was jammed with more than 500 on-lookers. The police were there to keep one traffic lane open for carriages and a few wagons.

When the time came for the race itself, the police closed off the street. Maud paced off the length of the hundred yards and positioned herself at the far end with two impartial judges who had not bet on either man.

Dutch was on the far end and watched the two contestants. Henry, their man from Harvard, was slender and strong, with powerful legs and a well developed chest. He wore pants cut off just above the knees and a white undershirt.

The challenger was a heavier man, sturdy and strong. He had won the last four races he had run in Denver and was the biggest foot race winner in Denver for several years.

The men shook hands, then toed a line Dutch drew with her boot across the dusty street. She made sure that there was an open space down the whole length of the race.

One side bulged in and she screeched at the police to push the people back so they could have the race.

When things were under control again she told the two men to get in their places.

"You'll start when I shoot off my .44, gentlemen. Do you both understand that?"

The two runners nodded.

"Get on your mark . . . get set . . ." She fired her six-gun.

Both men took off quickly. The larger man had a momentary advantage, but then the speed of the man from the east took over and he ran past the bigger man to win by over ten-feet. There were cheers and screams and men ran to each other to collect on bets.

Henry went with his cohorts, a team of four men who traveled with him and who did the work in the crowd taking bets against Henry. Maud and Dutch came back to the table and watched as the crowd began to fade away.

Maud had printed up new handbills about the El Dorado Casino opening the next noon time. She shrilled the message at the crowd as it broke up and soon the two of them went back inside the El Dorado Casino, through the new door with the stained and leaded colored glass art work, past the carpeted lobby with oil paintings and columns, and then into the casino itself.

They counted up their winnings.

"Almost $400," Dutch said. "Not bad for a morning's work."

"Let's take one of the dollar bills and put it in a frame as the first dollar we took in," Dutch said.

Inside they checked over everything. There was more painting to do, two new men to hire, and daytime and night guards to make sure of.

By four o'clock everything was ready. Maud sent all of the help home except the day guards. She talked with them, reminding them of what had happened last time.

"Somebody in this town doesn't like us, and they might try to hurt us again," Maud said. "Don't let it happen."

When the night guards came on at six o'clock, Buckskin was with them. They had two armed men inside the casino, and four men outside. The buildings on each side of them were the same height as theirs, so no problem.

Buckskin sat on a stool outside the main door in the shadow of the next building. He had his regular Colt six-gun and a sawed off 12 gauge shotgun. The loads were double-ought buckshot and could cut a man in half at fifteen-feet.

The first part of the evening went without incident, then a black buggy drove by slowly. When one of the guards walked out toward it, the rig scurried down the street.

By two A.M. things quieted down on the streets, and Buckskin leaned back against the wall on his chair and closed his eyes.

The sun woke him the next morning when it flashed in his eyes. He yawned, stretched, and looked at the other guards. All were awake and eager to be off duty. They had another hour and a half.

"Nothing happened, sir," one of the guards reported. "We figured you'd be working today, so you better get some sleep while you could."

A rifle cracked and a round slammed into the door beside where Buckskin stood.

"Take cover!" Buckskin barked and darted forward, zig-zagging across the street and down the block where he had seen a puff of blue smoke coming out the window of a three story stone building. It was the last window on the top floor.

Another slug slammed into the street near his feet. This time Buckskin spotted the rifle coming back inside the top window on the left. He darted on across the street and was out of sight of the window.

He ran up the street to the front door of the building. It was full of offices. He ran through the main hallway to the rear of the structure and paused before charging outside. He waited and after what seemed a year and a half, a figure slid onto an iron ladder that came from the roof of the back of the building and started down. The man carried a rifle.

Buckskin eased out the door, drew his six-gun and let the man get down to within ten feet of the ground. He shot him in the right leg, knocking the man off the ladder. He dropped the rifle and a revolver he was trying to carry and fell to the ground. He hit on his feet and crumpled to his left rolling toward the fallen hand gun.

"Don't try for it," Buckskin barked.

The man stopped.

"Sit up and look this way," Buckskin said, his voice deadly.

The man turned slowly.

"Good morning, J. Arthur Ihander. You're a poor shot. Didn't you trust one of your killers to do your work for you?"

"Bastard! You shot me."

"An eye-for-an-eye. I still have one shot coming. You shot at me twice. Where shall I put it? Right through your left eye, I think would do." He scowled at Ihander and shook his head.

"You didn't ask around about me, did you? I don't have an awful lot of use for the lawmen in this town. Sure, I could turn you in to them for attempted murder. You'd get a lawyer and I'd get called out of town, and you'd go free as a soaring hawk."

"You won't kill me right here."

"Good idea! Why didn't I think of that. Damn you're good, Ihander. All the best ideas. But I've got a better one. I'm gonna get my horse and tie your feet together and gallop up and down the streets dragging you by your feet until you don't have a square inch of skin left on your body. How does that sound, asshole?"

"I'm bleeding to death."

"There's another great idea. You're full of them."

"Get me to a doctor!"

"Why, so you can bushwhack me again? Not a

chance. I want the names of the two men who threw the buckets of coal oil through my front windows. Now!"

"I don't know who they were. They were hired out of a saloon."

"Bastard!" Buckskin walked up to him and scowled. "Get up."

Ihander struggled to his feet. Buckskin searched him quickly, found no knife or hideout. He punched him one stinging, powerful blow with his right fist and with all of his body weight behind it. Ihander's head snapped back, his eyes glazed and he did a half turn, then collapsed into a heap in the dirt of the alley.

"Hell, that wasn't much of a fight. Even so, I think I'm entitled to breakfast now."

Ihander's unconscious form made no objection.

Thirty-One

By ten A.M. there was a line and a crush outside the El Dorado Casino. The men began shoving and pushing. At five minutes after ten, everything was ready, so Buckskin opened the doors.

Dutch and Maud handed out the one dollar chips to the first 50 customers, then let everyone stream in. Business was booming almost from the first roll of the dice.

Buckskin was on hand in a suit and tie and white shirt, with his new low crowned Stetson of pure white. He had positioned six guards inside the hall and two outside.

Gamblers elbowed each other to get up to the tables to spend their money. The bar did a good business and after two hours the free snack trays were empty and more were sent for.

They had decided that any form of currency could be used at the tables to wager with: gold coins, silver coins, greenbacks or house chips. No other casino's chips would be honored.

Many of the more intense bettors liked to buy house chips. They were more convenient to use and to bet. At the craps tables chips were always used to pay off bets no matter what the currency used to bet.

The clientele was mixed. A few men wore suits and ties, more had on every day working clothes. Most of the customers were men with a woman or two here and there. A half dozen black men were sprinkled through the customers. Buckskin had seen six men who looked like town Indians. Right from the first there was a good number of Chinese in the room although there was a small number of Chinese in Denver.

The women bartenders were a novelty and drew a lot of comments and some rude suggestions. But the ladies reacted coolly and often a man customer at the bar would chastise the man who made the out of place comments.

The three women who circulated and sold drinks had a harder time, but they were young and resilient and learned quickly that a slap in the face was as good a weapon as any. Usually they went about their business and the gamblers went about theirs.

Denver reacted to a new gambling parlor the way San Francisco might. Buckskin looked at it with a note of caution and awe. It seemed to him that all over the West the people were caught up in a mania of gambling. He had found few men who didn't gamble one way or another, and the room in front of him was a small sample of the whole West.

Cowboys, miners, Indians, farmers, cattle barons, dance hall girls, preachers, store owners and a lot of housewives. It seemed to him sometimes that a man could earn a better living by being a professional gambler than in any other way.

Now he owned a piece of the pie, and perhaps it would let him move back to Denver someday and live in luxury.

Buckskin was surprised how quiet it was in the room. He estimated there were over two hundred men in the eighty-foot long by thirty-foot wide room. It was hard to crowd between them to get from one gaming table to the next.

Yet the sound of voices was a low murmur, outdone usually by the clinking of silver and gold coins in the bettors' hands.

Most of these men were looking for quick results—win or lose. The poker tables at the far end were nearly empty. They would move out some of them soon and put in more faro and monte tables and another roulette wheel or two.

By noontime some of the bettors were broke and wandered back to the street. Others were ahead. The room thinned out a little until it was less of a physical contest to move from one end to the other.

Maud sat behind a bank teller's cage, surrounded by heavy oak panels, where she sold chips. There usually was little worry about robbery in a casino. If a gang of thugs attempted to rob one, the angry clientele probably would rip them apart and throw the body pieces into the streets.

Maud sold chips at a steady rate, and didn't bother to count. She knew she would be buying back at least half of the chips later on during the day and at closing time. The signs said closing was set for 2 A.M. But they generally conceded that they would stay open until at least 3 on this first day.

Lefty Naidier, who ran the Denver Casino, came by on a courtesy call, and was given a tour by Dutch. Later on, Charles Eldridge, owner of the Western Casino, stopped in and Buckskin showed him around. Roger Herkimer of the Bonanza Gambling Hall came past later in the afternoon when he knew things would be slowing down.

By five o'clock there were no more than twenty or thirty men in the room. Some of the workers took a breather in a special back room where there were cots for them to grab an hour's sleep. The six ladies had their special room and Maud made sure they used it since it was going to be such a long day. She hadn't figured out yet just how long.

By six-thirty the house was jammed again with bettors and the wheels spun and the craps table was filled with eager hands reaching for the magic cubes that could make them rich with just a few lucky throws.

It was nearly seven o'clock when Buckskin realized none of their workers had had anything to eat since breakfast. He went to a cafe half a block away and ordered them to make two dozen roast beef sandwiches and two gallons of coffee and half a dozen pies and bring them to the back door of the casino as quickly as possible. He paid in advance and the man said they would be there within fifteen minutes.

Back on the casino floor he worked out a rotation plan so one man would be off while two others kept working. When the food came, he brought the first one-third of his people back for food and they cheered and ate quickly. Within an hour all but Maud had eaten and he took a sandwich, a big cup of coffee, and a quarter of a pie to her cage.

"Thought you had forgotten about me," she said.

Buckskin realized all of them were so excited, a little thing like going without food for ten hours wouldn't matter at all. But it did help.

They closed the doors at 2:30 and gradually shut down tables so the gamblers would have to leave. It was five minutes after three when they at last were clear of customers.

Buckskin went around and gave each worker a ten dollar bonus for the 17 hour work day, and told them to be back at 12 to go to work the next day.

As the new workers filed out the back door, Maud said they would have to hire another shift to work. "I'm gonna need someone to take my place in the cage too, you know. Somebody who won't steal us cross eyed."

As she talked she was busy totalling up the count. She began with $100 in change. First she figured that there were about $700 in their chips that had not been cashed in. Some would be kept as momentos, most would be used to play during the next few days.

Cash on hand in gold, silver and greenbacks, totalled a little over $12,000.

"There has to be some mistake," Buckskin said.

"No mistake," Maud said. "Except by the gents who think they know how to gamble. The house wins 90% of the time. We won't do this well every day. This was our grand opening. Still, we should average $6,000 a day, I would guess."

"My god! This is better than a gold mine."

"You bet, a hundred times better," Dutch said. "But what do we do with the money? The bank's closed."

"We'll be our own bank for a while," Maud said. "We don't even want the bankers to know how well we're doing. I'll put out a notice outside that we're interviewing experienced man for monte and faro and craps dealers. We have 15 men working now and our six ladies. We'll need that doubled or we'll work our people to death."

Dutch looked at the door. "Too bad we have to go to the hotel. We've got lots of space in the back room. It's two floors back there. Why don't we build ourselves a big apartment with a kitchen and everything? We can have three or four bedrooms and a big living room and parlor. Then we won't have to go to the hotel."

They all agreed, but not for a month or so. "Let things shake down a little," Maud said.

They put all of the money in the big safe. Maud

and Buckskin were the only ones who knew the combination. It wasn't written down anywhere.

Buckskin knew there wasn't a chance to find a cab this late at night so they walked briskly back to the hotel. He had his six-gun in his hand all the way. No one even came within sight as they slipped in the front door of the hotel and found their rooms.

That night Buckskin slept in his own room, falling on the bed without undressing. Not even his shot left arm hurt him that night. He didn't wake up until nearly ten o'clock the next morning.

When Buckskin went down to breakfast alone after shaving and giving himself a quick wash basin bath, he found Navaro sitting in the lobby. She gave him a quick smile and a shy, subdued handshake.

He chattered away a minute, then pointed to the dining room. "Breakfast? *Comida?*"

She nodded and they went in for breakfast. He ordered for her, eggs and country fried potatoes, and a stack of hot cakes, toast and coffee.

Maud straggled down and joined them and hugged Navaro, then chattered at her in Spanish and both laughed and smiled.

Buckskin left a ten dollar bill on the table and told Maud to take care of their food, then he hurried to the casino. The four guards on night duty said all was quiet. He unlocked the front door and went in locking it behind him.

The casino needed a good sweeping and cleaning. They would have to hire janitors to report in after they closed to clean up. One more detail.

$12,000. Most of that was profit. At least $11,000. He had seen one shabbily dressed man lose a hundred dollar chip on one turn of the roulette wheel. He had shrugged and walked away. That was probably a third of that working man's wages for the whole year!

He found a wide broom and swept the place down quickly and arranged things as best he could. The door rattled and he let in the barkeepers, the three women who had to get everything set up for the coming day. They brought in more whiskey and cases of bottled beer, and rolled in beer kegs from the back room. They would make money off the bar.

Buckskin was sure that they would hear from J. Arthur Ihander again. A little problem like a burned down casino and a shot leg wouldn't stop him in his continued try for revenge. Maybe he had sailed off to another town to try his luck. Buckskin hoped so.

The rest of the workers began coming, most a half hour early. They seemed pleased to be there, glad for the job and the excitement. Buckskin paid them ten percent more than the going rate for dealers and house men, and he was pleased with the quality of workers they got.

Navaro was here. Good. This was all part hers. He had no idea what she would do, but they would find something. Dutch had agreed to spell Maud in the cage. That would work out well. Each would know how well it went.

Buckskin had watched the house men. Soon they would need a floor manager. Especially when Buck wasn't there, which would be most of the time.

Dutch and Maud and Navaro came and they began keying up for the opening at 12. Already men were waiting outside. Maud went out and posted her sign about wanting more help. At once, two men came forward and said they had experience dealing. She took them in and had them talk with Buckskin.

By eleven-thirty all of their people were there and they were ready to begin. Dutch said she'd take first turn in the cage, and Maud briefed her on what to do and how to sell the chips. Each was marked by color and amount.

Just before they opened the doors, Maud went outside and stood by the sign. Then they started business and the men streamed inside, as eager as they had been the day before. A new gambling hall always attracts the men for a time, Buckskin knew. Then gradually they settled down to a favorite place to wager their money.

The tempo picked up and Buckskin talked to the two new dealer applicants. He hired one of them and rejected the other one. It was just a feeling he had about the man but he couldn't explain why.

They had been open only about 15 minutes but already the hall was nearly full. Then a man came rushing in wide-eyed and screaming.

"Somebody come quick, a woman's been shot! I think she works here."

Buckskin shouldered his way through the men and charged out the door.

Maud lay against the new facade, her right

hand over her upper chest. Blood seeped through her fingers and ran down to soak into her new dress.

"Sorry, Buckskin, some bastard pulled a gun and shot me."

Her eyes closed and her head rolled to the left.

Thirty-Two

"No, Maud!" Buckskin bellowed. "You can't die. Everything is going so well."

He pointed at two men nearby. "You and you, run and find a doctor and bring him back here as fast as you can."

They hurried away.

He eased Maud down to the sidewalk next to the casino building and moved her hand off the wound. Her dress was bloody just below her collar bone. He touched her throat and felt a heart beat.

Buckskin could see that she was breathing. Thank god! He took a white handkerchief from his pocket and folded it again and pressed it against the wound in her upper chest. It had almost stopped bleeding. The bullet was somewhere inside her yet.

"Where's that doctor?" Buckskin screamed.

A man on the other side of the street strode through the dust to where the crowd formed.

"Let me through, I'm a doctor," the man called. The people gave way and he knelt beside Maud.

"Gunshot," Buckskin said. The doctor examined her a moment.

"Lift her up so I can see her upper back," the doctor said.

Buckskin lifted her and the doctor nodded.

"Bullet didn't come out. Can you carry her to my office. It's a half block down the street. Carrying her now won't hurt her any."

Buckskin picked up Maud and carried her as the doctor led the way.

"Tell them inside where I've gone and that Maud's been shot but she's still alive," Buckskin called to the crowd. Two men hurried inside.

A half hour later Buckskin still paced in the small outer room at Dr. Theodore Lipskee's medical offices. He and a nurse had been working on Maud.

When the doctor came out he was smiling.

"That's a terribly tough lady in there. I managed to get the bullet out before she regained consciousness, and I was patching up the wound when she opened her eyes and started swearing." He laughed. "She has a remarkable vocabulary.

"She's going to be fine. The slug missed the top of her lung, nicked a rib but didn't break it, but she's going to be sore for quite a while. It must have been an underpowered forty-five caliber cartridge because the lead stopped short of her back. I want to see her in two days to check the wound, and put some clean dressing on it. It should heal leaving only a small scar."

Buckskin gave him $20 and the man shook his head.

"I don't have any change."

"You don't need any. Thank you doctor. Just mark off one of the bills somebody else owes you."

Maud came out of the door behind them. She was walking by herself, pushing away the nurse who tried to help her.

"Let's find the bastard who shot me. I'll know him anywhere. He ruined my new dress!"

The doctor and Buckskin both guffawed.

"I'll buy you another new dress," Buckskin said. "I'm taking you back to the hotel for two days of rest like the doctor ordered. Don't try to argue, or I'll sic Dutch on you."

Maud looked up at him and snorted. "Two days? Not a chance. I will take it easy the rest of the afternoon. I got to go on shift in the cage by five o'clock."

"We'll see," Buckskin said, putting his arm through hers and heading for the door. Outside, Buckskin hailed a light buggy for hire and the cabby took them to the hotel.

Maud made up new tortures all the way there that she would use on the gunman who shot her when they caught him.

"What did he look like?" Buckskin asked.

"Small, about five feet tall, clean shaved with a mop of red hair. Bastard had a gold headed walking stick. Looked like a derringer he pulled out of his jacket."

"The little son of a bitch!" Buckskin snarled. "That was J. Arthur Ihander, the former owner of the Lucky Lady Casino. The one that mysteriously got burned down. I'll be paying him a social call as soon as I can find him."

"Do that, and I'll go with you," Maud said. "Now you get yourself back to El Dorado and mind the business. This Ihander can wait a day or two. We got a good start with the casino, next two or three days will tell whether we can keep it going."

"I should stay with you."

"Not a chance." Maud got down from the buggy by herself. "Hell, I been shot before. Not a damn crisis. Now keep the cab and get back to the casino. I'll see you later."

He was torn. "You sure you'll be all right?"

"Fine, fine. Now get out of here." She stepped to the boardwalk and went into the hotel.

Ten minutes later Buckskin had returned to the casino, told Dutch and Navaro what happened and that all seemed to be fine. The place was packed again.

Buckskin circulated, took care of one small difference of opinion at the faro table, and got a high stakes poker game going behind the curtain. A house man monitored the game and took the house percentage.

By three o'clock, Dutch had assembled eight men who were interested in working, and Buckskin took them back to the unused poker tables and talked to each one. He hired seven of them, and told them to be there for work at seven o'clock that night. They were to wear dark trousers, long sleeved white shirts and black string ties.

Dutch had picked out three new barmaids from four applicants and they, too, would come on at seven. Buckskin went to the cafe and put in his supper order. This time he got 30 sandwiches of three different kinds, and told the cafe operator to bring coffee and iced tea as well. It should arrive at 4 P.M.

Back at the casino, Buckskin was getting restless. He should have charged right out and found Ihander and settled with him. The little rat might be halfway out of town by now.

But a board man got sick on the roulette wheel and Buckskin had to fill in for an hour. By the time the man could take over again they were rotating the dealers and ladies to the food table in back and the gambling seemed to pick up.

It was nearly three o'clock when Maud woke up from her nap in the hotel. At first she was uncertain why she hurt, then she remembered the shot and passing out from the surprise and shock of it as much as the wound itself.

Now she had work to do. She put her six-gun in her larger reticule, and wondered how to find out where Ihander was. She asked the hotel clerk if he could find out for her. He said he thought he could. Mr. Ihander was well known and had run the gambling hall.

She sat in the lobby for half an hour and the clerk came back with an address for her. She gave the clerk a dollar and went outside for a cab.

The cab driver knew the street and ten minutes later they arrived. It was a well to do neighborhood with stately houses. She told the cabby to wait and went up to the door and knocked.

A uniformed butler answered and told her Mr. Ihander was sleeping and couldn't be disturbed. She pretended to turn, then pulled out the six-gun and silently motioned the butler inside. Maud closed the door.

"Now, buster, you take me to where Ihander is, and if you say a word, I'll shoot your balls off, you understand me?"

The butler nodded.

"Move!"

The butler took her up a flight of stairs and down a hall to the third door. He pointed at the door.

"Don't move," she whispered to the man. She turned the knob silently and edged the heavy door open inward. It was a bedroom. The large room had a double sized bed on one side and two pieces of upholstered furniture. On the bed lay a man.

She pushed the six-gun muzzle into the butler's side and pointed him inside. He shook his head. She cocked the trigger and he blanched and slipped through the open door and stood to one side.

The body on the bed moved in sleep. He was fully dressed. She stared a moment at the shaggy red hair on the small man and snorted. He was the varmint who shot her.

She motioned the butler to stand against the far window, then moved up to the bed and put the gun muzzle under Ihander's chin.

"Ihander, you bastard, wake up!"

The man stirred, mumbled something, then his eye lids snapped open and he stared in terror. It only increased when he looked up at Maud standing over him.

"You slimy, no-balls, son of a bitch! You think you could get away with shooting me? You got one hell of a big think to try again. You got a choice how I kill you?"

Ihander croaked something, swallowed and tried again.

"I didn't kill you."

"You tried, you bastard. Now sit up so I can aim better."

Maud pulled the weapon away from him. "Why the hell ain't you out of town? You burned us, and you got your placed burned in return. You shot at Buckskin and missed. Then you try to gun me when I ain't even got an iron. You should have beat it out of town with whatever you got left."

"What . . . what are you going to do?"

Maud opened the top of her dress and showed him her bandage.

"That, Bastard Ihander, is where your round went. I'm putting one through you at the same spot. No lawmen involved. You had your shot on me, now I take one at you and we're all six, twelve a dozen and even. You got some troubles with that?"

"I lost my casino, you didn't."

"Wasn't your fault. You forgot about the fire station. Which evidently wasn't the case when yours burned. Like I say, we're even, soon as I shoot up your body. Then you can get out of town. I don't have a derringer, so I'll use my .44."

"You'll kill me."

"Not unless I try. Damn, I'm a better shot than that. You got your monkey here to see to you after I plug you. Now shut up so I can aim."

Ihander dove for the bed on his face, shaking with fear.

Maud put the muzzle of the six-gun under his chin and lifted him up to a sitting position. Then she backed off six feet and fired. It came so quickly it took Ihander by surprise. The round went in just under his clavicle and probably missed his lung.

The round pounded Ihander backward on the bed where he sprawled on his back screaming. Maud looked at the butler and pointed to Ihander.

"He's your problem now. A doctor would probably be a good idea. Just remind him when he comes back to this world that I could have, and should have, killed him. I never want to see his face again."

Maud turned and walked out of the bedroom and the house. The cabby roused from his short nap when she stepped into his rig.

"You back already?"

"Naturally. Now, take me to the El Dorado Casino. I hear that's the best place in town for real gambing action."

Ten minutes later, Maud got down from the cab at the casino and paid the hack driver. She had to wait a moment to get inside through the front door. Then she worked her way through the crowded room to the cashier's cage and stepped up to it.

"I'd like $10,000 in $100 chips," she said.

Dutch looked up. "You're supposed to be in bed."

"No time, I had to find the man who shot me. Now, I guess it's about time for me to take over for you."

"You're not going to stay in bed for even a day?"

"Not when there's work to be done."

"Maud, you look a little peaked. You go in the back room and lay down for an hour, and then I'll turn this cage over to you."

"Not tired."

"You will be, have an hour's rest. Come on. Pretend I'm still running our outfit."

"Okay, yes, ma'am, boss, sir." Maud grinned. "Oh, I shot the little bastard. The one who shot me this noon. He sure was surprised."

Maud turned and walked away to the back room leaving Dutch with her mouth open.

"You what?" Dutch said silently as Maud walked off.

Maud went into the back and found a cot and stretched out. Yeah, it did feel good, but she wouldn't admit it. She figured it would take about five minutes.

It was less than two minutes later that Buckskin boiled into the room and stared at her. "You what?"

"I found Ihander and put a bullet through him about where he shot me. He ain't dead or nothing and I left his butler with him to take him to a sawbones. An eye-for-an-eye, I always say."

"Law gonna come down on us?"

"I told him no lawmen. We're even."

"You must be feeling pretty good getting back at him."

"Yeah, about the way you did after you dropped those fire buckets into his place. Boss Dutch told me to get an hour's sleep before I take over the cage. Oh, a suggestion. That bank we use got any women tellers? If it does, why don't you hire one of them to come over here and run our cashier's cage. A banker woman would be honest and know how to handle money."

"Good idea," Buckskin said. "I'll get over there tomorrow and see who I can find."

"You do that. I'm having a nap."

Maud settled down on the cot and Buckskin found a thin blanket and put it over her.

Maud slept four hours until nearly eight o'clock and was mad as a wet cat when she walked into the casino.

Thirty-Three

Part of the dealers and house men worked two shifts that evening, but by the end of the night they had hired enough people to form two complete shifts. The regular hours would be from 10 A.M. to 6 P.M. and then from 6 P.M. to 2 A.M.

They hadn't worked out the eating periods yet, but in a few days they would get that scheduled. When the last gambler had left and the workers all departed, Dutch helped count up the money. They had a net income for the night of a little over $11,000. There were only about $500 in chips outstanding.

Buckskin went and found a cab and brought it around to the back door where the three women waited. Navaro was enthused about the operation and chattered with Maud, who understood some of it.

Maud was so tired she could hardly walk. Buckskin helped her up the hotel steps and once they got Maud into her room, Dutch made sure she got undressed and into bed.

When she came back to her own room, Dutch looked at Buckskin sitting on the bed. She began to undress as soon as the door closed and dropped clothes on the way to the bed.

She looked at him. "I hope you're too tired tonight," she said.

Buckskin grinned. "I'm way too tired. How about in the morning? Much better idea. We don't have to be to work until ten o'clock."

She frowned. "You realize we're working about eighteen hours a day?"

Buckskin chuckled. "Do you realize that the four of us earned almost $3,000 each for that work day?"

"Oh," Dutch said. "That makes it sound a lot better. Sometime soon we're going to have to split up our days there and get a floor manager we can trust. Two of us will be there in the first shift and two on the second."

"Good idea," Buckskin said and fell back on the pillow almost asleep.

Dutch slipped out of the last of her clothes and snuggled up beside Buckskin entirely naked. She liked to sleep that way, and tonight she wasn't surprised to find him sleeping by the time she blew out the light and pulled the sheet over them.

They woke when the sun slanted in their window the next morning about seven.

"Too damn early, Buckskin said and turned

over. Dutch heard the knocking on the door and got up and searched for a robe, found one and slipped into it and went to the door. She opened it and saw Navaro standing there.

"In?" Navaro asked.

"Sure," Dutch said wondering what she wanted.

Navaro wore a robe, too, and looked at Buckskin sleeping. She grinned.

"Long time, you, Buck love," Navaro said.

Dutch grinned. "Yes," she said. Dutch had never heard Navaro use that much English before.

"Navaro, too," she said.

"What?"

Navaro looked at her. "Buckskin do Dutch, Maud and Pris. He love all. Now love Navaro."

Dutch burst out laughing and grinned. "Why the hell not? We'll sneak up on him."

She nodded. "Both," she said touching Navaro and then herself and pointing at Buckskin. Dutch untied her robe and let it fall off her shoulders. She nodded at Navaro who giggled and slipped out of her robe.

Navaro was light brown in color, a little thick at the waist and hips, but with big breasts with still pink areolas and nipples. Navaro got on the bed on the wide side and Dutch slid in right next to Buckskin. She kissed him and began rubbing her hands over his chest.

He murmured in his sleep. Navaro pushed in close behind him, until she was spooned against him from breasts to thighs where he lay on his side.

Buckskin made some small noises and reached

for Dutch. Instead she pushed him over on his back and put his hands on Navaro's breasts. That satisfied him for a moment.

Dutch grinned and went to his crotch and worked on his flaccid penis, urging it to greater rigidity. Dutch kissed him, and then motioned and Navaro kissed his lips. Suddenly his eyes popped open.

"Oh my," he said gently. "It wasn't a dream. Two beautiful women in my bed."

He grinned at Navaro. "Your idea, Navaro?" he asked.

"Her idea," Dutch said. "Two for the price of one. Not a bad deal for a rich man."

"Or for two rich ladies," he said.

Then Navaro lowered a brown breast into his mouth and he stopped talking and savored the favor. Dutch brought him to a full erection and massaged him delicately.

Navaro came away from him and saw his erection and yelped in joy. She bent and took him in her mouth, depositing a coating of saliva, then surged over him where he lay on his back and gently lowered her hole over his lance.

"My god, this is service," Buckskin said. He moaned as he slid inside her sheath and Navaro began bouncing up and down. He looked at Dutch.

"What's your contribution to this threesome?" he asked. She edged Navaro's shoulders to one side and dropped one of her breasts into his mouth, and caught his hands and pushed them to her crotch.

"Now, close your eyes, I have a treat for you,"

Dutch said. She moved so she was just above his head, then she squatted and moved down so her pulsating, swollen nether lips were an inch over his face.

"Now, enjoy," she said.

Buckskin opened his eyes. "Christ, look at that. Hot, juicy, wide open pussy on a plate ready to be eaten."

"Go ahead, Buckskin, help yourself. How many times you been pumped good while eating a hot pussy?"

He caught her hips and pulled her down an inch, then his tongue darted upward and reamed her out and she groaned in a new delight. His tongue found her button and twanged it six times before she climaxed, spraying his face with juices and bouncing and rolling so much she fell away from him on the bed. His hand found her open crotch and he continued rubbing her until she let out a long high yet soft cry of total pleasure.

As Dutch climaxed, Navaro grinned and kept pumping up and down on his hardness. She didn't use any inside muscles and it took longer but soon she had him so excited he could barely stand it. He bounded up and toppled her over, hugging her to the bed, and a moment later he was on top of Navaro.

Dutch had slid away to the floor.

Buckskin came to his knees still inside Navaro and slammed into her pelvic bones so hard he grunted. Then she lifted her legs around his back and squeezed him. He slammed into her now six, seven, then eight times before he exploded and rained his fire down on her in great shots of jism that left him exhausted and drained. He fell on top of her and saw Dutch climb on the bed and drape herself over him, sandwiching him between two women.

They all rested.

Three times more they hooked up in combinations, and each time they thought it couldn't get any better. The final time Navaro squatted in front of the bed and took him in her mouth and he bent over the bed and the natural stroke brought him to completion well before he thought that it might.

Then they took the pitcher of water and the one towel and washed each other. Navaro put on her robe and hurried down to her room. Dutch put on her new dress for the day and Buckskin picked out a new shirt and string tie he had bought and put them on with a pair of his town pants.

Maud came to the door.

"Hey, you two, get it on one more time and then rush, it's past nine-thirty."

"Oh damn!" Dutch said and opened the door. "How did it get so late?"

"Your bed springs was making so much noise this morning when I came before, I could hear them down to the end of the hall. I had breakfast already. We'll send out for some for you two. Where's Navaro?"

"She'll be along soon, I'd guess," Buckskin said. He pulled on his shoes and did a quick job of shaving.

The four of them got to the casino ten minutes

before opening time and every one of the workers were waiting at the back door.

"So we're ten minutes late opening, they won't cause a riot," Dutch said.

"Today we start the new routine," Buckskin said. "No, damn, we can't do it yet. I don't have a floor manager picked out. Soon as we do, two of us will be on duty on one shift, and two on the other shift. That way we won't kill ourselves off in six months."

Maud nodded. "Makes sense. Navaro and I'll do a shift. I can talk some of that Mex."

"She knows more English than you think," Dutch said. "Try her."

They opened the doors on time and the men hurried in to a favorite table.

About an hour later, Buckskin noticed some excitement at the craps table nearest the door and he went to check.

One large man with a full beard and a top hat stood there with more than a dozen $100 chips on one square. He stared through smoke from his cigar at the chips and at the man with the dice.

"Let it ride!" he said softly. "This fine gentleman is going to make me rich."

The man with the dicce bet his $10 and threw the dice. They came up a seven, a winner.

People around the table cheered. The table man looked up at Buckskin as he pushed eighteen $100 chips over to cover the man's bet.

The man with the cigar looked at the young man with the dice who had taken back $10 of his winnings and left his original bet.

"The lad is backing off, not a good sign," the

cigar smoking man in the top hat roared. "But I still have faith in you, young man. Let it ride, the whole $3,600."

Many houses had "house limits" on any one bet, and now the man in the white shirt and string tie and green eye shade behind the table looked at Buckskin. He nodded and the house man grinned.

"Yes, sir, Mr. Moore, we let it ride. Get your bets down, gentlemen. We have to make some money here to pay off Mr. Moore. Bets all down. Throw the dice, sir."

The young man threw the dice and came up with a ten. There was a murmur around the table. Most people were not playing, just watching a man bet $3,600, as much as the average man made at his job in 12 years!

"The number is ten, the number is ten."

The man with the dice threw once and got four. His next throw brought him a six and the next a six and a four for ten.

"Point, the gentleman made his point." The people watched as the house man pushed 36 $100 chips to the winner. He pulled back some losing bets and looked at the big winner.

"Mr. Moore, your bet, sir."

The man knocked the ash off his cigar to the floor which was little more than rough planks. He took a long pull on the smoke and blew it out at the ceiling.

"Let it ride," he said softly.

Again the house man looked at Buckskin. The news of a big winner could be good for the house. Everyone in town would hear about it and rush here to play. On the other hand that would be $7,200 out of the coffers if he won.

Buckskin looked directly at the player. "Mr. Moore, let me congratulate you on your play. Of ccourse, you are more than welcome to let your bet ride. The management concurs with your decision."

There was a cheer around the table. The dice were still in the same man's hands. As long as he won he kept throwing the dice, house rules. He put another $10 on the $20 already on his bet and threw the square ivory cubes with the black dots. One rolled farther than the other. The first stopped with a one showing and the second rolled almost the length of the table before it stopped directly in front of Mr. Moore's stack of chips.

The second die came up a one as well.

"Craps," the house man said. His voice high and unnatural. "Sorry, Mr. Moore, but you lose." The house man swept the $3,600 worth of chips back to his side of the table and watched the other bettors putting down their bets.

"Mr. Moore, any wagering?" the house man asked.

Mr. Moore shook his head, held up his hands, showing that they both were empty. "Oh, well, I was rich for almost ten minutes. What more can a working man ask?" He turned and walked out the door.

Already the casino was buzzing with the story about the $3,600 winner. Most of them didn't say that he lost it all on the next roll of the dice.

Buckskin found his floor manager an hour

later. He was a man of about 40 now working one of the craps tables, who Buckskin remembered said he had worked at the bank for some time. They had a talk in the back and soon Buck promoted him to floor manager. The general rule on bets was that they be realistic, that the house never be put in the position of losing more than $8,000 on any one bet, and that if he had any questions he should talk with the partner on duty on the floor or at the cashier's box.

Buckskin put the man in charge of the floor and went to the bank with a deposit of $5,000, and to ask about a woman teller. The bank had a name for him and said he would have the woman, a widow in her thirties, report to him that afternoon for an interview.

Things were shaping up. He had a standing order at the cafe for them to bring food for 16 people twice a day, at 2 P.M. and at 10 P.M.

Yes things were settling down. Buckskin had just turned around when a man came up to him. At once Buckskin knew who he was. He was J. Arthur Ihander, the former owner of the Lucky Lady Casino, and the same man Maud had shot the day before!

Thirty-Four

"Mr. Morgan, I'm not here to cause any violence," J. Arthur Ihander said quickly. "No need for firearms. I am unarmed and alone. I come here so we can settle our differences once and for all with an unlimited stakes poker game between the two of us."

Buckskin Lee Morgan stared down at the five-foot-tall man wanting to pick him up, carry him to the street and skid him down the dirt as far as he could throw him. At once he knew that would not solve the problem.

"A poker game, the two of us? I'd rather sit down naked in a square box with a rattlesnake."

"Then you're afraid to meet me in a no-holds barred poker game?"

"I don't do lots of things I'm not afraid to do, Ihander. Give me one good reason why I should play poker with you?"

"To get rid of me. If I lose, I'll leave town and not bother your partners any more."

"I can do that much quicker. Just take you out in the back alley and put a bullet into you where it'll do the same thing."

"But you won't. You want to prove to yourself that you can whip me at poker. Poker is a thinking man's game. And you believe you can out-think me."

"I have so far. I have a casino, you don't."

"Yes or no, Morgan?"

"What kind of stakes?"

"I have a fifty thousand dollar letter of credit from my bank, which is also, your bank."

"Let's see it?"

Ten minutes later they were in the curtained room at the back. Dutch came in a few moments later to watch. No one else was permitted. Buckskin had a box with every $100 chip in the cage. The value was more than $50,000. He put the box on the table.

"Table stakes," Buckskin said. "I don't trust you for more. Next we will take off our jackets. My six-gun will be on the table. If I see you cheating, just one card, you're a dead man. Roll up your sleeves."

That done by both men, Buckskin took a new package of playing cards from his pocket and passed them to Ihander. He looked at them, checked the seal put on specially for gambling houses at the Pennsylvania printing plant, and broke it. He opened the box and found the backs to be a solid black that would show up any attempt to mark them at once.

"Satisfied?"

"Yes. Do you have $50,000 worth of chips there?"

"I do. Dutch has just returned from your bank and put a hold on $50,000 of your money. Which is your entire balance except for about $50.00."

"What guarantee do I have that you can cover those markers?"

"You checked our bank balance this morning. Our mutual banker confirmed that. Ready to play?"

Ihander had been shuffling the cards. He passed the new deck to Buckskin who shuffled them a few times, cut them and handed them back.

"Remember, I can cheat at cards as well, or better, than you can. I can spot a cheat a mile off. This is a thinking man's game." He took out his .45 and laid it on the table beside the box of $100 chips.

Ihander nodded. He bought $20,000 in chips from the box, and gave Dutch his marker.

He put $5,000 in the pot. Buckskin matched it.

"Draw, anything to open."

He dealt five cards face down to both players, put the deck down a foot from his hands and looked at his cards.

Buckskin had a rule when playing poker. Win the first hand, then ease back and check the other players. Now he had only one man to check.

"Open for $200," Buckskin said, sliding two

chips into the pot.

Ihander snorted. He put three chips in. "... and raise you by $2,000."

Buckskin put in another twenty chips and discarded two cards.

"Dealer will discard three."

He laid down his keepers and put the other three to one side. Then he picked up the deck and dealt two cards to Buckskin and took three himself. Buckskin watched him until he handed the deck to Dutch.

Buckskin had kept a pair of tens and an ace of spades. When he checked his new cards he found another ten and a five of clubs.

"Opener bets $1,000," Buckskin said and pushed in the chips.

"I thought we were playing poker," the smaller man said. "I'll raise you $5,000."

Buckskin met the bet and called him.

Ihander laid down his cards one at a time. Six of clubs, four of spades, deuce of spades, deuce of diamonds, deuce of hearts.

"Good hand," Buckskin said.

When Ihander smirked and reached for the pot, Buckskin laid down his three tens. "But I've got you beat."

Buckskin pulled in the chips and took the cards and shuffled.

They played for a half hour. Betting ranged up to $20,000 a pot. Each won his share and no one came close to going broke.

Then Ihander won two pots in a row. It was Buckskin's deal.

"Seven card stud, $1,000 ante."

They each counted out chips and pushed them in. Buckskin dealt two cards down to each player, then one up to each. Across the small round table an ace of hearts showed.

"This is not a thinking man's game of poker," Ihander said. He looked at his two hole cards, but showed no reaction.

Buckskin drew a king of clubs. "Ace bets."

He bet $100. Buckskin put down one small note. Ihander did not like stud games with no draw. Buckskin won that pot on a full house but it was a small pot.

Two hands later it was Buckskin's deal again. He went for a game of five card draw and Ihander relaxed a little. The ante was $5,000, and Ihander opened with $5,000 more. It was guts poker with nothing for openers.

The other man migght have a ten high and no pairs. It was a bluffer's paradise.

Buckskin kept three cards. He always did on draw poker. This time he missed matching up his pair of jacks and held only the jacks and three unusable cards.

Buck pushed the bidding and bluffed out Ihander on a final $10,000 bid. He folded and Buckskin didn't have to show his cards. Now Buckskin had sixty-percent of the chips. Ihander was down to about $15,000. He had drawn another $10,000 worth and now was up to $30,000 of his $50,000 limit.

On the next hand, Ihander won with three aces and two kings. Buckskin shuffled the deck face up and thought he saw something strange but didn't let on. The next hand Ihander won with four queens. As soon as Ihander put down his cards and reached for the pot, Buckskin's six-gun snapped off the table and the muzzle touched Ihander's chest.

"You're good, Ihander. You gave me just enough rope. I'm still not sure how you did it. Dutch, be sure to keep your hands in plain sight at all times and count the cards."

She did. There were fifty eight cards on the table.

"Isn't that strange, Ihander? Search him, Dutch. He probably has them in his crotch somewhere."

"This is outrageous. I'm not cheating. You set me up with marked cards."

"Then why are you the one winning?" Dutch asked him.

"We can prove you're cheating if you are. Before we played, Dutch opened that pack of cards and shaved one side of the bottom of the deck just enough. The old rocker shave. It won't show even if cards are not positioned all the same end down, but position them the way they came and the deck will rock to one side."

Buck grinned when Dutch came up with a small packet of cards from Ihander's fly. There were four aces left, three kings, and four jacks. They were a perfect match for the cards Buckskin had brought.

"We knew the same card makers sell cards to most gaming houses. It would be simple for you to find out what color backs we use and get a new pack to rob. But you got two packs. You're greedy."

By then Buckskin had sorted the cards and stacked them and as he tapped them into place there were six cards that were slightly larger than the others. Buckskin sorted out the larger ones, three aces, two kings and a queen.

"Unusual, Ihander," Buckskin said tersely. "Those were the exact cards you won the last three pots with."

Buckskin put his six gun down now and rubbed his eyes. "Damn, Ihander, I figured maybe you were serious when you came in and asked about playing an honest game."

Ihander shook his head. "No, no, you have it all wrong." He turned in desperation to make them understand. Then so quickly Dutch almost missed it, his right hand darted to his waist and he pulled a derringer smaller than Buckskin had ever seen before.

"But it won't make any difference now, will it?" Ihander said. "You'll be found dead here after I make my way out the back. This is a small caliber but deadly with a head shot." He began to lift the weapon toward Buckskin's head.

The report was loud and a dozen people ran back to the curtained area.

Dutch pulled her smoking gun from under the table where she had readied it. Her round slammed through Ihander's chest going upward, cut his heart in half and kept on going to lodge in his left shoulder.

Buckskin put his weapon back in leather and gathered up the chips but left them where they were stacked. Ihander had been thrown back in his chair and dangled over it like a puppeteer's dummy.

"Go get the Denver police," Buckskin told the first man past the curtain. "I'm afraid a cheater has been shot down before he could kill both of us."

Two hours later it was all over. The Denver police were a lot tougher than they used to be. A Captain Paulson had questioned them for over an hour. They showed him the letter of credit, the chips, the public challenge to an unlimited stakes poker game and how they challenged him and proved he was cheating.

The captain checked the cards and decided that indeed there had been cheating.

"We have no bad reports on the El Dorado yet, but we'll keep an eye on you. Our friend here, Mr. Ihander, had many complaints lodged against him. Only a month ago he killed a man who accused him of cheating, but that time the other man went for his weapon first.

"With an impartial witness here, Mrs. Smith, we'll have to rule self defense. Ihander was known to be handy with that little derringer. Smallest damn thing I ever saw." The Captain stood. "Well, I guess that ends it. I'll have the body taken out the back door to a funeral parlor."

When he left, they both relaxed and hugged each other.

"The $50,000 letter of credit?" Dutch said holding it up.

"We take it to the bank, and show his markers and collect our $30,000 and leave the rest where it is. The man might have kin somewhere."

Dutch kissed him. "I knew you'd know what to do."

The night after they closed, Dutch and Buckskin lay close together in her bed.

"We have a lot of work to do to put the El Dorado on a firm footing," Dutch said.

"And I know you and the others will do fine."

"What about Buckskin Lee Morgan?"

"Another week at the most. By then my arm will be healed completely and I'll be ready to move again. I'm still supposed to be going back up to Boise. I've got a horse ranch to run."

"Dumb. That's just dumb, Morgan!"

"You only call me Morgan when you're angry with me."

"I'm not angry, damnit, I'm mad as hell. You can make as much here in two days as you'll make all year with your horses up there in Idaho."

Buckskin laughed. "Probably. But I love horses, and I'm not so wild about chasing around after a bunch of wild-eyed gamblers for the rest of my life."

"Rest of your life? A year here and we can travel to France and Germany and England and even Rome and see everything the world has to offer. We'll be so rich we can buy half of New York City if we want to."

"This is all going to end someday—the gambling. Some cities back east have outlawed gambling. It'll happen here sooner or later."

"I'll bet on later. Every month could mean $50,000 or $60,000 profit. What's wrong with that?"

"Nothing. And it couldn't happen to a prettier, sexier lady."

"Promises."

After making good on his promise, they relaxed in the bed again and sipped at a bottle of champagne they had smuggled into the hotel.

"When?" she asked.

"Two weeks. We should have everything worked out by then. If we pay our people better than the other casinos, we'll get and keep the best people. We pay them well and we trust them —to a certain degree."

"Two weeks? You promised me six months."

"We said, maybe."

"Maud will swear for another week."

"Be good for her."

"Navaro thinks you're sexy. She'll miss you."

"Want to come to Boise with me?"

"Sure, but you wouldn't take me, even if I could get away. Hey, I'm the boss here. Everybody thinks so, anyway. Damn you! Two weeks, huh? Something else you've got to promise me."

"What's that?"

"Make love to me twice a day, every day, until you leave."

"Easy."

"Really?"

"Easy to promise. If I run out of ammunition, it'll be your fault."

"Yeah, I know. Come on. You owe me one more for today."

"What about this morning?"

"That was before the promise, didn't count."

Buckskin laughed and grabbed her. It was going to be a tough assignment, but he would do his best.

BUCKSKIN

The hard-riding,
hard-bitten Adult Western series
that's hotter'n a blazing pistol
and as tough as the men
who tamed the frontier.

_____ 2587-6 BUCKSKIN SPECIAL EDITION:
THE BUCKSKIN BREED $3.95US/$4.95CAN

#21: PEACEMAKER PASS by Kit Dalton
_____ 2619-8 $2.95US/$3.95 CAN

#20: PISTOL GRIP by Kit Dalton
_____ 2551-5 $2.95US/$3.95CAN

#19: SHOTGUN STATION by Kit Dalton
_____ 2529-9 $2.95US/$3.95CAN

#18: REMINGTON RIDGE by Kit Dalton
_____ 2509-4 $2.95US/$3.95CAN

#17: GUNSMOKE GORGE by Kit Dalton
_____ 2484-5 $2.50US/$3.25CAN

#16: WINCHESTER VALLEY by Kit Dalton
_____ 2463-2 $2.50US/$3.25CAN

#15: SCATTERGUN by Kit Dalton
_____ 2439-X $2.50US/$3.25CAN

LEISURE BOOKS
ATTN: Customer Service Dept.
276 5th Avenue, New York, NY 10001

Please send me the book(s) checked above. I have enclosed $_____
Add $1.25 for shipping and handling for the first book; $ .30 for each book thereafter. No cash, stamps, or C.O.D.s. All orders shipped within 6 weeks. Canadian orders please add $1.00 extra postage.

Name _____

Address _____

City_____State_____Zip_____

Canadian orders must be paid in U.S. dollars payable through a New York banking facility.   ☐ Please send a free catalogue.